Born in Anderson, Indiana, Gary  graduated with an accounting degree from Ball State University. He also studied at the University of Indianapolis for Computer Technology and the Gonzaga University for Organizational Development.

Gary uses his thirty-five years in the fields of forensic accounting, fraud examination, and internal auditing to write about corporate and social issues, and experiences that affect ordinary people in extraordinary situations. His experience spans the banking, retail, finance, education, and medical industries. He now juggles his time and residence between New Orleans and Gulf Shores, Alabama.

His first book, *Why Birds Fall*, is a mystery about corruption in the aviation industry.

Masquerade of Truth

Gary L Kreigh

AIA PUBLISHING

Masquerade of Truth
Gary L. Kreigh
Copyright © 2020
Published by AIA Publishing, Australia
ABN: 32736122056
http://www.aiapublishing.com

ISBN: 978-1-922329-07-3

Cover design by K. Rose Kreative

To the man in King's Square

Chapter 1

The French Quarter, New Orleans, Louisiana.
February 1956

The woman walking towards me wore black fish-net stockings under a white Chantilly lace skirt and a pink Elsa blouse. I dared not take a second look.

"I'm a man of the cloth," I announced sharply to ward off her advances.

I wasn't lying. I was a retired minister of a small Midwestern congregation. Surely her profession had some respect for mine.

"Oh, good," she replied. "I like a man in nice threads. We should get along just fine."

I sidestepped her. I didn't consider myself a prude, but such nonsense had no place with me. A young couple oblivious to the late-February afternoon chill provided a human shield behind which I could cross the street. I strode one block along Toulouse Street to Royal Street. Royal was out of my way, but the narrow thoroughfare was a safer route than Bourbon Street. It had high-end antique shops, clothing boutiques, and famous upscale restaurants.

Nevertheless, I pulled my suitcase closer and quickened my gait.

A Kaiser Darrin rolled past—a sporty two-seater in pastel lime. The driver honked his horn and waved at me; I suspect he did so for jollies and no other reason than to have me admire his car. But, then, he may have hit the horn because I stood out as much as his Darrin did on the historic street. In a different way, of course.

I was an anomaly. Most everyone walking in the Quarter was younger and trendier than me. I wasn't wearing a Gabardine bomber or Mackinaw bush jacket like the other, younger men. My corduroy sport coat with the flap pockets and leather elbow patches over my button-down shirt and long, narrow, plaid tie gave me away as one of their grandfathers.

A young woman, wearing (more than likely) her beau's lettermen sweater above a smart poodle dress and saddle shoes, turned and smiled as she and her boyfriend passed. She gestured a hello by fanning her fingers at me, then whispered something in her boyfriend's ear and giggled. Apparently, I was not only out of place but also humorously so.

More tourists walked in front of me, slowing my progress as they gawked at the revelry of the Quarter. They took in the aroma of French-fried food spiced with cayenne pepper and hot sauce that permeated the entrances to restaurants and outdoor cafes. Broken beads from Mardi Gras that had ended two weeks prior littered the streets, contributing to the stench of human excess that lingered in the tainted air. The tourists didn't seem to mind. Beads, stench, and French fried excess drew them to the Quarter in the first place.

I came to New Orleans for an entirely different purpose.

I came for the theater.

My good friend Charles Portier recommended a small, but highly regarded, theater in the French Quarter directed by a good Southern gentleman of excellent taste and quality—or so Portier touted. I realized there was a fine line between facts and embellishment with Portier, but he rarely steered me wrong with theatrical recommendations.

I carried my suitcase with relative ease as I made my way to Ursulines Avenue where my friend lived. I didn't require much. I lived frugally and my possessions were few, including clothes. I hadn't purchased anything since my wife passed away four years ago.

People who bumped into me as if I wasn't there didn't seem to notice my grip hitting their upper legs. My suitcase must've been even lighter than I thought.

Across Orleans Avenue past the back of St. Louis Cathedral, the raucous vitality of Bourbon Street gave way to musical soloists and flatfoot dancers striving to earn a buck. I enjoyed their performances for the brief moments I watched, but I tried not to stop, intent on reaching Portier's cottage as quickly as I could.

That changed when I heard a young man singing. He sat cross-legged against a stucco building and emitted a melody over the strumming of his guitar strings that I had never heard before, reciting lyrics I'd never hear again. I knew I would never forget the resounding tone of his voice.

I walked toward him, glimpsing beyond his scraggly frame to the humanness in his face—a young, timeless face with wispy bangs and clear, innocent features. Someone must have cared for him recently, I thought. His face lacked the ruddy complexion of someone who'd been on their own for any length of time.

Sparsely scattered coins lay on the bottom of his guitar case. I tried to walk past him, but the compelling sound of his voice brought a lump to my throat that I couldn't swallow.

3

I stopped and reached into my pocket, pulling out the first dollar bill I grasped. I dropped the bill into the case, then turned to walk away.

He responded with a barely audible, "Thank you."

I turned to see him smile at the windfall I'd bestowed next to his pittance of coins. He took the bill quickly from the case and placed it in a pocket. I knew then his need was real. I said a prayer and asked for blessings upon the young man. It was easier than turning around and talking to him directly about his need.

I turned onto Ursulines Avenue, giving the singer no more thought, and found Ursulines even quieter than Royal Street. The closer I came to Rampart, however, the more the traffic noise increased. Street cars and pedestrians stymied the progress of bumper to bumper traffic, increasing the chaotic energy I remembered from previous visits.

I spotted Portier's cottage ahead—a faded-gray façade in desperate need of painting. The poor building would never get what it needed, I feared, knowing my friend's inclination toward hoarding his pennies.

Someone sat on his front stoop. *Was that Portier himself?* I recognized his dog on the leash, but something appeared peculiar about the person holding it.

What in the world was he wearing?

When I drew closer, I saw that the person wasn't my friend. She was a large-framed woman, wearing a frock-like dress, bursting with color and pattern, and adorned excessively in cheap costume jewelry. Her blonde hair expanded from all sides of her head in curls, reminding me of Little Miss Muffet, only fifty years older. The tiara and matching colored bows added additional confusion to the conglomerate, but no more so than the heavy lipstick, rouge, and stark turquoise eye

4

shadow that blanketed her face and distorted the whites of her eyes.

I set my suitcase on the pavement to give Portier's dog, Bentley, a hearty scratch around his neck. He responded favorably, nearly swishing the woman's cocktail off the porch with his tail. The old Labrador hadn't changed much since I'd seen him last. Solid, well-tempered, and meticulously groomed, he sat obediently in stark contrast to his caretaker.

"That's it?" she asked bluntly—the woman's first words to me.

"Pardon?"

She pointed to my suitcase. "That's it?" she asked again.

"Yes. Something wrong?"

"Honey, that's no suitcase. It's a cigar box. I need a grip that big just to hold my nails and eyelashes. Chuck was right when he said you were religious, but I didn't know you were a monk."

I introduced myself and explained that the suitcase contained all I needed.

"That's sweet. Maybe you can give me some pointers on what to wear when I die. Otherwise, I'm counting on a helluva concierge service in Heaven for all my stuff. So what do you go by, puddin'?"

"Pardon?"

"Do you not hear well?"

"Yes, perfectly; I don't understand your questions."

She smiled, catching me off guard. "What do you like to be called? Do you have a name?"

"Oh, that. Please call me Richard. I was a pastor up north, and I'm used to being called Reverend Fountain, but please don't. I'd prefer Richard, and you?"

"Chuck calls me by my given name Genevieve. Genevieve Duval."

"What do you prefer to be called?"

"My stage name is fine. Genny. You may have seen stage posters of me on your way through the Quarter."

I shook my head.

"No? None at all?"

"I'm sorry. So you call Charles Chuck?"

She bellowed a hearty laugh. "Isn't it sweet?"

"I'm sure he doesn't think so. I don't see him responding much to Chuck."

"He doesn't. He hates it. He ignores me completely when I call him that, but I love him dearly. He's such a sweet neighbor to me."

"Are we talking about the same man?" I asked. My friend Portier had a crusty side to his personality. His glass was always half-empty, it seemed, and he had a cynical view of the outside world, especially of people.

Genny laughed again. "Oh, he's all right. Deep down anyway. He's a bit like an oyster, don't you think? Hard on the outside and difficult to open, but soft and mushy on the inside. He really doesn't mean what he says. Either that or I'm used to his insults. I live here in this cottage next to him, by the way."

"The bright yellow one?"

"Yes! Isn't it splendid?"

I scanned the front. I wasn't fond of the yellow, but by comparison Genny's home was much more appealing than Portier's.

"Is he in?" I asked, hoping to settle in before the evening's festivities.

"No, he met a client at the last minute, something about taxes and some sort of audit the IRS was doing. He didn't look

6

happy. He stormed out in a hurry and said, 'Here, watch the dog.'" She bent down to pat Bentley's soft beige coat. "Aw, you ain't no dog now, are you, Benny, you sweet thing. You're one of us now, aren't you?"

"Will he be long?"

"What, dear?"

"I asked if he'd be long. I'd like to settle in."

"Well, I don't know much about that. I don't expect him to be, but who really knows when it comes to things like taxes and audits and such?"

The look of disappointment must have been obvious on my face.

"Would you like to come in?" she asked as she stood. "I mean, to my place. Take your shoes off. Wash your face. Have a drink. I do have coffee if you don't want a martini."

I didn't have to ponder her invitation long before I accepted. "I'd like that," I said. "It's been a long train ride from Chicago. Coffee would be nice."

"Did you have a murder?"

"A what?"

"A murder. You came in on *The City of New Orleans,* didn't you?"

"Well, yes, but …"

"I've always thought *The City of New Orleans* would be a grand train for a murder, you know, like the Orient Express."

"Oh, I see. No, nothing like that happened, and I'm glad. I'm not much in for murder this trip."

Genny chuckled. "Then you came to the wrong city, sweetheart. Come on in. Make yourself at home."

I made myself comfortable in her small, eclectic parlor as she dawdled through a doorway into the kitchen.

7

"This is rather nice," I said to say something pleasant about the menagerie of furnishings.

"A little cluttered," she said, raising her voice for me to hear. "I got all my Mama's things when she died. I tried to fit it all in, but it's too much even for me, and Ben has to watch that tail of his, don't you, Ben? You knock everything I own onto the floor, don't you? Oh, I'd love to have room for a TV. See that spot over there?" she asked, walking to the doorway. "That's where I'd put it. I'd put it right there, but I first need to find a pot of gold. They're expensive! Have you priced them? They run two-hundred-fifty bucks at Maison-Blanche over on Canal Street. I can't afford that. That's why Bentley and I are such good friends. I offer to dog-sit at Chuck's house when Chuck's away so I can watch my favorite shows."

"Does the TV work at his place? The last time I stayed there, it sat idle, collecting dust. He said the picture tubes were burnt out."

"That's poppycock," she said as if disgusted. "I watch it all the time. No, it works. He just didn't want to turn it on. He hasn't watched much TV since Adlai Stevenson interrupted *I Love Lucy* with a thirty-minute political ad last year."

Although it sounded like my friend, I tried to defend him by saying it couldn't be true.

"It is! He says that's why he's voting for Ike in the election. No one interrupts his *I Love Lucy* and becomes president, so I hope you didn't come all this way to watch TV. Chuck mentioned to me that you two were going to the theater."

"Yes, we're taking in one or two shows. Some obscure plays in small theaters. That's what I want. Local performances by local performers. Will you be joining us?"

"I doubt it, seriously. Chuck and I are good neighbors, but in social circles, he keeps me at a distance."

8

"But you'll invite me to one of *your* shows, won't you?"

Genny emerged from the kitchen with a can of Community Coffee in her hands. "To one of my shows? Are you serious? You mean you'd come to one of my shows?"

"I'd love to. Why not?"

"You'll have to ask Chuck that question. He'll give you plenty of reasons why you shouldn't attend one of my shows, but, oh, that would be grand if you would. It really would. I could take you back stage. You could meet some of my friends, but, of course, I'd have to prepare you before you meet them."

"Prepare me?"

"They're a little odd—eccentric, you could say."

"That doesn't bother me. They can't be any worse than some of the poor souls I saw here in the Quarter along the way."

Her eyes softened and the gregarious features around her face seemed to empathize with my comment. She sat next to me on the couch and touched my arm. "You must come," she said. "I'm doing several benefits next month. I'm perfecting my shows right now. Those people you saw on the way, they need help. They come to New Orleans because it's warmer here than where they came from. They come without having a place to go, and they don't realize it can get downright chilly along the Gulf. If you want a mission field, Reverend, you've come to the right place. We have quite a need in our community."

"But my trip isn't about missions. I came to get away—to get a break from my life."

"I get that. I'm just saying—"

"I know what you're saying, and I agree. My work in the ministry should never end, not even on vacation, but I really do need a break, and I'm not seeking a mission right now."

9

Genny smiled as if I was being naïve, then stood to return to the kitchen.

"You don't think that's possible?" I asked.

"It's entirely possible."

"But you think less of me."

"I don't even know you. My first impression is that you're a very sweet, compassionate person. Unfortunately, we're a city divided by class between the haves and the have nots. It's entirely possible to enjoy your stay in New Orleans without ever noticing the plight of those around us. The upper crust seems to be able to do it effortlessly. I have no doubt that you can, too." She finished her trek to the kitchen.

I sat alone on the paisley couch of blues, greens, yellows, and purples, contemplating her words and thinking back upon the young man on Royal Street who sang his heart out to me, but I'd walked away, throwing a dollar in his guitar case to ease my guilt.

Chapter 2

Several firm raps sounded on the old wood door of Genny's cottage. I was about to put the steaming cup of coffee Genny had prepared to my lips when I heard them, and I nearly spilled the hot liquid over my hand and onto my lap.

"Good Lord!" Genny exclaimed as she set her cup on a table in front of me. She answered the door with hands on her hips.

I turned and saw my friend Portier standing just outside the doorway.

"You don't need to knock down my door, Chuck. Mr. Fountain will come willingly," Genny said.

"I'm here for Bentley," Portier grunted. "You can keep Fountain."

"Get in here."

Bentley's tail wagged fiercely at the entrance of his master, but the Lab received little more than a lackluster pat on his back.

I stood and greeted my good friend with a hearty handshake and a brief hug. Seeing me for the first time in months did little to change his foul demeanor. He took a seat across from me without saying a word. I looked at my friend's disheveled frame as he ran his stubby fingers through dark tangles of Brylcreemed hair.

"I won't stay long," he announced.

"You'll stay long enough to take that edge off. I'll not release man or beast to you until you do." Genny walked to an antique buffet table where she pulled out bottles of dark and white rum, grenadine, a can of fruit juice, and a shapely tall glass in which to pour the concoction.

"I don't want a hurricane if that's what you're making," Portier said.

"You're getting a hurricane," she spouted back. "Extra strong. I'm not spending an entire evening at the theater with you acting like this. You're going to mellow out first."

"Who said anything about you going to the theater?"

"I was invited."

"The hell you were."

"I invited her," I admitted.

"The hell you did."

I shook my head at my friend's indignation.

"Besides, there's been a change of plans," he said in his own defense.

"How so? I was looking forward to going."

"Oh, it's the theater, all right, but not in the sense you were hoping. I just came from my client. You remember Reed Alemand, don't you, Genny?"

"No." She handed Portier his drink and sat in a nearby chair.

"Yes, you do. Don't give me that. We were at Leroux's, and you were inhaling a roast-pork tenderloin when he stopped by our table."

"I don't remember. You just said I was eating roast pork at Leroux's. I so rarely get good tenderloin. I wouldn't interrupt a meal like that for one of your friends."

"He's not a friend. He's a client."

"Same difference."

12

"What about him?" I asked impatiently.

"*Dickies, Stocks, and Jabots.*"

Genny grimaced. "Oh, no."

"Don't listen to her, Fountain." Portier took a sip of the pink cocktail and puckered. "Good gracious, woman. This is pure alcohol."

"It's a hurricane. What did you expect? Drink and get happy."

Portier set the cocktail on a table. "Reed Alemand is my client. I've been his accountant for a number of years. He's from Breaux Bridge and is headquartered out of Lafayette."

I nodded. "I assume he has business in New Orleans."

"Baton Rouge and elsewhere."

"What does he do?"

"What doesn't he do is the question. Real estate, mostly, small business ventures. His business associate is Manny Lyons. You may have heard of the Lyons family."

I shook my head.

"Of Lafayette."

I shook my head some more.

"The freight and oil magnate."

I continued to shake my head.

"I haven't, either," Genny interjected.

"Yes, well, your friends are hardly magnates, are they, Genny? More like magnets attracted to each other."

"Move on, Portier," I said. "The name means nothing to us."

"Manny—I should say, Manfred—Lyons asked Reed to invest in a small stock theater company his brother founded. One of the first plays was one his brother co-wrote, produced, and directed."

"This *Dickies, Stocks, and Jabots?*"

"Yes. He's quite into the thick of it."

"As in heavily invested?"

"You could say."

"Is it in trouble?"

"Who said anything about trouble?"

"I assumed that's why you're in such a foul mood this evening. Was this investment against your recommendation?"

"No, nothing like that. I'm not his financial advisor in that sort of sense, just his accountant. I provide his advisor with the numbers to make the recommendations to his associate, Manny Lyons."

"And Manny's advisor advised against this venture, but Mr. Alemand made it anyway?"

"No, nothing like that."

"Then what?"

"The advisor is Manfred's father. His father is missing. He's been gone for six months now. No one can find him."

I shook my head in disbelief. "How does a freight and oil tycoon vanish for six months without being detected? I don't understand."

"Neither does the family, but apparently this isn't something out of the ordinary for the patriarch. That's why authorities are not taking the vacation seriously."

"That's what they're calling it? A vacation?"

"That's what authorities believe it is until there's evidence of foul play."

"Did this Manny fellow also invest?"

"I believe his hands are tied until his father returns."

"I don't see how this affects our evening plans."

"Are you going to drink your drink?" Genny asked.

"It's too strong, Genevieve. I need my wits about me."

"Then hand it here," she said. "I'll not waste good rum and grenadine on your tasteless palate."

He obliged, then said to me, "I would like to support the play by being in attendance if you'd be a good sport and join me. It's a Shakespearean parody, comical as well as educational."

"Educational?"

"If you're not familiar with Shakespeare, you'll get a crash course with the play. A quick lesson, let's say."

I turned to Genny whose tongue was already starting to turn bright red from her cocktail. "Is this why you turned up your nose a while ago?"

"I'm not much into Shakespearean parodies," she answered.

"I agree," I replied, not convinced I wanted to attend. However, I turned to my friend to give him the benefit of the doubt. "Local performers?"

"Yes, it's a stock theater."

"Very few local performers," Genny said. "I heard most of the actors came down from Philadelphia."

"Not enough money to bring them," Portier replied. "They were replaced with local talent."

"Hastily casted, ill prepared for their first performance," Genny added.

"Which was when?" I asked.

"Tonight."

"You mean tonight is the opening night? Never before performed?"

"Did you not hear me say it is a stock theater?" Portier said in defense. "That's how most work. They'll be on to a different play next week."

I shook my head. No. I did not want to attend.

15

"I'm appealing to your ministerial compassion, Fountain. Please attend with me. I told Alemand I would go and that I had a friend who has a great love for parodies. Alemand's a client. I'd like to retain his business."

I gave Portier a sour look, but eventually agreed.

"Well, count me out," Genny said.

"You were never counted in."

Portier stood, took Bentley by the leash, and led the dog to the door. "I'm leaving, as you can see. Stay as long as you want with this fine woman of exotic tastes, Fountain. The theater is within walking distance. I doubt we'll have to vie for seats tonight."

The play's venue was just as my friend said it would be. Seats were not assigned and were easily available.

A sparse number of smartly dressed people meandered the aisles, searching for a seat to their liking. Many of the women squeezed into velvet or satin gowns with their fashionable wasp waists, complete with accessories that were color coordinated from head to toe. The men, of course, wore what they wore to work—full-cut blue or grey vested suits with their front-pinched fedoras. Their attire was in stark contrast to the physical appearance of the theater still under renovation.

The stage was small, but the brocade curtain in a pattern of gold and silver threads expanded the full width of the building. It faced the audience in a majestic way that disregarded the lack of other aesthetics.

A quintet of two violins and one viola, cello, and bass each, could be heard in the orchestra pit warming up with scales and notes that often clashed against each other as if they were in the midst of a contemporary chamber piece.

"I prefer not to sit in the very front," I said above the squawking of one of the violins.

"This place is so small every seat is up front," Portier pointed out. "Let's move to the center, then."

I agreed. Decaying floorboards creaked under our feet as we made our way to our seats. Once comfortably situated, I glanced through the playbill to get a feel for the actors and the general quality of the production. The booklet wasn't very descriptive, and the biographies of the actors were practically void. Only the cover of the playbill captured my curiosity. Its black and yellow art-deco design was well done and professional even though it far from captured the feel of a Shakespearean parody.

I set the playbill in my lap with indifference and looked about the room. "What's the name of this place?"

"The Landalia."

"I didn't see a sign."

"It wasn't large."

"What was in this building before investors took it over?"

"I don't know exactly. I'm sure it was a residence from the late-eighteenth century through the early beginnings of this century. Most of these buildings were. As of ten years ago it was a restaurant—a very good restaurant in my opinion, but as restaurants go in this town, it couldn't keep up with its reputation. Service staff was difficult to retain. Quality diminished, patrons dwindled. Since about '52 it hasn't been much of anything. It's been a hodgepodge of insignificant businesses, if you ask me."

"I suppose that's how your client heard of the building, being in real estate and all."

"He's quite adept at finding gems in this city. They did a nice job on renovation, don't you think?"

I smiled courteously, but that was all I offered.

"I apologize for my foul mood earlier," Portier said in an attempt to smooth out his brash behavior.

"I couldn't tell the difference," I teased. "You've always been rude."

"I'm afraid Alemand's situation has put me in a much worse disposition," he countered. "I really am fouler than usual."

"It's Genny you should be apologizing to. You were very cruel to her, I thought. She doesn't deserve treatment like that. She admires you for some unknown reason."

"It's Bentley she admires. I'm just on the other end of his leash."

"It doesn't have to be that way, you know."

"I know. I said I was sorry."

"But what are you going to do about it and this foul mood of yours?"

Portier turned to me and, with a distinct air of finality, said, "I'm going to watch the play. Do you mind?"

The curtain rose. Mishaps began almost before the curtain made it to the top when one of the main actresses came on stage and tripped on a rug that had a corner flipped upward. The stumble must have unnerved her because she stammered through the first few minutes of her lines, adlibbing in a way that threw the other actors off cue. I stopped counting the snafus, miscues, and botched lines when I ran out of fingers. It was then I realized the audience was laughing more at the bloopers than the actors' scripted lines.

Portier turned to see if I was enjoying the performance. I'm fairly certain he didn't miss the disgusted expression on my face.

18

At one point, the set changed, and I was hopeful it was a turning point for the better. The actors and actresses had assembled on their proper marks. The quintet played a beautiful nocturne as the lights dimmed. The lead actor, however, was nowhere on stage. He finally appeared, fumbling with his costume. Safety pins, holding a doublet too large for him, came apart as he delivered his lines with exaggerated gestures.

Suddenly, at a time least expected in the play, the lights brightened, signifying the end of the first act.

"Thank God," Portier whispered to me. "I don't know about you, but I could use a glass of wine or champagne."

"Will they have any?"

"They better," he said. "I can't go through another act without a buzz of some kind."

We stood and turned to face the crowd of people, heading for the exit. A bottleneck at the door stymied our progress.

"No, forget this," my friend said. "Let's forgo the champagne and get the hell out of here. We'll have a nice dinner somewhere. My treat. I'll even find a pay phone and give Genevieve a call to join us. She told us this would be bad, but I wouldn't listen. It's the best apology I can offer her."

I agreed and watched as the attendees filed slowly out of the rows of seats and into the aisles.

Portier nudged me as we stood in queue and said, "That man looks very familiar to me. I can't place him, though."

"What man?"

Portier leaned to one side so I could take look at the gentleman.

I saw scraggly facial features under his fedora and glanced judgmentally at his wrinkled and unkempt suit, atypical for a night on the town in New Orleans. His walking cane, however, impressed me. A sterling-silver panther perched upon a carved mahogany stick, as if ready to pounce on unsuspecting prey. I'd never seen a walking stick so striking and exquisite. Its sophisticated flair didn't match the crude man who accompanied it.

Portier continued to stare at the man to try to place him. "This will bug me all night, you know."

Surprised, I said, "I don't want to judge, Portier, but he hardly seems to be the type of person you'd know."

"He may be a client from long ago; I can't remember. You wouldn't know him, I'm sure."

"I doubt that I would," I said, my attention diverted.

A woman in one of the doorways that swung open diverted my attention for several seconds. I couldn't see her face, but I found her silhouette striking—an hourglass figure and hair beautifully styled and adorned by a cloche hat that swirled to one side.

I noticed I wasn't the only one who'd been looking at her. The man with the scraggly beard saw her, too. Instead of admiration and awe, however, his eyes sharpened with alarm. The part of his face that appeared above his beard became pasty and grim. He peered around the people standing in line in front of him as if it was imperative that he got around them as quickly as possible. The bottleneck in the aisle made no place to maneuver. The longer he stood in line, the more agitated he appeared.

"Getting to the lobby is tedious, isn't it?" Portier asked.

I didn't answer at first. I glanced toward the doorway then back at the man. Although the woman's silhouette was gone, fear remained etched in the man's weathered face.

"Yes," I finally replied, "but at least the intermission has been interesting."

"It's quite all right, you know, Fountain," Portier said as I pulled out a chair at Leroux's for Genny to sit.

"All right for what?" I asked.

"A woman. I saw you gazing at that woman's silhouette in the theatre."

"Oh, please, don't start that again."

"You met a lady friend, Richard?" Genny asked.

"No," I replied emphatically.

"But if you had, it would've been quite all right, you know. Your dear wife has been gone now for, what, three years now?"

"Oh, I'm so terribly sorry," Genny said sincerely as she touched my arm.

"Please, you two, let's get something to drink and then order. I'm famished. Four years, by the way."

"But you saw a woman that piqued your interest?"

"As I told Portier, it was nothing like that. She stood in the doorway of the theater and her very presence awed me. That is all. I'm old, but I'm not dead."

"How sweet," Genny said as she turned her attention to the menu. "I had the roast tenderloin the last time, didn't I? I think I'll try something different, something with roux and loads of seafood. On second thought, maybe I'll have the fried chicken. I'm awfully fond of it, Richard. I attribute this luscious body of mine to my Mama's fried chicken. It's my trademark."

"Her fried chicken?"

She laughed. "No, honey, my body. My body is my trademark. Look at it. I like to say that I carry around my own Mardi Gras float."

"As attractive as that sounds," Portier said under his breath.

"Are you from here?" I asked.

21

"No, I'm originally from Mobile," Genny said with glee in her eye. "I loved it in Mobile, but I had to leave. If I was going to make a name for myself in showbiz, I had to go someplace other than lower Alabama."

"So you came here?"

"Not at first. I've been in San Francisco, Chicago, New York, you name it. I had a couple of stints here in New Orleans but thought I should be in a bigger city, so I left. I was wrong. I had to come back."

"Why is that?"

"They love me here. My friends back in Mobile said I was crazy. The crowds in San Francisco thought I was eccentric. Can you believe that? In San Francisco? Chicago said I was 'over the top', whatever that means to an entertainer dressed like a piñata. There wasn't enough work for me in New York; they said I was unemployable. But New Orleans?" Genny grinned and licked her lips flirtatiously. "New Orleans calls me wonderful! I'm always busy. I was the emcee to a beaucoup number of krewe balls this past Mardi Gras. Why, even Dorothy Lamour thought I was fabulous. She came back home to New Orleans for Carnival, you know. See these beads here? She threw them at me off a balcony at Bourbon and Bienville. I have pictures of her at Gallier Hall. Want to see them?"

"Maybe some other time," I replied. "It sounds fabulous. I'm glad you're doing well."

Genny tried to be cute and petite as she smiled, but it didn't come across well. Something about her gregarious features and the loud-patterned dress she wore was a far cry from cute and petite.

"Now tell him the truth, Genevieve," Portier said bluntly.

Genny looked at me, a pink tinge of embarrassment on her face.

22

"Tell me what?"

"Nothing," she said quickly.

"No; tell him," Portier insisted. "You might as well give him both sides."

"Very well, you old candy ass. Chuck would tell you that my life isn't all glitz and glamour. I tend to embellish."

"Not to worry. I'm not unborn as young people would say nowadays. Everyone embellishes. Besides, I suspect most of the people in this city aren't half of who they say they are anyway. Am I right?"

"How about we order some wine?" Portier said to change the subject.

"And fried chicken," I added. "I think I'll have some with you, Genny."

We ordered, and the food came to our table hot with an aroma that filled my senses and made my mouth water. More food arrived than I expected from an upscale restaurant, and it was the juiciest and most flavorful fried chicken I'd ever eaten.

"Don't be intimidated by the atmosphere in this place, Richard," Genny said. "It's perfectly acceptable to lick your fingers and wipe your face with your hands here."

"Don't you dare!" Portier exclaimed. "Perhaps in Mobile, but not at Leroux's. Don't tell him things like that, Genevieve. He'll take you up on it, and my reputation here will be tainted."

For most of the evening, we sat comfortably, ate bountifully, and listened to fine music without much conversation. We told Genny just enough about our evening at The Landalia to confirm her original thoughts about the play.

"I'm only going to say one thing," she said softly after a wing disappeared before my eyes.

"And what is that?" Portier asked.

23

"Pass the hot sauce."

"That's it?"

"No, it seems to me there's a sinister undertone behind your client's investment in this play."

I set down my fork to listen. Though on the surface Genny's life appeared irresponsible and her thoughts shallow, I respected her intuitive observations and judgments.

"Nonsense," said our host.

"Let her speak. What do you mean, Genny?"

"Doesn't it strike both of you odd? I mean, I see Chuck's client, that Reed Alemand fellow, as an independent businessman in his own right. He's wealthy, but certainly not to the degree of his business partner, this Manny guy, and his brother. Think about it. The two brothers are members of the Lyons family, one of the wealthiest families in Louisiana."

"As I mentioned to the two of you before," Portier said, "their funds are tied up while their father is missing."

Genny snorted. "Do you believe that? Can you actually sit there with a straight face and tell me those two grown men have no money of their own by their own means? Do their siblings not have any money, either? You mean to tell me that all their money is tied into their father's accounts and unattainable until he returns? No, Chuck, I think someone's spreading the apple butter too thick on your biscuit if you believe that."

My friend returned to his etouffee without comment.

"What are you suggesting?" I asked.

"Well, I'm no astute businesswoman, as Chuck will tell you, and my friends aren't exactly the most reliable when it comes to their own money, but I've learned something from them, and this cockamamie story of Chuck's client lights up the tilt sign for me. You see, Richard, the poor in this city are

24

pretty good at exploiting each other and taking advantage of those who don't know any better. I would venture to say the rich are just as good at it."

"So you think the Lyons brothers are taking advantage of Reed Alemand in some way? What motive would they have?"

"I have no idea," she replied. "It would be something we'd have to look into."

Portier set his spoon into his dish with such a clang that the people at the table next to us lifted their heads and looked our way. "There'll be no such thing," he said with authority. "Mr. Alemand knows what he's doing, I can assure you of that, and the Lyons family isn't swindling him. We will consider the matter dropped. We'll not delve into the Lyons' finances or Alemand's relationship with them. I want to hear no more of this unfortunate evening and the insinuations being derived from it, do you hear?"

Genny opened her mouth to speak.

"Do you hear?" he asked louder.

She closed her mouth wisely.

Chapter 3

My friend meant it when he said he wanted to hear no more of the prior evening's events.

The next morning, I made a brief comment that *Dickies, Stocks & Jabots* was written so poorly that the actors didn't have a snowball's chance in New Orleans to make the play a success. Not only were my comments met with silence, but Portier took his coffee and beignets into his private study and closed the door.

"Bentley," I said to the eager Labrador, "I think this will be a good time for me to take a walk. No, sorry, boy, I'd love to take you, but I can't. Your master would never forgive me if we left the house without his knowledge, and I'm afraid he's not speaking to me to ask for his permission. Some other time."

I stepped onto Ursulines Avenue with a light jacket and not a clue as to where I would walk. The street was quiet. I heard only the buzzing of traffic along Rampart. Perhaps eight o'clock was too early for the French Quarter. It wasn't too early for me, but I realized long ago that retired Midwestern ministers were on a different time table than the rest of the world.

It was fifty-two degrees when I left Portier's cottage, and those on the streets were wrapped securely in winter wear. Granted, it was the coldest fifty-two degrees I'd ever experienced combined with the humidity off the Gulf of Mexico, but it wasn't winter-clothing weather by any means.

A cup of good hot coffee was in order. I turned onto Bourbon Street to reach the Clover Grill, a favorite of mine for breakfast. The coffee was indeed hot and to my liking. I drank two cups at the counter, paid my bill, and meandered onto Dumaine towards the river.

I wondered if the young man I'd met yesterday afternoon would be at the same place on Royal Street. Although I suspected he wouldn't, I walked towards Royal just in case. Sure enough, he wasn't there. When I walked one block further towards Chartres Street, however, I saw a young man slouched against a building. I recognized him as soon as I drew close enough to see his face.

He recognized me, too, looking at me with hopeful eyes as I approached.

"Were you here all night?" I asked.

He shrugged. To his left, a jacket and an old blanket covered a metal grate over the sidewalk that emitted heat from under the street. "My place was full," he said.

"Where's your place?"

"Everywhere."

"Everywhere where?"

He hesitated to answer. "Sometimes St. Roch, sometimes the Bywater, sometimes the Marigny. Most the times Labreville."

I couldn't mask the look of sorrow on my face when I realized his first answer was the most accurate. Everywhere. I imagined home was anywhere he could find a place to stay safe and warm.

"You wanna Lucky?" he asked as a gratuitous gesture.

I noticed that his pack of cigarettes was almost empty. Even if I smoked, I wouldn't have taken one of his last Lucky Strikes. "Are you hungry?" I asked.

He looked down. I followed his gaze and saw a paper cup a quarter full of a café au lait and a sack of powdered sugar remnants from Morning Call. "Nah, I'm good, but thanks."

It seemed unlikely that a young man who slept all night on the sidewalk of Chartres Street spent his hard-earned money on Morning Call beignets and café au lait.

"You buy the beignets, or did someone buy them for you?" I asked.

"I had help. Did I see you last night?"

"Yes, I put some money in your guitar case. You were singing something really good."

He didn't look convinced.

"No, I mean it. It was good."

"I remember. Not many folks give out dollar bills."

"Do you remember what you were singing? Do you remember the name of it?"

"No, I was just playin', buddy, sorry."

The thought of someone singing something that creative while 'just playin' blew me away for a second. I wanted to ask him to play me another tune that came to his mind, but I realized his guitar wasn't with him. "Where is it?" I asked.

"Where's what?"

I strummed my hands near my chest.

"Oh, my axe. Yeah, well, I think I left it at Miss Cora's."

"Miss Cora? She a relative?"

He smiled as if it was a stupid question.

"I don't know a Miss Cora," I said, defending my question.

"First of all, she's very old. Second of all, she's very Negro, so I doubt we're related, but she lets me come over to get warm

28

and talk. She's 'bout as close as I have to someone." He looked up to meet my eyes and added, "Someone I trust."

"Does Miss Cora feed you?" I asked intent on learning more about his story.

"When she can."

"Did she give you that sack of beignets?"

He shook his head.

"Someone else you trust gave them to you?"

He nodded.

I reached into my pants' pocket and pulled out two one-dollar bills. "Here's for lunch. Get something good, okay? You can trust me, too."

"I know."

"How do you know that? You don't know me."

"You look me in the eyes. People you can't trust don't look you in the eyes."

His reply sounded genuine, coming from someone I suspected could trust very few.

I bid him well and walked a half block away before turning around to see if our conversation had a positive effect on his morning. To my surprise, he wasn't there. The young man's belongings were gone, too.

I turned onto Decatur Street toward Esplanade and walked past the iron-clad setting of the old U.S. Mint building. Several men and a few women had made temporary homes from cardboard boxes around the bushes surrounding the iron fencing. I stepped over a large man who blocked the sidewalk. He looked contorted on the concrete but snored loudly as if he didn't mind. Another man slumped over the side of a park bench, his head drooping down, his chest against the iron arms of the bench. How uncomfortable his position appeared to me, but he slept soundly as his arms reached lazily toward the sidewalk.

I didn't want to be oblivious to the individuals' plights, but under the circumstances and the time of day there seemed to be little I could do. I walked down Frenchmen past Washington Square then south again, stopping along the banks of the mighty river to watch freight and cargo barges maneuver with amazing accuracy between the river banks.

A strong breeze blew from the flowing waters of the Mississippi. I tucked my jacket closer to me, but I warmed quickly as I walked, and the jacket became more of a nuisance than a comfort.

Algiers Point, the second oldest part of the city next to the French Quarter, sat on the other side of the river. I'd heard on the train coming to New Orleans about a restaurant in Algiers I should try. If Portier ever talked to me again, I'd ask him to take me there.

Ah, yes, Portier. I remembered.

How odd about his client and the predicament he was in with the rich Lyons brothers and their small stock theater. Even odder was my friend's reaction to Genny's hypothesis that there was something deeper to the situation than a simple bad investment. Portier accepted comments poorly. In fact, he seemed to be outright offended that she would make such a suggestion.

I hoped reflecting alone in his den this morning would change his outlook on the situation and give Genny the benefit of the doubt. She didn't mean to be disrespectful. She was only trying to make sense of a perplexing situation.

I'd walked enough, I decided. The best use of my time was back at the cottage on Ursulines to make sure my friend was well and our friendship intact.

A stone footpath near the Mint building provided a small shortcut to my destination. Of course, it meant walking through the battlefield of those who'd lost their fight against consciousness the night before.

I stepped again over the large man on the sidewalk—he continued to snore—and walked again past the man slumped over the arm of the park bench. This time I stopped. A sense of something unnatural alarmed me.

"Are you okay?" I called. "Sir, I'm asking if you need help."

I straightened my posture and, being careful not to touch him, took a closer look at the old man, his belongings, and his surroundings. Only then did I notice coagulated blood on the back of his head. I looked closer at his face. His pallor was dull, pasty, and lifeless. Small, uneven gasps for air rose and fell from under his wrinkled sports coat.

The man needed help.

I spun around in a panic, looking for someone—anyone—to tell me where I could find the nearest phone.

Tourists ignored my pleas as they walked past, and I realized that waiting for assistance was going to be futile. I ran into a small shop across the street that hadn't opened for the day, but was preparing to do so. The shopkeeper gave me a dirty look when I requested him to call for an ambulance. Something in the look of his eyes told me he knew why I was there. He knew the ambulance was for someone across the street, but he didn't care. He had probably seen the old man slumped on the bench all morning, but did nothing.

"Do it anyway," I said.

He picked up the receiver next to his cash register and dialed a number he'd memorized.

I ran out of the store and back across the street to the man. He hadn't moved and was still breathing, but his breaths were shallow and raspy. His throat gurgled.

"Hold on, sir," I pleaded. "I have help coming. Hold on. Just a little longer."

I could do nothing more than talk to keep him alive until help arrived. I said a prayer and looked to the Heavens, knowing that the Holy Spirit didn't mind being on a dirty, cracked street among the uncaring. I pleaded, prayed again, then turned to the man and told him to hold on a little longer.

I sensed someone standing behind me. Someone had actually stopped—maybe to help. I glanced behind me.

"You a preacher?" the woman asked.

I ignored the question.

"You sound like one."

"Do you know him?" I asked.

"Why the hell would I know him?"

"I'm just asking. Will you go for help? That store across the street. Ask the storekeeper if help is coming. Hurry, please."

She remained standing behind me, immobile and unwilling. Instead of assisting, she walked beside the bench, reached under the hedge, and pulled something out.

"What is it?" I asked.

She ignored me.

"It could be important. What is it?"

"It's none of your business, that's what it is."

I gave her a dirty look and turned back to the man. I was about to tell him to hold on again when I felt a knot in my throat I couldn't swallow. I couldn't tell him to hold on any longer.

"What are you doing?" she asked.

I didn't know. Instead of words of encouragement, I leaned closer and whispered, "Do you see Him?" Of course, no response and no reaction came from the old man. "It's okay, you know; I mean, if you do."

"What's okay?" the woman asked. "What are you talking about?"

"You can hold on if you want to, buddy, but it's okay to let go. It's not mine to say. It's your life. All I'm saying is that if you're ready to go, if you see the Lord's hand, it's okay to take it because God loves you. God wants to take you home where you belong."

The woman drew nearer. I took a deep breath.

Another person stopped to see what was going on. "What's he doing?" they asked.

"Shush. He's a preacherman."

I waited, but the old man continued to breathe slowly. "You may want to take His hand," I said. "You may want it more than anything else in the world right now, but you're not sure. You may have regrets about your life, about what you've done, about what you didn't do, about what God might think, and about what He'll do to you when you meet Him face to face, but you don't have to worry about that. All of that has been taken care of for you. He's paid the price. All you have to do is believe you're forgiven and take His hand. It's all by grace. It's really okay. Nothing else matters anymore. The only thing that matters is that you're holding His hand, and He's going to take you home."

Suddenly, everything that surrounded us became peaceful and timeless.

I'd seen death many times and had been around those seriously ill when they died. This experience was no different.

The man slumped farther over the park bench. He took his last breath and entered eternity with a cleansed heart.

"You killed him," the woman said.

Closing my eyes didn't make her disappear.

"What did you say to him?"

I turned and gave her a dirty look. It took every ounce of diplomacy within me not to call out her ignorance and lack of compassion. I glared at her and noticed the sound of rushing water behind me.

Having passed away, nothing constrained the man's bodily functions. He peed heavily through the slats of the bench onto the pavement below. Instinctively, I grabbed his backpack and pulled it aside so it wouldn't get wet. I didn't have to rummage through his things to find something that caught my eye.

"What is it?" the woman asked. "What are you looking at?"

A playbill, rolled in a tubular fashion, was stuffed into a side pocket of the backpack. I immediately recognized the yellow and black, art-deco cover with the name of the play printed in bold Broadway lettering. *Dickies, Stocks, and Jabots.* The words, *A Lyons and Alemand Play* sat below the title

How curiously odd, I thought to myself, that a man such as this might have been at the same play that my best friend and I had attended the night before.

Did I recognize him?

I looked closely. Blood had matted his hair and dripped across a part of his face, hiding his most distinguishable features. I wasn't sure if he'd been at the same theater or just happened to pick up the playbill along the street that someone had carelessly dropped.

I slipped the playbill back into a side pocket of his backpack and stepped from the body in time to see a white,

34

late-model ambulance appear from around a building on Esplanade and roll to where I stood on Decatur.

The paramedics, dressed in white, walked to the old man and made a quick assessment. There was no sense of urgency or alarm, not because they didn't care, but because there was nothing to be done.

A policeman spotted the woman and me, standing off to the side.

"Are you the one who called in?" he asked me.

"Yes, sir."

"Do you know him?"

"No."

"What happened?"

"He killed him," the woman blurted out.

The officer gave her a side glance before turning his focus back to me for a response.

"He died as I was talking to him," I explained.

The woman stepped closer, but the patrolman intercepted and requested that she step away.

When she was out of earshot, I said, "I'm a retired minister. I tried to encourage the man to hold on. I could see he was injured badly, and I've been with the dying long enough to know when encouragement is not what the person needs—or wants."

"What did you do?"

"I gave him the Gospel. He must have welcomed it because he went home almost immediately."

"Home?"

"Heaven, officer."

He raised his eyebrows briefly. "What's your name?"

"Richard Fountain."

"You're from out of town?"

"Yes."

"Visiting?"

"Yes. I have a friend who lives here in the Quarter. I'm visiting for just a few days."

"How did you come here?"

"You mean to this spot where the man was?"

He nodded.

"I was coming back from a walk along the river when I spotted this man and that other man asleep on the sidewalk. I figured the man on the sidewalk was okay, but the man here on the bench—well, something was peculiar about him. He was slumped unnaturally over the side of the bench."

"That's it?"

"He had a gash on the back of his head by the looks of it."

"Or he fell," the officer offered.

"Yes, he could have fallen," I replied, "but he didn't. You'll notice his backpack has been rummaged through as if he was robbed."

"Anything else?"

"Not that I can think of."

"If you wouldn't mind, put your name and the address where you're staying on this report." He handed me the piece of paper. "Sign at the bottom, please."

I scanned what he'd written and asked, "Is that all you need?"

"For now. We'll do an investigation. Was that woman with you the whole time you were talking with him?"

I turned to look where the woman was standing. She was talking indiscriminately to anyone on the street who would listen to her story.

"She was never with me, officer," I replied. "I don't know her, and I wouldn't put much credence into her witness testimony. I didn't kill the man."

The officer thanked me again after I returned the report to him. He left and walked toward the woman who continued to talk like a celebrity.

I looked at the man who was being lifted off the bench and onto a stretcher. His pale, contorted face was more vivid now. He didn't fall, I was certain of it, but it was not mine to determine what did happen. Still, simply doing my civic duty wasn't very satisfying, and I turned away with an empty feeling in my gut.

Rather than walk through the crowd that had gathered, I turned back the way I'd come along the iron-clad fence edged by bushes. I hadn't walked far when something shiny caught the corner of my eye. There, amongst broken glass, rotting oak leaves, and a few stray strands of faded Chinese beads was a silver object. I reached down and grasped the find in my hand.

My heart raced.

An ornate, silver panther, ready to pounce upon its prey, glared back at me. I recognized it as the finial from the walking stick of the scraggly man at the theater the night before. Where the finial was, surely the mahogany cane was nearby. However, eager to tell the officer of my find, I didn't look for it. I walked to where he'd finished his interview with the woman who'd stood next to me as the man died.

"Excuse me," I said.

He looked at me, but said nothing.

"I think it wouldn't hurt if you checked the bushes along the walk close to where he died." I pointed to the exact location.

He looked at me as if to say he knew how to do his job, but asked instead, "Why's that?"

"It looks like there's been a commotion near the bushes. It could have been where he was assaulted and robbed."

The officer looked at me skeptically before saying, "That woman says you went through his things."

"What?"

"She says you pulled his backpack from under the bench and pulled something out of it."

"I could say the same of her. She pulled something out of the hedge."

"I'm asking *you*. Did you pull something from his backpack?"

"Yes, sir, I did."

"Do you mind telling me what it was?"

"Not at all. It was a playbill. After the man died, he began to urinate on the sidewalk. I moved the backpack out of the way so it wouldn't get wet. In so doing, I saw a playbill rolled up in a side pocket of the pack. I pulled it out to look at it."

"For what purpose?"

"Because I'd been to the exact, same play the night before. It was a strange coincidence that we could've been in the same building less than twenty-four hours ago."

"That's all you took?"

"I didn't take it. I just looked at it."

"Then you put it back?"

"Why, yes, sir. After my curiosity was satisfied, I slipped the playbill back into the side pocket. Why? What did she say I did with it? Other than the playbill, I didn't touch anything else in the backpack."

He looked down at my hand. "What's that?"

38

I looked down. I was still clutching the silver finial. I lifted it so he could get a good look at it before I placed it in my coat pocket.

"It's mine," I replied. "I had it here in my coat. I don't know why I pulled it out."

"What is it?"

"A finial."

"To what?"

"A walking stick."

The officer hesitated as he studied my face.

I hoped he was pondering whether someone like me or someone like the dead man was more inclined to carry a walking stick with an ornate silver finial of a panther. Suddenly, he nodded as if he bought my story.

I sighed with relief. I should have felt guilty, but I didn't. There wasn't an ounce of remorse in me from telling the fabricated story or for taking the finial from out of the debris. There should have been. Every bit of my teaching in the church, every sermon I'd ever delivered admonished what I'd done, but I decided justice would be better served at my own hands. I didn't doubt that the police's investigation would be of little substantive value. After all, the unfortunate man was poor, neglected, and homeless. The finial would be of no use to them. For me, however, I hoped it was everything I needed to bring closure to the old man's life.

The officer returned to the ambulance, and I turned to continue back to Portier's.

Just then, a young man raced toward the attendants who were placing the man's body into the ambulance. "Mr. Montgomery!" he yelled. "Mr. Montgomery!"

The officer stopped him before he could go any further.

My God! I said under my breath. I raced toward the officer and the young man who I recognized as the boy who sang and collected coins along the street. I grasped the youngster by the arm and placed my hand on his shoulder. He was arguing profusely with the policeman about approaching the emergency vehicle, wanting to see who was inside. "Stop!" I said to the boy. "Please!"

He looked at me wildly. "Is it Mr. Montgomery?"

I turned to the officer and apologized, assuring him I would take care of the young man. He appeared relieved when I steered the boy away from the ambulance so that he could finish his routine. We moved to a secluded spot on the sidewalk.

"Was he Mr. Montgomery?" he asked again. "Someone said he was. Someone said he was dead."

"Wait. First, tell me your name, then we'll talk about Mr. Montgomery."

He frowned, as if his name were immaterial or insignificant.

I reiterated that I needed to know.

"Donnie," he mumbled eventually.

"Is that your real name or a cover-up?"

"Real."

"Okay, good. Let's calm down now. Here, sit on this ledge for a sec."

"No, I just need—"

"You need to sit down."

He did so, but I looked at the crowd of people who gathered around the scene even after the ambulance and police had pulled away and realized that the ledge wasn't the best place to calm anyone down, let alone to obtain meaningful information.

"Come on," I said. "Let's get a real breakfast in your belly."

We found a corner table in a small café nearby. Only two other patrons were seated. We sat away from them.

"Ham, eggs, crispy bacon," I told the waitress. "Grits, toast, lots of coffee, and some home fries. Yes, for both of us, please. One check." She left, and I leaned toward the young man. "Now, Donnie, tell me about this Mr. Montgomery of yours?"

He looked up, and for the first time, he seemed irritated at my impertinence.

"What's the matter?"

"He's not *mine*."

"Just a figure of speech."

"He was everyone's friend."

"Okay, everyone who?"

"Everyone in Labreville."

"Labreville. Where's that?"

Donnie took a deep breath and exhaled. I could tell he was exasperated by my invasive questions, but I wanted to know as much as I could. He started to answer but stopped when the waitress sat two cups of coffee and cream on the table in front of us. Although she didn't care what we were talking about, the young singer wouldn't speak in front of her.

"Look," I said. "I'm not asking these things to pry into your life or into the lives of your friends. Okay? But I may have seen or know of this Mr. Montgomery myself. Something bad happened to him, and it isn't right that a crime against him should go unpunished."

"What's it got to do with me?"

"For some reason, out of fate or destiny, I met you last night, and I don't think it was any small coincidence that I did

41

because you know this man, too. You know him better than I do. You're my only link to this man."

He sipped his coffee and stared blankly at the black and white speckles mixed into the gray Formica tabletop.

"Help me find out what happened to him," I pleaded.

Donnie's face twitched. "Labreville's in the St. Roch area, not far off Elysian Fields and St. Claude."

"Okay, I know where that's at."

"Farther lakeside, though. Down near Urquhart."

"Did he live there with all of you?"

He shook his head, ensuring that his eyes didn't meet mine. "He had his own place, I think."

"A place?"

"Yeah, his own place. Not far away, but not with us."

"Like a shotgun house or something?"

"I don't know," he replied, getting irritated again. "He never took us there. He came to us. He always came to us. He helped us. He seemed to know what we needed, and he helped us. Food, blankets. One time he gave me a toothbrush, said I needed to smile more."

"A good guy, then."

"He was okay."

"Sounds more than okay."

"Some neighbors didn't like him helping us, 'specially when he came with blankets and food."

"I don't understand. Why's that?"

"I dunno. They wanted us to move on, I guess. They didn't want us to stay in the neighborhood. They treated us like stray cats and thought if he fed us we'd just hang around and wait for the next time he came."

"Did you?"

"Some did, some didn't. I never did. I always sang in the Quarter for some money. I could sing and play the guitar. Some of them didn't have that."

The waitress interrupted Donnie's story to set down the plates and bowls of food that I'd ordered. She started to walk away.

"Ma'am."

She turned abruptly.

"Ketchup?"

She looked at me as if I had three heads.

"I'm a Hoosier. I need ketchup."

She left, and I bowed my head to say grace. Donnie dug into the food immediately and didn't stop eating even when I asked him to continue with his story.

"Not much more to say," he replied with his mouth full.

"Oh, I think there is. Tell me about Mr. Montgomery as a person."

He shook his head.

"Why not?"

"Nothin' to tell."

"Didn't you get to know him?"

"Sure, but, you know you older Clydes."

I frowned. "No, tell me."

"You old guys, you keep things pretty close to yourself. Y'all are private. You don't let things out, and it's hard to get to know you."

"We're kind of bad in that way, I'll agree. So Mr. Montgomery was like that?"

Donnie suddenly stopped eating and looked off to the side.

I turned to see who or what was there, but I didn't see anybody or anything. It was just a window to the outside. Nothing else.

"What is it?"

"Nothing."

"I think it is."

"It's just, well, it's just, that woman, you know, that woman that was there with you and Mr. Montgomery."

"You mean the one that talked with the police after I did?"

Donnie nodded. "She was outside there, lookin' in through the window."

"Was she looking at us?"

"Dunno."

I didn't believe him. I think he did know.

He looked into my eyes and must've seen my apprehension because he said, "I don't think she could see inside that good. She went on."

"Don't worry about her. She's nothing," I said. "Tell me more about what you were saying of Mr. Montgomery. He kept his life private?"

"Yeah, but somethin' was botherin' him. He never talked about it, but I don't think he could hide the fact that something wasn't right. He still did nice things and all, but lately he was quiet, distant, short with us sometimes. He'd help us then leave; didn't stick around to shoot the breeze like he always did."

"Was he the one who brought you coffee and beignets this morning?"

"Yeah, he was that way. He knew where I hung out. He dropped it off, but he didn't stop to talk. He didn't say two words to me this morning. That's not like him. He acted like he had to go. He had to keep movin'."

"Was he being followed?"

"That's what I thought. I looked down the sidewalk when he left, but I didn't see anyone. That's how he acted, though. It was like he was tryin' to get away."

"What time was this?"

"Early. Still dark."

"Was he carrying anything when he dropped off the food?"

"You mean like that backpack he carries?"

"Yeah, exactly."

"Yeah, he had it with him."

"How about a stick? Did he have a walking stick?"

Donnie smiled.

"Is that a yes?"

"Yeah. He always had that walking stick with him."

"How did you hear about Mr. Montgomery being on the park bench?"

"I dunno." He appeared bewildered. "Someone I know from the clubs, I think. I get names confused. Memphis told me. Her name is Memphis. I reckon that's where she's from. That's all I know her as."

"Where was this?"

"On St. Peter. That's where I was when I found out. There were three of us."

"Then what happened?"

"I ran here. I had to see for myself."

"What about the other two?"

"I dunno. They ran back into the Bywater, I guess. What does it matter? Are you writing a book? What about Mr. Montgomery?"

"Your friend was right, Donnie, I'm sorry. Mr. Montgomery didn't make it."

The young man set his fork down and stared out the window.

"You have to go to the police," I said.

"Why?"

"Because what you just told me could be important. You said he acted as if he was being followed, as if his life was in danger."

"I don't know that. I'm just sayin' that's what it looked like."

"I know, but it might light a fire under the detective to look into it. Otherwise, I'm not sure anyone is going to care."

He looked towards the window again. An intensity radiated from his eyes.

I looked, too, but saw nothing.

He wiped his chin with the back of his hand and looked down at the floor as if he was counting steps to the quickest way out.

"Don't go," I said. "Please."

"I'm not. I just—I just gotta go to the john."

I took a deep breath. I didn't want him to get away from the table, but I couldn't keep him from going to the bathroom. I nodded for him to go.

He pulled his chair back and rose slowly. Just as I feared, he ignored the sign pointing to the restroom. Instead, Donnie bolted out of the front entrance like a gazelle being hunted.

Chapter 4

"Where the hell have you been?" Portier demanded as soon as I stepped through the doorway of his cottage.

I received a good five-minute lecture from him, but I listened to very little of it. "I'll remind you that you were the one that gave *me* the cold shoulder, Portier. You shut me out of your den and ate your breakfast in private. That wasn't a sign that you were ready to play together on the monkey bars, so please save your disagreeable comments for Genny. She handles them better than I do. Besides, you're not the only one who's had a rough morning."

My friend simmered down as Bentley crept sheepishly toward him for a pat on the head and reassurance our argument was over.

"What's wrong? Not a good walk?" he asked.

I assumed it was his attempt at making amends. "Not one of my better ones, no."

"Do you want to tell me about it, or shall I guess?"

"Oh, please, be my guest," I responded sarcastically. "If you guess it correctly, I'll buy your dinner."

"Very well. I don't suppose that commotion on Decatur Street near the old Mint building had anything to do with *you*, did it?"

"How did you know about that?"

"Who didn't? I was the last to find out. When you hadn't returned, I stepped out onto the front stoop, debating whether to go looking for you when Genevieve came out of her cottage at the same time. She asked me if I'd heard what was going on. Normally, an ambulance taking a drunk away is no big news in the Quarter, but her friend said this time it was. The situation was different."

"Genny received a call? That's interesting, that someone would call her."

"She has a number of friends. They know each other and look out for each other; apparently someone died this time, and they called to make sure it wasn't someone they knew."

"I see. Well, I'll admit that I was at the center of the commotion you heard about."

"Someone died?"

"Someone did."

"And you were involved?"

"I was there. If you listen to a certain woman who stood behind me as it happened, she'll tell you I was the one who killed him."

"Good God, Fountain."

"I only found him, though. He was practically dead. I just talked to him a bit. He died peacefully."

"Good, I mean good that he died peacefully."

"But he died from a violent injury."

"Murder?"

"I seem to be the only one who thinks so."

"Say no more," Portier said, standing. "I'm not sure I can listen to anymore without a good, stiff drink."

"It's too early for that."

"You forget what city you're in. Time is well on its way to one o'clock in the afternoon. We're behind schedule. Come. I could use a Sazerac."

As if Bentley understood every word his master said, the Lab stood, raring to go.

"Not this time, either, Ben," I said, remembering that I had already turned the pup down for a walk.

"No, let him come," Portier said. "He could use some fresh air."

We walked a few blocks to a small pub with wide doors that opened to a lavish wood bar. Bistro tables adorned the outside of the pub where a man reading a newspaper sat.

"Inside or out?"

"It's a little chilly," I said.

"Sixty some degrees. It's warmed up nicely. There are people out."

"They must be from Minnesota."

"Nonsense. We'll sit in the sun. It'll give Bentley more room."

I obliged and sat at a table next to the man reading the paper so that Portier and Bentley could have space on the other side. We ordered two Sazeracs, and my friend handed Bentley a couple of dog biscuits to bide his time.

"You say it was murder?" he asked me.

"I believe it was, yes."

"What did the police say?"

"Well, you know the police. Even if they agree with you, they're not going to show their hand because they don't know who they're talking to. I mean, for all the officer knew, I could have been the murderer."

"Do you think they'll investigate?"

I shook my head.

49

"Good," he said emphatically.

"Good? How can you say that?"

"You don't need a murder while you're here, Fountain. You're here to relax."

"It's a little too late for that."

"Besides, you don't want to get involved in this town. Trust me, you don't."

"I don't believe you. I don't believe New Orleans is like that."

"I don't care what you believe. You're not from here. Contrary to what you said last night at dinner, you *are* unborn. You haven't lived here like I have. You have to trust me."

"I have to follow my moral conscience, Portier."

At that, I reached into my side pocket and pulled out the silver finial. I took a napkin and wiped spots off the panther that kept it from gleaming as it should. Then I set it on the table in front of my friend for him to see.

"What's this?"

"The reason I can't take your advice."

"No, I'm asking you seriously. What is this?"

"You don't recognize it, do you? Didn't you see it last night? It's a finial from a mahogany walking stick I believe a gentleman we saw at The Landalia had in his possession as we exited the theater at intermission."

"How did you get it?"

I didn't answer. I was hoping his focus would be on the man at the theater.

"You took it," he said accusingly. "When? This morning? Don't tell me it belonged to the dead man. Oh, my god, Fountain, don't tell me you took a dead man's walking stick."

I looked to my left at the man reading the newspaper to see if he was listening. He was seemingly engrossed on the

50

front page of his paper. "Would you keep your voice down?" I requested.

"What if it's the murder weapon?"

"I only found the finial. I didn't see the cane to know if it was. Don't you recognize it?"

"I wouldn't tell you if I did. I don't want to be an accomplice."

"It's nothing like that, Portier. Seriously, I need you to remember. Last night, there was a man you thought you recognized. Remember the man?"

"I don't know."

"Yes, you do. The man in front of you. He had a scraggly, unkempt beard, wrinkled suit. He was well mannered, but out of place. That man."

"Yes, of course I remember. Get to the point."

"Do you remember where you recognized him from?"

"No, I've long put that man out of my head. I've no idea, and I certainly can't remember before my drink."

On cue, a young woman with long, flowing hair brought our two cocktails and set them on the table. She also set a bowl of water on the sidewalk for the pup.

"Cheers, my good man," Portier offered. "We need something of good cheer during this visit of yours."

"If you could only remember," I said, "that would be a start."

"I can't. Besides, why is it so important?"

"A person's life was snuffed out this morning. It's important to me. I don't care what he looked like or how he smelled. He died before my eyes, and I can't rest."

A long lull in the conversation ensued. Portier studied me carefully. I could see the wheels turning in his head; so much so, he didn't even touch his drink. I glanced back periodically, hoping his expression would change, but it didn't. I knew what he was thinking. I wished he wouldn't speak of it out loud, but he did.

"This is beyond a quest for human justice, isn't it?" he asked. "There's someone else involved. You want to make amends."

I wanted to disagree, but I couldn't.

"Whoever it is you're wanting to protect, Fountain, you can't, just like you couldn't protect that boy back in Indiana."

"I could've tried harder. I should've asked more questions."

"It wasn't your place to ask questions."

"Why? Because it wasn't appropriate to question foster parents on the care they were giving? Because it wasn't my place to put my nose where it didn't belong? Is that what you're going to say?"

"No, because it wouldn't have done any good. Toby Markle was a lost soul in a system that didn't care about him. There's nothing you could've done."

"And I'm to accept that? I'm to go on with my life oblivious to the suffering around me, masquerading my compassion with an air of *que sera sera*?"

Portier's eyes softened and the creases around his lips diminished.

"I've been in New Orleans less than twenty-four hours," I added. "I've met some individuals who've crossed my path more than once who are interconnected that should otherwise not know each other at all. I don't take interpersonal connections like that lightly, and when one of these individuals dies in front of my eyes, I take it even more seriously. Quite to my surprise then, a young man who I met on the streets runs up and seems to know the man as well. It's not coincidence, Portier, and it's my personal duty to get to the bottom of this

52

matter. I should've asked more questions about Toby Markle, and, by damned, I should ask more questions now." I sat back in my chair and took a deep breath. "Pardon my French, by the way."

"Who is this young man?" Portier asked.

"I met him yesterday afternoon as I walked through the Quarter to your home. He's a singer. He had a nice voice, and I was taken in. I saw him first on Royal Street and then again today on Chartres."

"He was panning for money?"

"Yes, I guess you could say that."

"There you go. That's your answer. That's why you were taken in. That's how they scrape their living together. It wasn't a divine awakening you had, Fountain, or Toby Markle coming back to haunt you. That kid saw a sucker coming down the street. He made you feel sorry for him, and you were taken in."

I was ready to counteract and opened my mouth to spout my rebuttal, but Bentley started barking at a middle-aged man walking on the sidewalk. There was nothing striking about the gentleman, and no apparent reason for Bentley to bark. The man simply walked with hands in his pockets, eyes focused ahead towards his destination.

My friend grabbed his dog's leash to pull back on the animal's aggressive stance. "Whoa, boy, sit! Sit, Ben, sit!"

Bentley would have nothing of it.

The man continued his trek along the sidewalk while the loyal pup barked incessantly until he passed, letting the man know he was not welcome, and he was not to return.

Portier patted the dog's ruffled hairs and calmed him into a sitting position.

Bentley looked at his master, hoping for a word of praise, but resumed his recumbent position on the sidewalk when the pats on his back were his only reward.

"Did you see that?" my friend asked.

"What in the world got into him?"

Portier peered at me with conviction. "That man was a bad apple."

"Bad apple?" I asked, surprised and bewildered. "He was an ordinary person. He was just minding his own business, walking down the street."

"No, dogs are intuitive. They know bad character just by the scent of a person. That person may have appeared to be unassuming, but dogs know a bad apple when they come across one. I'm convinced of it."

I shook my head, not because I didn't believe him, but because Bentley's behavior was so sudden and aggressive that I was startled and couldn't believe what I'd just seen.

"You need to be more like Bentley," my friend said. "If you had a similar instinct, you wouldn't be taken in by people on the streets. More importantly, you wouldn't be in this predicament with a dead man."

I ignored his comment by watching the man sitting at the table beside us. He got up from his seat, put some coins beside his paper, and walked away.

Bentley disregarded him.

"A good apple?" I asked of the man who left.

"Just not a bad one," he replied. "Dogs are much better than pastors about their intuition of people, I can assure you."

"Is that an opinion about this Donnie kid?" I asked.

"Donnie is his name? You're on a first name basis, are you?"

"His name is Donnie, yes, but I'm not about to debate you on his character. There was something about him, Portier.

There was just something about him. It's a connection of sorts."

"To Toby Markle?"

I ignored the question.

"I suppose you gave him money."

"That's my business if I did."

"So you trust him—just like that?"

"I didn't say there was a trust. I said there was a connection."

"Ah, a connection. That's one way to spin it."

I told Portier I wasn't spinning anything. Trust had nothing to do with giving money to someone in need.

"Do I dare ask what you have up your sleeve now?" he asked.

I stood to go. What I wanted to do was to knock on the door of Genny's cottage to see if she was home. I hoped she could tell me what her friend called her about this morning, and if she had any additional information that she could share with me.

"Sit down," he implored. "Finish your drink first. It takes hours for Genevieve to make her hair that big, and then she has to decide how many bangles she's going to wear. You've got time to finish your drink."

I agreed. There was no use rushing a long shot.

As I pulled out my chair to reseat myself, I looked at the table next to us where the man had abandoned his *Times-Picayune.* The newspaper was folded into quarters. The portion of the front page that was visible from where I stood had a photograph of a man. I picked up the paper and allowed it to unfold on its own, revealing a bold headline of a Louisianan socialite, missing for months. I sat down and studied the photo. The ashen pastiness of my face must have alarmed Portier.

"What is it?" he asked.

I tossed the paper over our tabletop so that both of us could see. "Wasn't that him?" I asked, pointing directly to the photo. "The man from last night?"

Portier didn't answer.

"At the theater," I said impatiently.

"Stop. I know what you're talking about. Let me think."

"There's hardly anything to think about, Portier. That's him!"

My friend didn't disagree. He sat back in his chair and lifted his drink slowly to his lips. "I can't say for sure."

"What do you mean you can't say? Portier, it's as plain as day."

"That's an old photo. It's such a stretch."

Yes, I had to agree it was a stretch that the man we saw at The Landalia the night before was the man in the *Times-Picayune* being touted as missing. The likeness, however, was indisputable to me. "That's why you recognized him at The Landalia," I said. "He's that missing magnate you talked about last night at dinner."

"No, listen," he responded. "That couldn't be Roger Lyons. It makes no sense."

"Of course it doesn't. That's why you didn't recognize him. You didn't expect to see him at a cut-rate stock theater, looking like a cut-rate gentleman. That's why it didn't register."

"It just can't be him. It still makes no sense."

I scanned the article to find out more about the socialite who was missing. His whereabouts were unknown to his family, I read. They were searching everywhere between Houston and New Orleans to no avail. I turned the page to read more about the family, who was involved, and the business activities in which the family had interests.

The end of the article displayed another photo of Roger Lyons, dressed in coattails and a top hat, at a charity gala in his hometown of Lafayette, Louisiana. It was the last-known photograph of the magnate before he went missing.

I studied the photograph carefully. It wasn't his apparel that caught my eye. It wasn't his gray, manicured hair or the distinguishable features of his face that captured my attention. What gave me goosebumps was an ornate silver finial on top of a mahogany walking stick that he carried in his hand. I recognized the panther immediately.

Chapter 5

Portier tried to argue with me again.

"No," I said with conviction. "I'm sorry, but this is him. This is the man who died on the park bench this morning!" I was so anxious that my voice almost squeaked as I uttered the words.

Bentley listened to my fragmented voice, tilting his head from side to side with bewilderment.

"We're being hasty," Portier said, trying to be rational. "Calm down. Let's think this through. It makes no sense."

"It makes perfect sense," I said. "This is where he's been hiding—in New Orleans."

"As a derelict, sleeping on a park bench, carrying a simple duffle bag, and getting clobbered by an unknown assailant? Now I know you've lost your mind."

"I agree, it doesn't make sense on the surface, and I don't have the answers yet, but it's possible. Just think. If you're someone who wants to be lost even for a little while, where can you go where no one will find you? Where can you go in this world where no one even wants to look for you?"

Portier sipped his drink, but remained silent.

"You become homeless, living in smelly, dilapidated, rat-infested boxes," I said. "No family like the Lyons family is going to search in those box and tent communities even if they suspect that's where he is. You must agree with that."

"Yes, I would agree, but I don't agree that he'd purposely and consciously make a decision to do that on his own. No one chooses to be homeless. Why would someone do such a thing?"

I stopped to think. "I guess that's the real mystery."

Portier huffed as he drank the rest of his cocktail. "Have you finished yours? I'm ready to go."

"I don't want it. I want to keep my wits about me. I think we're onto something."

My friend grabbed Bentley's leash in his hands and looked at me with an angered expression. "No, you get this straight. We're not onto anything. I, particularly, am staying out of it. I suggest you do the same for your own good." He stood, and, with a one-syllable command to Bentley, set off down the street before I had a chance to get up and follow.

I folded the newspaper and tucked it securely under my arm. I didn't want to lose the picture of Roger Lyons who I knew to be Mr. Montgomery, and I certainly didn't want to lose the evidence I had of Mr. Montgomery holding his ornate mahogany walking stick.

I watched Portier march towards Ursulines with his loyal companion leading the way while I decided what I should do. My friend was right. Talking to Genny about her call this morning would be fruitless. No, I wanted to be more direct. I wanted to get results and have some closure to the traumatic event that had happened to me.

I walked the short distance to the French Quarter-Marigny Triangle District office of the New Orleans Police Department. The door to the block and brick building was heavy to open. One would think being in the thick of the French Quarter that the District office would be buzzing with rowdy drunks and officers trying to calm the chaos, but it was quite the opposite.

The hall was quiet. My shoes clacked against the linoleum and echoed off the tiled walls. I thought someone would emerge from an adjacent office to determine what the noise was all about, but I continued to walk undetected until I found a counter with an officer sitting dutifully on the other side up to his neck in reports and loose-leaf papers.

"May I help you?" he asked.

"Yes. My name is Reverend Richard Fountain." I decided to add "Reverend" for credibility, but the look of the officer's face gave me no indication that it helped. "I was on Decatur Street this morning near the U.S. Mint Building and—"

The phone rang.

"Hold on," the officer said, lifting a finger for patience.

He picked up the receiver, replied in one-syllable words to what the person on the other end wanted to know, then hung up abruptly. "Now what? You were on Decatur?"

"Yes, sir, and I came across a gentleman on a park bench who passed away. A report was written by an officer this morning as the ambulance took him to a hospital or to the morgue somewhere. I was wondering—"

"Somebody died and you want to report it?"

"No, it's already been reported. I would like to speak with the detective assigned to the case."

The officer pursed his lips and turned in his seat. "Hey, Dominic, you hear about a stiff over on Decatur this morning?"

I couldn't hear the answer.

"What's going on with it?"

More muffled words from the male voice I couldn't hear.

"Yeah, who? Ahh, okay, gotcha." The officer behind the counter turned to face me. "That would be Detective Robicheaux."

60

"May I see him?"

"I'll ring, but he hasn't been answering."

"Is he not in?"

"I said he hasn't been answering. He may be in. He's not answering." The officer lifted his hands as if they were tied. "I'll try again."

"Thank you," I said as he did so.

He hung up quickly. "He's not answering."

I exuded a grunt loud enough for him to hear. "Is there a possibility to leave a message? It's important. A man is dead."

The officer gave me a sarcastic look as if they'd never seen a dead person in New Orleans before and he'd get right on it. He must have seen the disgruntled look on my face because he said, "Look, I saw the report when it came in this morning. Looked pretty cut and dry to me. It was a case of an accidental fall, resulting in trauma to the head."

"Are we talking about the same case?"

"The stiff on Decatur?"

"Yes, sir."

"He was dead before help could arrive."

"No, I was there when he died. He was alive when I found him, and he died later. I'm not mistaken."

"Sorry. Don't know what to tell ya."

"Officer, his wound didn't look like a fall. He'd been bludgeoned."

"You have new evidence?"

"What?"

"New evidence or information that would confirm that?"

"No."

"Then I'm not sure what more can be done. Detective Robicheaux will look into it."

"Is there a Detective Robicheaux?"

The officer looked into my eyes to see if I was trying to be a smart aleck. I changed my expression immediately to look like a concerned citizen.

"Look, Reverend, sir," he replied, "Robicheaux's a good guy. I'm sure if there's anything to the man's death, he'll look into it promptly and thoroughly."

I nodded and thanked the officer, then left the building with an empty feeling that Mr. Montgomery's report was going to fall deeper and deeper into a pile of paperwork on Detective Robicheaux's desk—if it even got there.

~

The next morning, I awoke early. I made a cup of chicory and sat on the back terrace as the sun snuck through the leaves of the satsuma tree that sat on Portier's boundary with Genny's property. The day felt chilly, but not uncomfortable. I read my devotions and studied a few verses from *Ephesians*.

Portier soon joined me. He seemed in a much better frame of mind than the morning before, and I invited him to sit with me.

Bentley followed close behind, yawning. The Labrador plopped down beside me, grunting as his tired body hit the paving stones.

"It's a new day, Fountain," Portier announced. "I should think today will be much brighter than yesterday. What shall we do to start it off? I won't have you taking any more walks in the Quarter if that's what you're thinking."

"You won't need to," I announced. "I have a full day planned."

Portier sipped on his coffee and pretended not to be intrigued.

I returned to my devotion book.

62

"Doing what?" he finally asked.

I looked at him apologetically and said, "I'd rather not say. I doubt you'd approve very much."

"Dear Heavens, you've signed with Arthur Murray to learn the rumba."

I laughed. "No, much worse, I'm afraid."

"Then it must have something to do with Roger Lyons' disappearance."

"I plan to go to Lafayette."

"Lafayette's a good two to three hours by car."

"I'm well aware of that."

"For what purpose?"

"I have an invitation to the Lyons' home."

Portier nearly dropped his cup of hot coffee into his lap. "Say that again?"

"I was invited."

"No, tell me the part where you explain what the hell you're going to do at the Lyons' estate?"

"Convince them to come to New Orleans to identify the body of Mr. Montgomery."

"They invited you to talk with them about a dead body? Seriously?"

"I gave the Lyons estate a call yesterday evening without your knowledge. Their butler wouldn't hear me out, but I was able to talk to a kind young woman by the name of Angelle. I believe she said her last name was Lyons. Not sure exactly. I was more concerned about getting my foot in the door."

"You talked to Roger Lyons' youngest daughter?"

"Apparently. I told her what I had to say, that I believe I had met her father, that he was living in New Orleans, but I was sorry to have to tell her that he'd passed away."

"Are you out of your mind?"

"Not at all. The police aren't going to tell them. Somebody has to."

"You don't even know if it's him."

"I most certainly do. I have his finial."

"That damn finial proves nothing. Did she ask you any questions? Did she verify your credibility?"

"She asked a few questions."

"I dare say she didn't ask enough. You can't go, Fountain. You simply can't go."

"And why not?"

"I won't allow you to make a fool of yourself."

"I'm fairly astute on matters of social etiquette, Portier. I'll do fine in their presence."

"I'm not talking about social graces, you dimwit. I'm talking about what you're going to say to them and what you're going to ask them to do."

"I'll worry about that when I get there."

"Is Miss Angelle the only member of the Lyons family you'll be talking to?"

"She said that her sister, Joyce, will be home. She wasn't sure about her brothers. She was probably referring to that Manny and Andre fellows you spoke of the other night."

"Joyce Lyons Nicolet will chew you up and spit you out, Fountain."

"Do you know her?"

"I know of her. I know enough about her to know you're no match for her."

"You should probably come with me then, being so familiar."

"I'll do no such thing. I've met the family, including Joyce Nicolet, on various occasions through my client,

Reed Alemand, but I'll certainly not meet them under your circumstances. I suggest you not, either."

"It's too late. I've accepted Miss Angelle's invitation."

"How do you plan to get there?"

"That's what I was just thinking. That young man who oversees the garage where you store your car. What's his name? Gregory? Surely he drives. Do you think he'd be available?"

"Not for the whole day, and his name is Jeffrey."

"Would you mind checking?"

The wheels churned in Portier's head, and his eyes glared even more.

"I plan to go whether you help me get there or not," I said. Still no word.

"Does Genny have a car?" I asked.

"She has an old Packard under tarp in Treme' somewhere. I wouldn't depend on it."

"Then I'll hire a Checker. Do you have Checkers in this town?"

"You'll do no such thing."

"Then you give me no choice," I said. "I don't know why you're being so hateful about this. Your mood from the other night hasn't improved at all."

"You know why. I told you and Genevieve the other night at dinner. I'll have no one looking into the Lyons family or my client Reed Alemand."

"This has nothing to do with your client."

After some thought, he reluctantly said, "Very well, take my Studebaker. No, I insist. I'll see if Jeffrey will drive you. If he can't, then I'll have him pull it out of the garage and park it out front for you. But you have to promise me one thing."

"What's that?"

"You keep Joyce Nicolet's fingernails away from my Studebaker's paint job."

Chapter 6

Portier's mechanic, Jeffrey, was indeed available to drive me to Lafayette.

I didn't ask how much my friend paid to have him available. All I needed to know, Portier contended, was that Jeffrey was willing to drive me.

He arrived at Portier's doorstep in his olive one-piece mechanic's overall, clean and pressed. A well-groomed young man, he had a lean, solid frame, and hair combed fashionably into a jelly roll. A deck of cigarettes tucked in the pegged sleeves of his t-shirt protruded through his overalls, and he walked with a self-assured, almost arrogant, skip that many young men in their early twenties possessed.

"All gassed and ready to go, sir," he said with confidence.

The Golden Hawk was hand-washed to shiny perfection, the chrome glittering in the morning sunlight.

"You went to a lot of trouble," I said.

"No trouble, sir, not for Mr. Charles. Do you have a grip, sir?"

"No grip, Jeffrey. It's just for the day."

"You better get going," Portier said as he stepped onto the stoop. "The sooner you go, the sooner you can get back."

"I appreciate you changing your mind about this trip," I said to him.

"I haven't changed anything. I still think you're a fool for going, but I can't stop you."

"But you'll be anxious to hear what the Lyons family has to say just the same, won't you?"

"I already know what they're going to say."

"And what's that?"

"Not a damn thing. They're not going to tell a perfect stranger one iota of what's going on in their lives, and don't think you're going to go there to change that."

I took a deep breath and reached for the Studebaker's door handle.

"Fingernails!" he spouted one last time as Jeffrey revved the engine. "Watch out for the fingernails!"

"What did he mean by that?" Jeffrey asked as we crossed the Huey P. Long Bridge over the Mississippi.

"Nothing. He's not fond of the people I'm going to meet. I suppose he's right about me going, but I'll not give him the satisfaction of saying so. I plan to go through with this visit despite his cynicism."

The trip didn't take as long as I thought it would because Jeffrey didn't go through Baton Rouge. He took the U.S. Highway south to Terrebonne parish then west to Lafayette through the Bayou.

"You been this way before, Reverend?" Jeffrey asked, steering with one hand on the Neckar knob.

"Yes, spent a week for several summers here with my father as a teen. He rented a fish camp with Portier's father near Pierre Part from some crusty old Cajun. Can't remember his name. What I remember the most were the nights, sleeping in that old camp. I bet Portier remembers them, too. Hot as all get out. My sheets were soaked with perspiration. I wasn't used to the heat, and it didn't let up. And the bugs. The bugs were as big as bats hitting the screen over the windows. I could hear critters sloshing in the water underneath. I spent the night wondering if any of them could climb the pylons up to the front door. You think our fathers were any comfort? They slept like babies all night long. Snored like bears. Portier and I did a lot of praying those nights, Jeffrey. I give Louisiana a hand for getting me into the ministry."

"What about the fishing?"

I laughed. "Well, now, the days were a complete opposite from the nights. It was heaven during the day. The fishing was fantastic—the best memories of my life! Fishing in the Bayou with my Dad and Portier and his father was something I'll never forget. It was total elation during the day and absolute horror at night."

I noticed a smirk cross Jeffrey's face—one he tried to hide.

"What is it?" I asked. "What's so funny?"

"Nothing," he said. "I was just thinking about Mr. Charles being a kid and all. I thought of him being an old, crotchety eight-year-old. So you say he was actually a kid once?"

"Oh, yes, yes, he was. He even laughed, played pranks, got his hands dirty and everything."

Jeffrey grinned again and shook his head.

I figured I knew what the other grin was about. "So you're wondering what happened, aren't you? Well, I wish I knew the answer to that. I'd like to say the betrayal of a woman he loved or a colleague embezzling from his practice and plunging him into financial ruin turned him sour, but I can't. It doesn't matter, really. I had great times with Portier when we were kids, especially when we were fishing with our fathers."

Jeffrey smiled genuinely this time. "They still have some of those camps around here."

"Do they now?"

"Probably not in any better shape than when you were here."

"Good," I said. In a way I was glad to hear that. Knowing the camps still existed in their rustic condition preserved my fond memories a bit longer.

"Do you still fish?" Jeffrey asked.

I shook my head. "Sadly, no, I must say. I haven't since my dad passed away. You see, my father only had one arm from a thrashing accident so when we were fishing, it was more than just a day of me being by his side. I was his other arm. There was something very powerful and spiritual in that for me. I haven't picked up a rod since."

"I doubt Mr. Charles has, either," Jeffrey added thoughtfully.

I looked at him as if he was on to something. "I suppose you're right. I bet those times meant a lot to him, too."

We soon arrived at the Lyons estate. Jeffrey whistled at the sleek expanse of the white mansion with its antebellum columns, supporting a veranda with wrought iron railings. Manicured evergreen shrubs in various geometrical shapes adorned the walk to the front door.

"Perhaps Portier was right," I said, eyes peeled to the house. "I may be a bit out of my league."

"Just remember to stick your pinky out when they give you coffee or tea. That'll impress 'em."

A gentleman answered the door. He wasn't a butler of sorts, but he also didn't announce he was a member of the family. He was expecting me and called Miss Angelle to the foyer.

Angelle Lyons glided into the room. There was no other accurate way to express her entrance—she glided. Her approach expressed such a simple elegance that it nearly took my breath away. She extended her hand to mine and thanked me for coming. Even the palm of her hand was delicate and soft as rose petals. If she'd worked a day of hard labor in her life, she hid it well.

"Shall we go out to the veranda, Mr. Fountain?"

I stepped back for her to lead the way as the gentleman held the door.

She wore a belted swing dress in pastel blue that floated around her as she stepped into the breeze. "Would you like some coffee?" She pointed to a cushioned chair and pulled her cardigan closer to her body. "I think I would like to have some."

"Yes, that would be nice."

"Regular or chicory?"

"I'm fond of chicory."

"So am I." She turned to the gentleman. "Henri, do you mind?"

He bowed and returned to the house.

"It's not too chilly for you to be out here, is it?" I asked.

The young heiress shook her head. "No, it's actually quite nice. I prefer it out here."

"I appreciate you taking the time to see me. I take it my visit wasn't received well with the other family members, however."

"My brothers haven't been here today so I wouldn't know about them, but my sister was less than enthusiastic as you can imagine."

"Is that Joyce?"

"You know her?"

"No, only what my friend's colleague has to say. You may know him. His name is Reed Alemand."

"Oh, yes, Reed. Nice man. I don't know him well."

"Does he not come around to visit your brother Manfred?"

"He does," she said, "but I don't pay much attention to him."

"Did your father?"

Angelle turned from me suddenly to look toward the street as if she was no longer interested in our conversation. "Is that your driver?"

I looked toward the Golden Hawk where Jeffrey wiped the windshield and spit-polished the chrome.

"Handsome young man," she said.

"But about your father."

"My father, yes, Reverend Fountain, I'm very grateful you called. He's had us terribly worried, you know. He's done this before, don't get me wrong, and you'd think we'd be used to his eccentric travels by now, but one never knows when one disappears for an extended period, do they?"

"This time was different?"

"Yes, extremely so. He's been gone much longer this time. It's been much more secretive, too, if you ask me."

"Is he with your mother?"

Angelle smiled. "My mother?"

"It's a fair question."

"In any other household, perhaps, but not ours. No, my mother isn't with him. She's here in Louisiana or Portugal or Bolivia, somewhere. Who knows? All I do know is that my mother never went with my father when he disappeared in the past. You can trust me when I say she didn't go with him this time, either. You see, she's just as erratic as he is with her travels."

"Would she have an idea where he went?"

"I doubt she cares."

"Do you care?"

She cocked her head as if it was a curious question.

72

"Did I say something wrong?"

"No, it was just insensitive."

"I apologize."

"No apologies are needed," she replied. "You had your reasons for asking, I suppose, given our family situation. Yes, I do care, but I learned at a very young age that my father will do what my father wants to do despite our caring."

"What about your siblings?"

"My brothers and sister are ready for him to come home. Their hands are tied financially as I understand. I don't understand why. We have our own money, but the operation of this house has been my father's responsibility."

Silence descended as she took to admiring Jeffrey once again. Without warning, however, she turned with a sudden change in demeanor. "So you say he's dead. Is that true?"

"If the man I met in New Orleans is who I believe he is, then, yes. I'm sorry to tell you that I believe your father is dead."

Tears welled in her eyes. "And what makes you say that?" she asked. "You made it sound on the telephone that he was practically a derelict. Why would a man like my father be living under such conditions on the streets of New Orleans when he's worked tirelessly day and night all of his life to build a legacy that is the exact opposite of what you describe?"

"That's what I encourage your family to find out, Miss Lyons—to see for yourself and to determine if the man in New Orleans is actually your father. You need to do that for closure."

Angelle took a deep breath and dabbed her eyes with a handkerchief she pulled from a side pocket.

Henri came out of the house and handed us our coffees.

When he left, she said, "I believe you're being sincere. I have no reason to doubt that you're here for no other purpose than to see that our father—if this man is our father—is properly laid to rest. Joyce is skeptical of your motives for being here, but I believe you're being genuine and sincere."

"Then you'll encourage your family to come to New Orleans?"

"I'll see what I can do."

We sat in silence for a couple of minutes, sipping the hot chicories before she set her cup on a side table and stood. I stood with her. "Let me talk to Joyce," she said. "Will you excuse me, Reverend Fountain?"

"Certainly.

"I'll call for you if I've made some progress."

After she entered the house, I walked to the end of the walk and told Jeffrey I hoped to have one more conversation before we returned to the city. I thanked him for his patience, but he waved me off as if the wait was no bother. He seemed to enjoy leaning against the car as he smoked a Kool.

Angelle soon emerged with a broad smile. Her sister would receive me inside, she said. "You'll be pleased, Reverend. She seems very interested in what you have to say."

I stood for several minutes alone with Angelle in the library. Custom oak shelves and trim, crown molding, and portraits of distinguished family members and politicians decorated the room. I took a framed photograph of light-hearted people in costume from the shelf and looked at it closely.

"Is that you?" I asked, pointing to one of the characters.

Angelle laughed. "Yes, isn't it delightful? Silly, of course, but it was the most fun."

"Mardi Gras?"

"Yes, the Krewe of Acadia Ball. Our family has been a member for generations. We had a wonderful time even without father."

"I take it these are your siblings around you?"

"And my mother."

"She was in Lafayette for Carnival? Not off to Monaco or someplace more exotic?"

She laughed again. "No, she surprised us by coming home to celebrate."

"Very attractive woman," I remarked. "You and Joyce have a strong resemblance to her."

Angelle's smile disappeared. She turned towards the door. "I wonder what's keeping Joyce."

I replaced the photo back onto the shelf and waited. The suspense of Joyce's entrance was meant to break my spirit, I was convinced of that, for when she finally entered the room and greeted us, Joyce Nicolet was pulling long, white satin gloves onto her arms while juggling an expensive handbag. She reminded me immediately of Jean Simmons from *Footsteps in the Fog* as she peered from underneath her wide-brimmed hat.

"I was about to step out," she announced. "I apologize I can't be long. You must be Reverend Fountain."

"Yes, very kind of you to take the time to meet me, Mrs. Nicolet."

"Yes, but I haven't much to say to you."

"That's all right. It's I who would like to talk with you."

"About my father?"

"Yes, if I may."

"You may, but from what I gather from Angelle, the man you describe couldn't possibly be our father."

"And why is that?"

"What would he be doing on a park bench in the early morning hours of the Quarter as if he had slept there all night?"

"That's what I hope you'll find out by going to New Orleans and identifying him."

She laughed. "My dear man, you seem very sincere just as Angelle told me you'd be. You were very kind to come, and we appreciate it tremendously, but I can assure you I have no desire to traipse all the way to New Orleans to identify the rotting remains of a perfect stranger." Before I could say anything, she added, "And I doubt my brothers will be interested, either."

"I should be interested," Angelle interjected.

Joyce turned sharply to her sister. "You'll do no such thing."

"Glen could drive me."

"That boyfriend of yours has no business driving, and you know it."

"I have many reasons to believe that the man I discovered is actually your father, Mrs. Nicolet," I said.

"I'm sure you do or else you wouldn't have come, but I'm telling you the man isn't him."

"But Joyce," Angelle pleaded.

"It isn't him," she said sternly. "It couldn't possibly be. I won't hear of it, and you won't be going to New Orleans to find out, Angelle. Do you hear me?"

Angelle cupped her hands in front of her and lowered her head.

Joyce Nicolet turned to me after being satisfied of her sister's acquiescence, and replied, "If there's nothing more, Reverend, I thank you once again and bid you good day." She called for Henri who appeared in the doorway on cue. "Fetch

76

the car for me, would you, please, Henri? Now, if you two will excuse me, I must be going."

Joyce left the room ceremoniously, leaving me with Angelle Lyons alone in the library once again.

"I'm terribly sorry," Angelle said.

"Oh, please, don't be. I was more surprised when you said she was willing to see me than I was over what she actually had to say."

"I'll show you the way out."

Before we could exit, a young woman, around twenty or so, petite with black, cropped hair and eyes larger than her face should allow, entered the room and looked around. She looked surprised to find us standing there. "Isn't Joyce here? I thought I heard her voice," she said.

"You did," Angelle explained. "She just left."

"Gone again?"

Angelle turned to me and tried to smile, but she did a very poor job of it. "Reverend Fountain, this is Joyce's step-daughter, Carmen."

"Pleased to meet you."

"Likewise," the young woman said. "A reverend?"

"Former pastor."

"Then it's true," she said.

"What's true, my dear?"

"He's dead. Grandfather is really dead."

"We're not sure of that."

"Then why is this pastor here? Why didn't you call for a priest? Grandmother won't like a Protestant pastor, you know."

"I'm not here in an official capacity," I said.

Carmen didn't look convinced. She studied me intensely. Finally, quite by surprise, she said, "It's not like it matters very much."

"Pardon me?"

The young woman looked at me as if I had lost my manners. "Just as I said. It doesn't matter if he's dead … or just gone," she said snidely.

"Carmen!" Angelle said.

"Oh, please, save the dramatics, Auntie, dear."

"It's a horrid thing to say."

"Nothing we all haven't thought in our heads these past few months."

Angelle turned to me and apologized. "I'm terribly sorry, Reverend. We're not as barbaric as she would make us sound."

"I didn't think anything of the kind," I replied. "I must be going. I've stayed long enough. It was nice meeting you, Miss Carmen. Angelle, it was a pleasure."

I passed Carmen and smiled at the young woman. A closer look at her revealed it wasn't cosmetics that gave her eyes such a large, lifeless appearance. It wasn't even her disagreeable personality that accentuated her macabre features. She had a natural look of unpleasantness about her.

When I stepped into the entryway, a gentleman, deep in thought, walked hastily from the entrance towards us.

"Oh, Andre," Angelle called. "I'm surprised to see you here."

He stopped to address her, but seemed perturbed that she was there. "Yes, I'm sorry for not phoning ahead, dear, but I needed to come home."

"Something wrong?" she asked. "Oh, I'm sorry, Reverend. This is my brother, Andre."

"Yes, I thought it might be."

"And who are you again?" Andre asked, extending his hand.

"Richard Fountain. I should say I'm a friend of Charles Portier, Reed Alemand's accountant."

Andre Lyons looked suddenly alarmed. "Reed sent you?"

"No, no, sir, I'm here on an entirely different matter, but I thought mentioning Mr. Alemand might give you a perspective of who I am."

"He may have found father," Angelle said.

"Father?"

"It's not pleasant news," I said.

"No, no, of course not. I say, yes, maybe I … would you have time for a quick chat, Mr. Fountain? Did I hear my sister call you a reverend?"

"Former. Please call me Richard."

"Yes, of course. Step in here. I consider this to be my den. Joyce and father use that one across the hall. Joyce is my sister."

"I've met her."

"You have?" he asked as he closed the solid oak door behind us. "Ah, then you're acquainted. I hope she was on good behavior. Sweet woman when she wants to be."

"She was delightful."

"Good, good. My father, you say?"

"Yes. Have you seen him lately?"

"I haven't seen him in months."

"He wasn't at your play the other night? *Dickies, Stocks & Jabots?*"

Andre paused before answering. "*Dickies?* You know about that? You've heard of it?"

"I was there. I thought I saw a gentleman matching your father's description at intermission."

"It couldn't have been him."

"Can you be sure?"

79

"As sure as the two of us are standing here. You see, my father wasn't much into my plays. He thought they were a waste of his time."

I shook my head and tried to look confused. "But I was so sure I saw him. Perhaps he wanted to surprise you."

Andre laughed. "Yes, his appearance would've been the ultimate surprise." He stepped back and gave me the once over. "Did you know my father?" His question seemed to indicate that he knew I didn't.

"A little." My answer wasn't entirely fabricated.

"Then you'd know my father wouldn't have been at The Landalia to see my play."

I tried to smile to convey that I understood.

"But how about you?" he asked. "Did you enjoy it?"

I stumbled for words and was able to mutter some descriptive pleasantries that eventually evaded the question.

"Say no more. I get it. It was terrible, a flop. The Landalia's a flop. That's why I came home. I had to get away from New Orleans."

"I understand Mr. Alemand is a partner in The Landalia."

"Why, yes, he invested, but he's not a partner. Why? What did he say about it? I can't imagine what more he could say that he hasn't said to me already."

"About what? The play?"

"The play, The Landalia, my taste in champagne during the intermission, you name it." Andre Lyons suddenly stopped talking and eyed me curiously as if he realized he was talking to a perfect stranger. "Who did you say you were?"

I hesitated before answering honestly. "I'm an acquaintance of Reed Alemand through my friend Charles Portier."

"Yes, I know Mr. Portier," Andre said.

I didn't know if that was good or bad.

"Was Mr. Portier with you at the play?"

I acknowledged he was.

Andre sighed then looked for a chair to sit down. "Well, then, I'm sure he'll find out soon enough."

I stepped closer to him. "Find out what?"

"Alemand and I had an argument yesterday afternoon. I owe Alemand a great deal of money. You probably know that if you know him. He's afraid he'll never see any of it. He may be right, you know. Unless father turns up and has a change of heart, there may not be any money."

"Then you haven't heard."

"Heard what?"

"I called yesterday evening and talked with your sister Angelle, and I spoke with Joyce just moments before I saw you. I believe I found your father in the French Quarter yesterday morning. He was badly injured, and before help could arrive, he passed away."

"What?"

"I encourage you to come to New Orleans to identify him."

"That's insane. In the Quarter? In the morning? What was he doing there?"

"That's what I hope your family will determine."

"I'm not planning to go back until tomorrow or the day after."

"It's your father I'm talking about."

"Allegedly my father."

"But if it happens to be him, it will put some financial closure on his death. I understand that your family's funds are encumbered by his absence."

Andre Lyons laughed. "Without going into detail about my father or my family for that matter, the idea of gaining financial closure from my father's death is a moot issue."

"I don't understand."

"I'd rather not to go into my or my family's business, if you don't mind."

"I wouldn't expect you to, but Angelle is the one who mentioned it to me, and you're the one who mentioned it doesn't matter."

"Very well. I will tell you so that you can reassure Mr. Portier as Reed Alemand's accountant that I'm doing everything in my power to keep The Landalia afloat, but I've been embattled with my father for many years over my interest in the theater. He doesn't approve. Choose any other business, and he would've invested in my success at the drop of a hat. Choose the theater, and he'll have nothing to do with me. He wouldn't even co-sign a loan for me. I had to seek investors from men like Reed Alemand. Now those men like Reed Alemand want their money. They want to see a return on that money. I don't have it, and I don't see any way of getting it."

"But if the man in New Orleans is your father, and he's dead, Andre, I assume there will be a matter of a will."

"It won't concern *me,* though. That's what I'm trying to say. My father did prepare a will, make no mistake, but his offspring have all been omitted from it."

I nearly gasped at the information. "Are you absolutely certain of that?"

"Who can be absolutely certain about anything in life, but I wouldn't put it past him."

"That's all the more reason to come to New Orleans, Andre, to see if this man is actually your father."

The rejected heir plopped into the leather chair behind his desk and rubbed his face with the palms of his hands. "Let him rot in hell," he spewed forth. "I mean it. He didn't believe in me when he was alive, why should I believe in him when he's dead?"

Chapter 7

I rode back to the city without speaking. Jeffrey was respectful and let me sit in silence. I dreaded facing my friend Portier. The thought of groveling at his feet to tell him he was right about the Lyons family made me cringe.

The Lyons family appeared to be uninterested in what I had to say except for two people. Angelle Lyons was curious to see if the news about her father was true, and Carmen Nicolet was hopeful that it was. Joyce Nicolet and Andre Lyons, the two who could make the identification happen, were not interested in the least.

"What you need is a good meal," Portier said after I told him what I needed to say about the trip. "A good, solid meal, that's all you need. I'll call Arnaud's. Go freshen up. Let's see what we can do to salvage some of the evening that's left." He could've left his comments at that, but he added, "You wasted a good day in traveling we could've spent doing a number of other things."

"You're not going to give me any slack on this, are you?"

"You don't deserve any slack," he replied. "You've consumed every minute of our time with your *Hercule Poirot* stunts. I'll give you slack when you stop finding bodies and stop chasing heirs and get back to why you came to New Orleans in the first place."

"How can I? It wasn't my fault I came across a dying man."

"But it's your fault you continue to delve into the poor man's death. That's the job of investigators."

"This is too much for you, isn't it?" I tried to say with compassion. "I apologize, Portier. I sincerely apologize for being the worst guest ever. I should find a boarding room until this blows over."

"You'll do no such thing. You've made your bed here, Fountain. You'll stay put. I'll go about my business while you go about yours. If you're content with this half-ass goose-chase you're on, who am I to interfere? I take responsibility for some of this fiasco. I shouldn't have dragged you to The Landalia to watch that horrible play. If we hadn't gone to the play, then finding that dead man wouldn't have been quite so intriguing to you."

"Then you believe the man I saw at the theater was the man in the park."

"I didn't say that. All I'm trying to do is apologize for being so brash. I know you must do what you have to do. I just don't want any part of it, that's all."

I was ashamed of myself almost immediately. I had consumed our time together with this adventure, if one could call it that. I didn't know now how to make it up to my friend, especially when I didn't want to stop my pursuit of ...

"Murder."

"What?" I asked, coming out of my trance.

"You were mumbling over there," Portier replied. "I could hear you. You were mumbling about Roger Lyons, and you were about to say he was murdered. I said it for you."

"Oh, I didn't realize my thoughts were coming out aloud."

"They were."

I zipped my light jacket and turned toward the door.

"Now where are you going?"

I shrugged. "I don't know." It was the truth. I just wanted out. I needed to leave before I inadvertently made more comments that shouldn't be overheard.

A nippy breeze met me at the door. I stepped onto the stoop just as Genny exited her cottage. Dressed in her usual array of bright colors, cloaked in infinite layers of fabric and costume jewelry, she smiled the moment she saw me, but then changed her expression almost immediately. "Oh, my, Richard, you're the face of doom and gloom this evening."

"A long day, Genny."

"Is it because of Chuck? Is he in one of his moods again?"

"No, I'm afraid it's me this time."

"You can't be all to blame. Where is he?"

I pointed to the cottage.

"Are you hungry?" she asked. "I'm going for catfish. Will you join me?"

I said I would be delighted, but I exaggerated. I wasn't that hungry.

"This'll be a good time to warn you about my friends," she said.

"Excuse me?"

"My friends, darling. You said at one time you'd like to see my show at the club. Remember? Then I said that would be great, but before you do, I'll need to explain my friends. If we see any of them you'll have to swallow a lot more than catfish, trust me."

"I'll be fine, Genny. There's no need to explain them. You and Portier must think I'm socially inept."

"No, just out of your element."

"That's not true. I'm very much in my element here in the French Quarter. This is what I do. I see human suffering, and I do something about it."

86

Genny laughed heartily. "Oh, dear Richard, that's why I love you to pieces. You're as dramatic as I am."

"Yes, that was a bit dramatic, I admit, but you know what I mean. You're more in tune to those around you than Portier. He's oblivious and chooses to be."

"You can't fault him entirely. When you live here day after day, you tend to be numb to the needs people have or the choices they've made. It's our way of coping. Come now. Let's be like Chuck and be oblivious, shall we? I'm hungry. I could use a good plate of Mississippi catfish, and I think you could, too."

Genny was right. I was starting to get hungry, but she was wrong on another account. I couldn't be oblivious.

We walked towards the river as she talked about her singing and acting career. She spoke as if she were on the verge of a breakthrough to Hollywood, but her climb to success sounded more like it was fledging and difficult. She talked and I tried to listen, but my mind was on how I could find that young singer Donnie to learn more about the identity of Mr. Montgomery.

Before I knew it, we had walked to Decatur Street not far from the park where I found the dying man.

I stopped at the corner.

"Oh, I'm terribly sorry, Richard. I was jabbering away. I didn't mean to bring you this way. We could've taken another route. I wasn't thinking, or I'd have turned on Dauphine."

"It's okay, Genny. This is quite alright. You don't mind if we head towards the park, do you?"

"I don't think it's a good idea. You're not in a good frame of mind, Richard. I could tell you weren't listening to a word I said. Let's go and get something to eat."

"No, I must do something first." I ignored her request and turned toward the park.

Genny hurried to catch up with me, panting and exclaiming that her running wasn't a pretty sight.

I stopped in front of a storefront and looked through the display window.

"What're we looking at?" she asked, gasping for air.

"This is the store where I called for help. I thought I remembered seeing them."

"I don't see anything but drab old army blankets."

"Precisely," I replied, stepping closer to the window.

"What do you want with those?"

"It gives me an idea. Look at the sign in the window. How late are they open?"

"Late. All these stores stay open late. They try to get as much of the tourist foot traffic as possible."

"Good. We'll have time for dinner then." I turned and began to walk back the way we came. "Are you coming?" I called as she continued to stand in front of the store window. "I thought you were hungry."

Genny ran to catch up to me again. She led me into a narrow restaurant that opened to a large entertainment area in the back. "This is the club where I sing," she said. A full bar sat on one side of the room, tables for dining on the other. A stage served as the focal point with a black-and-white-checkered linoleum dance floor in front. Carnival colors of purple, gold, and green still decorated the ceiling and walls. Christmas lights twinkled overhead. A decorated artificial tree stood in the corner.

"Christmas tree?" I asked surprised. "Really?"

"Mardi Gras tree. We keep it up from Christmas, but after Epiphany change the color of the lights and decorate it in beads and bows."

"Fat Tuesday is over, though."

"Yes, it really should come down, but it looks wonderful, don't you think?" Genny gestured toward a specific table in the middle of the dining area. "This is *my* table," she said.

It was front and center, providing an excellent view of the stage, and more importantly, providing an excellent view for patrons to see *her*.

"So this is the club where you sing," I said, taking in as much as I could see.

"Oh, honey, I do more than sing. I dance; I act; I do standup; I emcee events. You were right, though. There wasn't one placard board on the street about my shows. I'm going to talk to my manager. The scoundrel is going to hear about it. You might want to stuff a napkin in your ears, sweetheart. You won't like what I have to say to him, being a preacher and all."

"I doubt I'll hear anything I haven't already heard in my life, Genny, I assure you."

She patted my arm, her bangles rattling loudly. "Oh, you dear, sweet, naïve little man. You really are dewy-eyed, aren't you?"

She called for a waitress, and a woman about Genny's age approached. She scowled upon seeing Genny at the table. By the looks of her face, Genny didn't look all too pleased to see her, either. I surmised the women had butted heads before.

"What do you want to drink, darling?" Genny asked me. "Sazerac? Hurricane? Old Cuban? The bartender is Cuban, you known. He makes the best."

"Iced tea."

"Sweet tea?"

89

"Plain."

"This is Loosiana, honey."

"Sweet tea."

"I'll have a gimlet, dear," she said to the waitress. "I'll be watching, so don't spit in it."

The waitress raised the corner of her lip at Genny then walked towards the bar.

"Beautiful gal, isn't she?" Genny said. "She's not one of my favorites around here."

I took a quick glance around the club. The patrons were as eclectic as my hostess. Most wore costumes or headdresses in a variety of colors and styles. No masks, though. Masks were only for Mardi Gras, Genny explained.

"I seem to be overdressed," I said.

"Nonsense. We'll tell everyone you came as Rudy Valentino. They love Valentino here. Oh, I should have come as Gloria Swanson. That would've been a blast. Yes, a fat, loud-mouth Gloria Swanson and a skinny, gray-haired Valentino."

I must've grimaced because she glanced my way.

"Oh, now, don't be that way. Let's have fun."

"It's rather difficult to have fun right now—not with Donnie out there knowing something that could help me. I need more information. I can't get this whole Mr. Montgomery affair out of my head, and Donnie's my missing link. I'm sorry if I'm ruining your evening."

"Look at me. Do I look like you're ruining my evening? One thing you need to know about me, sweetheart, is that no one ruins Genny Duval's evening if I don't want them to. Got that? I'll be fine. You worry about yourself. Ah, look who's back with our drinks. That was fast, dear."

"Not that busy tonight. Tomas is bored at the bar."

"It'll get better. It's still early yet."

"You know what?" I said to the waitress. "Have Tomas fix me a gimlet as well."

She looked at me as if she couldn't believe I was going to make her walk back to the bar.

Genny bellowed with glee. "Now you're talking! Well, just don't stand there, sweetheart. The man wants a gimlet!"

When the waitress left, I looked at Genny and tried to smile. I must've presented a sorrowful expression instead because she replied immediately, "Stop thinking about Donnie."

"It's not just Donnie. I need to find someone that might know where he is."

"Don't look in this place."

"Why not?"

"These people don't have much, but they're not homeless."

"But they might know something."

"No, they won't. You're going about finding him the wrong way."

"That's why those blankets are necessary."

Her mouth contorted into several positions while she thought.

"I see," I said. "You don't think any higher about what I'm doing than Portier does."

"Don't put me in the same boat as Chuck."

"But you are. For different reasons, of course."

"That's not true. I don't see how blankets are going to help you."

"They're for the homeless. Donnie is homeless. I hope to find him."

She shook her head. "I just don't want to see you get sucked in."

"Sucked into what?"

91

"I've already told you, Richard. You're not as savvy about this city as you think you are. You don't fully understand the culture, the history, the politics, the law, the class system, and everything else that makes this city tick. You don't even understand the people you want to help."

"What does that mean?"

"It means not everyone around here needs or wants your help. I don't care what they look like on the outside to you."

I lowered my head, realizing she was more astute than I wanted to admit.

"And one more thing. Not everyone wants you to help these people, either. Not just in New Orleans, there's backlash everywhere about helping people in need for fear of enabling them. It happens even where you're from, I bet."

"So you think I should stop what I'm doing."

"No. I just think you should be smarter about how you go about it. Otherwise, you're going to get yourself killed or in legal trouble."

I frowned. "You don't believe that."

"I do. You don't fully understand what it is you don't know."

The waitress approached our table and set my gimlet in front of me. She turned and walked away without saying a word.

I lifted my glass. "Prost."

Genny responded more enthusiastically, then remembered the waitress left without asking if we wanted any food. "Oh, that burns my ass," she said as she rose from the table. "That woman did that on purpose, not asking what we wanted to eat." Genny suddenly looked at me and said apologetically, "Oh, I'm sorry, Richard. You probably don't use the phrase 'burn my ass' very often, do you?"

"No, not often," I said.

She laughed and went in search of our waitress.

I picked up my drink and took a sip. It was tasteless.

The room began to fill gradually, adding to the buzz of conversations. I watched people closely, wondering if any of them had information that could be useful to me.

Genny soon returned, waving to a couple near our table dressed as George and Martha Washington. "Can you believe it?" she asked, sitting down. "They were George and Martha last year, too. I wouldn't be caught dead wearing the same costume two years in a row. New Orleanians may not have enough sense to wake up in the morning, but we do remember what costumes people wear."

"Don't look now, but here comes Cleopatra," I said.

Genny glanced behind her, then turned quickly back to face me. "That's not Cleopatra. She's Moline, Princess of Rokavia."

"Oh, how I could use a cigarette right now!" the princess said in a shrill voice.

"Don't bother us, sweetheart. Can't you see we're talking? Where's Victorius? Go bother him."

"Oh, darling, he doesn't have any Picayunes."

"Those nasty smokes? I thought it smelled better in here than usual."

The princess pouted. "I can't tell you how disappointing he's been to me lately."

Genny looked at me and said under her breath, "Victorius is her boyfriend. He's a Roman god from the island of, what island, dear?"

"Tedius."

"Oh, yes, Tedius—appropriate name. Apparently, the only access to Tedius is by his personal yacht." Genny used her

93

index finger to circle her temple as if the man was crazy. "That's him over there in the toga. Not attractive, is it?" She took a sip of her drink and glanced at me to see what I thought of her description of the disillusioned character. "But he does know Aristotle Onassis," she added.

Moline groaned. "He doesn't know Onassis."

"He doesn't?"

"No, Genny, he barely knows Jack Shit. Can you believe that? He lied to me about Onassis."

"Some things never change, Moline, except for that costume of his. He's got a new toga, doesn't he?"

Moline jerked her head to look at Victorius. "No, he doesn't have anything."

Genny laughed. "Calm down, sweetheart. I only noticed his new costume. I'm not after him."

"He doesn't have anything."

"Why, he certainly does. That's a new sash over his shoulder and a new gold cord around his waist. And where's your other arm cuff, darling?"

A gold serpent coiled around Moline's right wrist. Genny pointed to her left arm.

"Oh, that. I, uh, I gave it to Victorius. He lost one of his. He's wearing mine."

I turned and looked at the Roman god. He wasn't wearing anything on his arms.

Moline saw the confused expression on my face. "It's true," she blurted before I could say anything. "Look, Genny, will you do me a favor? Will you buy me a drink and lend me a cigarette?"

"No, Moline."

"Seriously?"

"Do I look like I'm joking?"

94

"Why won't you?"

"Cigarette paper is only a dime. Get some Durham and roll your own."

"I need one now, Gen. Why wouldn't you help your dear friend?"

"Because I'm a lady, Moline."

"So am I."

"No, not *your* kind of lady. I'm a properly bred and behaved Southern woman of distinction. Women of my caliber pay for nothing. I'm here to be admired for my grace and beauty, and I plan to keep it that way."

"Not even for friends?"

"Especially not for friends, dear. You know the rules."

"Won't you bend them a little?"

"Not one bit."

"And why not?"

"Because I don't have to."

"You're exhausting, Gen. You're simply exhausting. You haven't a kind bone in your body." Moline sulked for a few seconds before turning her attention to me. "Perhaps your gentleman friend would like to show how much of a gentleman he is by buying an equally refined woman of distinction a drink and giving her a cigarette."

"Perhaps he would." Genny shrugged. "I'll leave that up to him. Be my guest, Reverend Fountain."

"Reverend?"

"Yes. He's a preacher, Moline. You're hitting on a preacher man. Reverend, please meet my friend, Moline. She's not from Rokavia. There's no such place. She's from Illinois or Iowa. I don't know which, but I suspect it's Illinois, someplace close to Moline."

"Oh, you think you're so smart," Moline retorted. "And how do you figure I came from Illinois?"

"Because I've sung everywhere, sweetheart. I know my geography. The Quad Cities consist of Moline, Rock Island, Davenport, and Bettendorf. You picked Moline because Bettendorf is a lousy name for a princess."

Moline ignored Genny. Instead, she extended her gloved hand to me and smiled superficially, revealing yellow, jagged teeth and a tongue white as snow from consuming more alcohol than was good for her. "Pleased to meet you, Reverend. Is that what you'd prefer to be called?"

"No, honey," Genny interjected. "He'd prefer to be called from over there. Bye, bye. We'll talk later."

Moline placed her hands on her hips and wrinkled her nose.

"I mean it, dear. Give Victorius a hug for me, but don't have him come over here."

Moline didn't move.

"I said bye, bye."

Moline gave a huff, then flittered away, discouraged and empty handed.

I gave Genny a dirty look. "I wish you wouldn't have sent her off like that."

"Oh, is she your type? Do you go in for heavily sedated and cosmetically transfigured women, Reverend Fountain?"

"Certainly not, but perhaps she knows something about Donnie or Mr. Montgomery that could be useful."

"She doesn't. Trust me, she doesn't."

I glared at Genny as she sipped her gimlet.

"Look," she said. "We're not that much different, the two of us."

My eyebrows rose. "I beg your pardon."

96

"You and me."

"How's that?"

"A man behind a pulpit isn't any different than an entertainer behind a microphone. We deal with the same type of people. We deal with people who show us what they want us to see and tell us what they want us to hear."

"I'm not following you."

"Then listen to me. As I told you before, just because Princess Moline hasn't got a pot to piss in doesn't mean she has information on every Tom, Dick, or Harry who is down and out on the street. If you want information like the kind of information you're seeking, you need people who are really down and who are really out. You need the ones who've been there and the ones who are there. People like Princess Moline of Rokavia are down, but they're not out. There's a difference." Genny paused to let her words sink in. "Don't look at me like that," she said seriously. "I know what I'm talking about. Underneath this atom explosion of hair and make-up is a woman who knows her stuff around this town."

I couldn't hide my disappointment and frustration.

"Let me get Tomas," she replied. "You look like you need another drink."

"Have him put alcohol in it this time."

"Oh, did you get one without?"

"It tasted like it."

"Must've been reserved for the anglers."

"Anglers?"

"That's what I call them—women just waiting to reel a bloke in."

"But why wouldn't it have alcohol?"

"Oh, you are naïve, aren't you? It's so cute. Look, a hostess around here—and I use the term hostess loosely—asks a man for a drink. He buys her one. The drinks arrive at the table. His has plenty of alcohol so that he'll lose his senses. Hers has no alcohol to keep her senses sharp. Besides, the house isn't going to waste alcohol on an employee. You get it? Before you know it, he has no money, and she has no buzz, but she's walking away with his cash. Tomas gave you the wrong drink. You say you want alcohol in it?"

"Yes, if I'm going to pay for it."

"Exactly. You're catching on to this town. Hey, do me a favor; don't let anyone eat my catfish if it arrives. I'm going to have a talk with that cheap-ass bastard who made your drink." Genny turned to me with another look of apology. "Oh, I'm so sorry, Richard. You probably don't say words like 'cheap-ass bastard', either, do you?"

"No, not often."

"I'll be more careful."

"Please don't," I replied. "I learn the most interesting things when your mouth is unfiltered."

Chapter 8

The catfish was just as Genny said it would be—crisp, hot, and flavorful.

I patted my belly and looked at my watch. Nine-thirty. Time to get going.

"You go on," Genny said. "Things are starting to pick up around here. Do you mind if I stay?"

I didn't. What I wanted to do was best doing without her.

I paid the tab and walked toward the park on Decatur Street, hoping the shop with the blankets was still open. The lights were still on although I saw no customers as I walked into the store. The owner looked at me, appearing to raise his guard, as I approached the counter. I sensed he recognized me from my experience with Mr. Montgomery.

"May I help you?"

"Yes, do you have many of the blankets I see in the window?"

He didn't answer at first. "How many do you need?"

"About twenty probably."

"Twenty? You have a car or cart nearby?"

"Excuse me?"

"Twenty of those wool outdoor Army blankets will be quite a load. Do you have a cart to carry them away?"

I hadn't thought about needing a cart because of the blankets' weight. "No. What about ten?"

"Ten." He looked me over, and I sensed he thought even ten blankets were too heavy for me. "I have another brand in the back," he said. "It's a polyester blend; still warm for the outdoors, but not as bulky. It'll save you some money, too."

"Maybe I should just start out with five."

The shopkeeper nodded and walked down a crowded aisle to a shelf in the back. He pulled five gray blankets and placed them on the counter in front of me. "These okay?"

"Yes, perfect. Thank you."

I paid for the blankets and picked them off the counter. The shopkeeper was right; I was barely able to hold the five, let alone twenty.

Back on Decatur, the fog started to roll in off the Mississippi, saturating the air with a cold, damp mist. I knew I didn't have much time before the fog thickened, and I wouldn't be able to see, let alone talk, to anyone.

I quickened my step. Within thirty minutes, I had given away four of the blankets and talked with several individuals about people they knew in the area. Some were cooperative, but most were not. I assumed they were more interested in hunkering down for the night before the chill got the best of them.

None of the faces I saw were Donnie's, and none of the stories I heard included Mr. Montgomery.

I mentioned Montgomery's name as I bent down to give an old man my last blanket. He lifted his back from against the stone ledge on which he rested and started to say something but stopped when he turned to glance down the deserted street.

"What's the matter?" I asked.

He shook his head, grabbed the blanket, and leaned back against the ledge.

"What is it? Do you know who I'm talking about? Montgomery. Do you know a Mr. Montgomery?"

He shook his head again.

I stood and looked down the street in time to see a man standing in the fog. He turned and walked around the corner of a building. "Who was he?" I asked.

The man didn't answer. He pretended to close his eyes and fall asleep.

I walked away from him unsatisfied. I didn't know what I expected to gain from any of the individuals I'd met on the street. I'd hoped at least one would be willing to talk to me. My consolation was that five people would be warmer this evening. Nevertheless, it would be another example Portier would use to prove that my quest to identify Mr. Montgomery was futile.

I walked through the fog down Dumaine Street toward Portier's cottage. A cat yowled through the mist. Someone closed their shutters. I heard nothing else until what sounded like a tin can was kicked behind me. I shivered and turned, sensing someone near. To my surprise, no one was there. I waited a few seconds for signs of movement, but no one emerged from the shadows cast by the streetlights.

I continued onward and reached the Clover Grill at the corner of Bourbon and Dumaine. Customers filled the tables along the windows, but several spots were still open at the counter. I wasn't hungry, but the thought of a hot cup of coffee and the company of others appealed to me.

I sat alone at the counter, wrapping my hands around a white diner cup. Steam rose above its rim. I lowered my head just enough to give the tip of my nose the benefit of its warmth as well.

It wasn't long before someone climbed onto the stool next to me and ordered a cup of coffee, also.

"Cold out there," he said.

Still shaken from my walk in the fog, I wasn't in the mood for conversation, but I muttered, "It could be worse for February."

"That doesn't matter to the people you were helping tonight, does it? It's cold enough for them."

I lifted my head and got a glimpse of the man sitting next to me. The collar of his dark overcoat and the brim of his fedora covered most of his face, but I could see bushy brown eyebrows and thick stubble on his chin.

"You've been following me," I said.

A waiter placed his black coffee and tab in front of him. The man thanked the waiter, but ignored my comment.

"Why?" I asked.

"Let me ask you first. What do you hope to gain by talking to these people?"

"Who are you?"

He sipped his coffee and said he needed a good hot cup. "Hits the spot, doesn't it?"

I reached into my pocket and placed a dime on the counter.

"Don't go," he said. "We're not done talking."

"I don't like how our conversation is going." I stood, intending to walk toward the door, but he stuck his arm out in front of me and said, "Perhaps you'd rather talk about Mr. Montgomery."

I sat back down. The blood rushed from my head, and for a split second I felt lightheaded and confused. "I don't know what you're talking about."

"No, of course not." He smiled broadly, exposing a missing eye tooth.

"Why do you ask?"

"I thought you wanted to know. That's who you've been asking about this evening as you passed out those blankets, isn't it?"

"What if it is?"

"Then I say you didn't get very far. Those people on the streets aren't going to talk to you. You're not one of them. You're not even from here. They don't know you. You have no credibility. Didn't Miss Duval tell you that?"

"We'll leave Genny out of this. I want to know who you are before we talk any further."

"There's no need to know who I am. I'm just here to help, Mr. Fountain."

At hearing my name, I once again stood to go.

"Sit back down," he commanded.

I pursed my lips in displeasure, but sat on the edge of the stool, prepared to bolt for the door if need be.

"You should drink your coffee," he said. "It's getting cold."

"Did you know this Montgomery?"

"No, never met him."

"Then why should I listen to you?"

"I didn't say you had to. All I'm saying is that I may know of someone who did."

"Someone who knew Montgomery? Who is it?"

"Not so fast. If I give you a name, I need to know something. What do you hope to achieve? Why are you so interested?"

"If you're asking, then my reason is probably the same as yours."

The man turned away and pulled a coin from his pocket.

"You're not going to tell me?" I asked.

He looked at me, his dark, penetrating eyes glaring from beneath his eyebrows. "There's a woman. She lives in the Ninth Ward just over the Industrial Canal off St. Claude. She goes by the name of Miss Cora. She knows most of what goes on with people like your Mr. Montgomery. She might be able to help. She might know something."

"How can I get a hold of her?"

"I just told you. Her name is Miss Cora."

"But that's hardly an address."

He slapped the coin on the counter and tipped his fedora to me. "Good night, Mr. Fountain."

~

The next morning, Portier didn't ask any questions when I asked if Jeffrey knew his way around the Ninth Ward. I supposed he didn't want to know. He also didn't answer my question directly. He simply dialed a number, said a few words, hung up, and went about his morning routine.

Jeffrey arrived fifteen minutes later.

The young mechanic didn't ask any questions as he drove me through the narrow streets of the Bywater near the river. I asked if he knew where he was taking me.

"Ninth Ward is all Mr. Charles told me. Upper or Lower?"

"Excuse me?"

"Upper or Lower Ninth Ward? One's on this side of the Canal, the other's on the other."

"Oh," I replied. I didn't know.

"What's the address?"

"Miss Cora."

"No, I asked for an address."

"I heard you. All I have is her name. Miss Cora."

Jeffrey yanked on the Neckar knob and stopped the car along the curb. "That's it? You mean, that's what Mr. Charles asked me to do, drive you all over hell's creation looking for a Miss Cora?"

"She's on the other side of the Industrial Canal. I remember now. That would be Lower, right?"

Jeffrey put the Hawk in gear and sped from the curb. He drove me across the Canal and stopped in front of a small market on St. Claude.

"I'll go in and see what I can find out," I offered.

"Yeah, that might be a good idea. That's why I stopped."

To my surprise, the woman behind the counter did know a Miss Cora and gave me directions. I returned to the car. We passed Jackson Barracks when I asked Jeffrey to turn around.

"How do you know I have to turn around?"

"The woman back there said if we got to Arabi we've gone too far. We're about to Arabi, aren't we? Just turn around, please. She'll be riverside of St. Claude."

I'd been to New Orleans enough times to know what riverside meant and how to use it in conversation. Due to New Orleans' geographical location, the city was virtually surrounded by either the Mississippi River or Lake Pontchartrain. Riverside meant toward the river; lakeside meant toward the lake. North, south, east, or west was immaterial.

We drove several blocks back the way we'd come before I asked him to stop by an elderly man rocking on his front porch, enjoying the morning sun. He responded cordially as I approached and asked if a Miss Cora lived in the neighborhood. He didn't answer at first.

"You know her?" he said after a moment.

"No, sir, but we have a mutual acquaintance that I need to tell her about."

He nodded, but it was a half-hearted nod as if he wasn't sure whether he should tell me or not. Finally he looked down the street and pointed to a smoky blue shotgun house with a porch. "She's sittin' out front, she is. You tell her Mort said hey, and she'll talk to ya."

I thanked him and returned to the Hawk where Jeffrey had rolled down the passenger window to hear the conversation.

"Okay, I can take it from here," I said to him. "Thanks for the lift."

"Are you kidding me? No, I'm not dropping you off and leaving. I'll park right here until you're done."

"That won't be necessary. I'm going to that blue house."

"Well, then, you walk down to the blue house, and I'll follow, but I'm not leaving you. Mr. Charles would have my ass if I dropped you off and left."

I walked to the house to which the elderly man had directed me. Miss Cora, who looked to be as old as he was, rocked on a swing, her head against the back, her eyes closed. The metal gate squeaked as I opened it, making just enough noise to jostle her from her dozing. She watched me carefully as I made my way up the walk while she dabbled the back of her hair to freshen it.

She didn't smile, but her face was kind. Years of toil were etched into the wrinkles of her black face. Gray and silver strands scattered through her hair. They glittered in the sunlight and blew about in the light breeze. She had a gracious, gentle air about her, with a sophistication unlike her modest surroundings.

I introduced myself as a pastor, mentioned Mort and Mr. Montgomery's names, and asked if I could sit with her for a while.

She moved to one side of the swing and patted the cushion beside her for me to sit. "Then it's true; Mr. Montgomery is dead," she said, seeming to know what I came to talk to her about.

"Yes, I'm afraid so. I was wondering what you could tell me about him. I heard you knew him."

"Who told you?"

"I'd rather not go into that."

"Because you don't know, do you?"

When I didn't answer, she smiled. "I'm old, Reverend, but not daft. There isn't much you need to hide from me."

"I'm not so young myself, Miss Cora. I'd rather not take the time to discuss what doesn't matter."

She smiled. "Well said. Perhaps we should get right to the point, then. What do you want to know?"

"I'm the one who found Mr. Montgomery on Decatur Street near the Mint Building. I was there when he died. Someone at the scene said his name was Montgomery, but I haven't been able to substantiate it."

"Why do you want to?"

"I have reason to believe his name isn't Montgomery at all. His family has a right to know what's happened to him."

"Then it seems our conversation will be short."

"What do you mean?"

"Well, like you said, what's the point of discussing something that doesn't matter? His family didn't matter. They weren't interested in him."

"But I think his life was very significant. It might not appear that way on the surface, looking as if he was homeless

107

and all, but I think there's more to the man than what I could see as he was dying."

"That's interesting," she said. "I mean, by the way you worded your impression of him."

"Then I'm not off base?"

"Oh, no, you're as right as day."

"Then will you tell me, Miss Cora, will you tell me honestly? Was he leading a double life? I mean, was he really homeless?"

She smiled again, as if the question amused her. "He was as homeless as homeless could be, sir. He was homeless in every sense of the word. Did he have a place to go home to at night? I couldn't tell you. He never told me that, but it didn't matter. In his mind and by his actions, he was every bit as homeless as anyone I've ever known. He was one of them, Reverend. Whether he had a home or not wasn't important. What was important was that he was one of them."

"Where'd he concentrate his efforts?"

"There's a makeshift community on the other side of the Canal lakeside of St. Claude. It's called Labreville, named after St. Benedict Joseph Labre, the patron saint of the homeless. Mr. Montgomery helped create that community for those unable to go to a mission."

"Unable to go? Why's that?"

"Some of them got kicked out of the mission for various reasons and can't go back. You know what I mean. Even missions have rules and standards. For those people who couldn't go to them, Mr. Montgomery gave 'em food and shelter at Labreville. He talked to them, mostly men, mostly young men. They face addiction, you know, behavioral problems, or run-ins with the law and can't find work. He knew there was no place in this town for men like that. They either get killed or kill themselves. The lucky ones get thrown into the cooler. At least there they get a meal and a bed."

"Was there anyone you can think of that didn't appreciate what he was doing who would want to harm him?"

"You mean someone that didn't appreciate him helping the unfortunate?"

"Yes, something like that."

"Oh, sure, Reverend, all the time. Some folks hated it, said he was actually promotin' homelessness in this city by creatin' more blight and invitin' more people from up north to come down here so they could eat and get warm, but I can't say there were many of 'em. They weren't as angry about Labreville as they were about what he was doing at Charity."

"Charity?"

"The hospital. Where folks go when they can't pay. You know what I'm talking about."

"Yes, I know of such hospitals, but I'm not sure why people would be so adamant against him working at one."

"Because it was the polio ward he helped. Them folks in the polio ward are treated like lepers, they are. Folks didn't like him workin' in the ward then comin' into their neighborhoods. Mr. Montgomery wasn't afraid of no polio. He didn't care what the neighborhood thought. He just wanted to help people—even those in the iron lungs."

"How did he manage to get in? I thought no one could enter the polio wards."

"He saw just the ones in isolation, not the ones quarantined or nothin'."

"Still, that doesn't make sense, Miss Cora. I minister to such patients and their families in Indiana. Only very close relatives are allowed in the wards, such as the mothers and fathers of the children."

"I'm just sayin' it like I hear it, like he tells me, Reverend. If you ask me, he gets in 'cause he does more than just volunteer. I wouldn't be surprised if they someday name a wing after him."

I sat back and thought for a second. "A wing? You mean a wing of the hospital? If they'd name a wing of the hospital after him, then he must've contributed a lot of money to them. He must be very wealthy."

Miss Cora rocked and lifted her eyebrows as if I was on to something.

"And you know the name the hospital would dedicate the wing to, don't you?"

She shook her head. "No, sir, I don't know nothin'."

"I think you know it wouldn't be Montgomery."

"Don't have a clue, but it don't matter no more. He's gone. His work is done, too."

"Isn't there someone who'll look after Labreville?"

"I couldn't tell you. I wish I knew. I worry about that."

"Yes, I imagine you would. You seem to be the type of person who looks after others, maybe even worry about them a bit."

"And you as well, sir, you as well. That's why you're asking all these questions, isn't it? There's somebody you're worried about."

I wondered how she knew. Was it evident on my face? I couldn't lie so I didn't try. I said honestly, "Yes, there's a young man. His name is Donnie for all I know."

She didn't have to tell me she knew the boy. Her eyes gave it away immediately.

"He sings, doesn't he?" I asked her.

"Like no angel I've ever heard, Reverend, and, believe me, there are a lot of mighty good singers around here."

I hoped my silence would encourage her to continue, but it didn't. She just looked at me. She studied my face, then smiled gently and repositioned herself on the swing. "He's not a bad kid," she finally said.

"I never thought he was."

"Then you don't know him very well, do you?"

"I don't know what you mean."

"Some would disagree."

"He needs help, that's all he needs."

"Oh, I agree, but he won't get it 'round here. He's tried to get a job—a good job—but he can't. No one will hire him."

"Why not?"

She looked at me as if to determine by my expression if I really didn't know. "He's a thief," she said bluntly.

I looked at her with disbelief.

"Or so he was accused," she added. "That's why his folks kicked him out of their home up in Kentucky. They didn't like what the neighbors thought of havin' a thief livin' next door. He got put away for a while at the reformatory in Lagrange, I understand. Then when he got out, his folks told him he had to leave home and get a new start. That's when he came to New Orleans. Somewhere along the line someone told him he could get a job singin' here. He heard that no one would care about his past here."

"But they do care, don't they?"

"They care very much, Reverend, yes, indeed, they do. Once there's wind you're a thief there's no job for you in the shops, the eatin' places, or the clubs in this town, and you know New Orleans is full of shops and eatin' places, and clubs."

"He's anxious. That's why he needs help."

"You'd be anxious, too, Reverend. Lord, we all would."

111

"No, I'm not using the word loosely. I mean anxious in the clinical sense. He doesn't appear to have addiction issues from what I can see aside from nicotine, but he has an emotional issue. That can lead to alcohol."

"Or drugs. You don't need to be tellin' me. I know all about that, but I'm gonna tell you somethin'. His good fortune's about to run out. He's not gonna get very far with that young woman he hangs with."

"There's a girl?"

"I don't remember her name. I think he calls her Miss Karen or Miss Connie or somethin' like that. I don't approve of her. I try not to speak ill of no one, but she carries an ill spirit with her, mark my words. It don't make sense."

"Make sense how?"

"Why she dotes on Donnie like she does."

"He's a likeable fellow."

"That's not what I mean. No, she's the type of person, Reverend—and I've seen this type of woman in this town before—that latches onto to a man for one purpose whether it be money or power or to get from here to there. They chew him up just to spit him out. Don't think they don't exist."

"I can't see that happening to Donnie. I mean, I can't see him being attracted to someone like that."

"Don't you, Reverend? You don't know young men, then. Donnie's had a bad lot in life. He's got a record. His own parents have kicked him out of their home. He has no one, but out of the blue comes this pretty young thing takin' an interest in him. He's mesmerized by her. I can see it plain as day. That boy is head over heels for her."

"What's in it for her?"

"Beats me. I've tried to figure that one out myself. She dabbles in drugs. You can tell it in her eyes. When she doesn't have make-up on, you can tell it by her skin, too."

"But Donnie doesn't have any money to pay for drugs."

"Maybe she's not using him for his money."

"I'm not following you."

"He's a thief."

"Or so she thinks."

"Exactly. If she doesn't have the money to do what she wants in this town maybe Donnie will steal it for her. If he gets caught, she still has the drugs, but doesn't have to do the time. A boy like Donnie won't snitch on a young woman like her. I'd bet the farm on it. Like I said, she'll chew him up long enough to spit him out. That's what I don't like about her."

Suddenly, I didn't want to talk anymore. What Miss Cora said was probably true, and if it was, the need to find Donnie was even more urgent.

"What's the matter?" she asked. "You don't look too good."

"I need to find him."

"If you think you're gonna stop him from seein' that girl, you're headin' down a dead-end street, Reverend."

"I still need to find him. He knew this Mr. Montgomery. I need to know what he knew about him. In so doing, maybe I can help Donnie where Mr. Montgomery left off." I sat on the swing and rocked for a few minutes, thinking back on Toby Markle. I sighed before saying, "I've taken enough of your time." I stood to go.

Miss Cora didn't look at me or say good-bye. She focused toward the street.

I turned to look. Donnie strolled down the sidewalk, hands in his pockets, looking down at the old, cracked cement. He

113

turned to come up the walk, lifted his head to see Miss Cora on the swing, but saw me instead, and stopped.

For a fleeting second, we both looked at each other—dumfounded by what we saw. I couldn't speak. I didn't know what to say. He didn't try to speak, either. Instead, he bolted down the street the way he'd come.

I turned to Miss Cora. "Where's he running to?"

She wouldn't answer.

"Does he come here often?"

Miss Cora nodded. "He checks on me. He's a good boy."

"So please tell me. Where's he running?"

"I don't know."

"I think you do. He came from that way and ran back that way. I need to talk with him. Why won't you tell me?"

Miss Cora straightened her back defiantly, but didn't say a word.

I didn't argue. I didn't see the point. Instead, I walked briskly to the car that Jeffrey had running for me.

Chapter 9

I was surprised when I opened the door to the cottage on Ursulines to find Portier standing in the parlor with one arm outstretched toward me, the phone receiver in his hand. "It's Angelle Lyons. She's in town and would like to see you," he said.

After taking the call, I wasted no time hurrying to the small café where she said she would be. I found her sitting at an intimate table in the corner, nursing a French 75 under the canopy of a wide-brimmed hat more suitable for summer than late winter. She smiled when she saw me and gestured for me to sit across from her. I did so, but by the time I had made myself comfortable her smiled had faded, replaced with a look of deep concern. She sipped her cocktail and offered me one, but I refused, preferring a cup of chicory, instead.

"It was kind of you to see me," she said when my coffee had arrived.

"Not at all, Miss Lyons. I would drop everything to see you."

She smiled again, but it was short-lived. "Have you heard anything more about my father? I'm sorry. Perhaps I should've referred to him as the man you found in the park."

"No, not much time has passed since we last spoke. You could've called me rather than make the long drive if that's what you wanted to ask. It would've saved you a trip."

"I make the drive often. I keep myself busy while in the city." Angelle picked up her drink and sipped it gently—so gently that I doubted a drop of alcohol reached beyond her lips. "I've thought a great deal about our conversation, Mr. Fountain. I know you didn't get much out of my siblings, but I believe you. I believe you're being genuine when you say the man you found was my father."

"Then I urge you desperately, Miss Lyons, to encourage your family to come to New Orleans to identify him. Better yet, we could go now, and you could identify him yourself."

She shook her head as she reached for an embroidered hanky that lay across her lap. "That would be impossible. I couldn't do it."

"Someone must. If the man isn't your father, at least we'd know."

"If he isn't my father, then what a cruel task to put me through."

"That isn't my intent, Miss Lyons."

She dabbled at the corner of one eye and gathered her composure. "I know it isn't. Accept my apology. I wish my brothers would to do it themselves."

"Do you mind telling me more about your brothers?"

She looked at me skeptically and asked why.

"Because you're upset right now. I get the feeling that knowing for certain if your father is dead or not will help alleviate your anxiety. I don't understand why your family is so adamant about not wanting to learn the truth."

"Adamant isn't the right word. There's nothing we're adamant about."

"I don't believe that's entirely true. I met Andre. He seemed rather angry at your father."

She shook her head. "You call it anger. I call it a spoiled tantrum. Yes, Andre's put out. He's always been put out with father. He feels like a step-child compared to Joyce and Manny, but he needn't feel that way. He brought his poor financial situation on by himself. I don't know what he's told you, but that's exactly how my father saw his predicaments."

"How did your father respond?"

"How any strong-willed parent with high standards would respond. He saw my brother, Andre, as a grown man. He believed Andre was astute enough to find his own solutions."

"Was he?"

"Absolutely. My father expected all of us to approach our challenges thoughtfully and methodically. He expected the same out of his daughters as he did his sons. That's why Joyce is such an independent thinker. Father encouraged it. Granted, she takes her independence to extremes at times, but my point is that Andre was afforded the same opportunities as the rest of us to be successful in our own right. He made bad choices. I don't feel sorry for him at all."

"He's in quite a bit of debt, isn't he?"

Angelle laughed. "That's putting it mildly. He badgers my boyfriend, Glen Balfour, about it all the time. It's very awkward."

"Why your boyfriend? Does he have money?"

Angelle lost her jovial expression. I suspected she'd said more than she wanted to reveal.

"Does Glen Balfour come from money?" I repeated.

She shook her head. "No, but he's rather creative at coming up with ways to obtain cash now and then."

This time, it was I who laughed.

"Glen's adventures are exciting, that's why I'm attracted to him," she said, avoiding eye contact, "but they're far from being funny. They're becoming frightening, and I don't find it humorous that Andre continues to request funds from Glen. It only encourages him."

"It was explained to me that your brother Manfred can't help Andre because the money from your father is restricted in some way by your father, but is that the real reason?"

"I don't know. I believe Manny could find some money if he wanted to, but he's more like my father in that way. He's very good at business. He and his partner, Reed Alemand, have done very well, but Manny watches his money closely. I don't think he's crazy about throwing good money into bad projects."

"And Reed respects that?"

"Oh, implicitly. Reed has always respected my brother's wealth and decisions. I've never had any inkling to the contrary. Manny has issues with mother and father, don't get me wrong. He cringes when they go at it with each other, but he keeps his distance. He keeps his wife and children away from the house unless he can't avoid it. He doesn't want his family to be subjected to my parents' behaviors and lifestyles."

"Is it that bad?"

She smiled and took a sip of her cocktail without answering the question.

"What's your mother like?" I asked, approaching from different angle.

"I can answer that question in two words: boy crazy. I probably shouldn't be telling you this, but that's why father cut her off. She likes the company of men. I say boy crazy because these men don't have to be mature, they just have to be wealthy. Father let her behavior go on far too long. He didn't want a scandal, but her escapades were already scandalous around Lafayette. You don't need to look at me with pity, Mr.

Fountain. My mother and I are not close. We're nothing alike, and I'd prefer to separate myself from her behavior as much as possible."

"Except for Glen Balfour."

Angelle's expression turned grave. I suspected she thought I was passing judgment on her for being with a man like Balfour. It wasn't judgment on my part as much as it was a hunch. After all, I hadn't met him yet. Nevertheless, Angelle didn't answer my question, and I didn't press the issue. Instead, I asked, "What about you?"

She eyed me with distrust. "What about me?"

"Tell me more about you."

"Is that a roundabout way of asking more about my boyfriend?"

"No; it was a genuine question."

"Then I'll give you a genuine answer. I don't have much in my life I can hang my hat on. I guess you could say my life has been filled with men like Glen Balfour. If you don't already know, although I suspect you do, I've had a couple of failed marriages. My father hasn't been proud of me because of that. I suppose in his eyes I'm not much higher on the monogamous scale than my mother, but it wasn't anything like that. They were simply poor choices. We all make them. I just happen to make them over and over with the same type of men." She twirled the swizzle stick inside her glass and said bluntly, "I blame my father for that."

My eyebrows rose involuntarily at the statement. "In what way?"

"He was never home. I'm not sure how a young woman can gain the proper perspective of what to look for in a man when she has no role model to look up to. I so wanted my father's attention. The only way I got it was to marry badly.

119

Oh, believe me the men I married got his attention very quickly. It was a costly and devastating way to find out how much he loved me, but it did the trick."

"Does your father's disappearance bother you?"

"Why should it?" she retorted quickly in what I believed to be an honest reflection of her thoughts. "He was never there for me before. Why should his absence bother me now?"

"Because I think it does despite what you say."

Angelle Lyons grasped her glass boldly and finished the rest of the cocktail in one swallow. "I love my father," she said. "I just don't know in what way. Do I love him because he's my father? Do I love the idea that I have a father who comes to my rescue when I need him? Or do I simply love the wealth and influence that comes with a man like my father?" She captured the attention of the waiter and ordered another drink then turned to me and said, "That's the mystery, Mr. Fountain. That's the real mystery about my father's disappearance as far as I'm concerned."

"Oh, and who do we have here?" a male voice said from behind me.

Angelle and I were so deep in conversation that neither of us noticed the man entering the café and walking toward us. The stench of cigar and hard liquor preceded him to our table.

"Glen; where have you been?" Angelle asked.

"Out and about, my dear kitten, out and about. I have colleagues to see, business to transact."

Angelle gave me a side glance before saying, "We don't want to hear about it."

On the contrary, I was very interested in hearing what he had to say.

She introduced me to Glen. He shook my hand, entwining his fingers awkwardly in mine, having had too much to drink to shake my hand properly.

"A reverend, you say?" Glen bellowed. "Whoa. Better watch my step, huh, babe?"

"Glen, sit down."

He did so, accidentally kicking the chair in which he'd chosen to sit, scooting it farther away. He tried to hide the embarrassment by embellishing a cockamamie story about his colleagues and what sounded like a legitimate business deal in the making. "The future of this city is in pies," he said. "Wouldn't you agree? I mean, look at Hubig. They make pies. That's all they make. How easy is that? Sounds cool, doesn't it?"

Angelle's drink arrived at the table, and I asked for mine to be topped. Balfour continued to ramble.

When I'd listened long enough, I stopped the conversation by saying to Angelle, "I want you to look at something." I reached inside my coat pocket and pulled out Mr. Montgomery's finial. I held it in my hand in the middle of the table for her to get a good look at it in the light.

The finial glistened.

Her eyes widened.

I let her focus on the intricate piece for several seconds before asking if she'd ever seen it before.

She shook her head, but it wasn't convincing.

Balfour leaned toward me to get a closer look at the finial, too. The acrid odor of his breath nearly curled my nose hairs. I ignored him, hoping he would return to an upright position his seat. He didn't budge. I saw him try to glean Angelle's reaction from the corner of his eye.

"I'll be damned," he said under his breath.

"What about?" I asked.

"Nothing," Angelle stated, replacing her hanky inside her purse as she stood to go.

Balfour also stood, nearly falling on top of me as he did so. "Where did you get that?" he asked.

"Do you recognize it?"

"Are you coming, Glen?" Angelle asked.

Glen pointed at the finial but didn't say anything.

"Glen, it's time to go. Now."

I put the finial back in my pocket. Although I didn't receive a definitive answer as to whether either one of them recognized the piece, I suspected Angelle's reaction and Balfour's dumbfounded comments were all I needed to draw a proper conclusion.

The two left the café as quickly as Balfour could stumble towards the door.

I paid the tab and exited the café, deciding to stop by the club where Genny worked. I didn't know if she had time to review with me the latest information I'd gathered, but it was worth a try. I had no one else to turn to as a sounding board.

The club where Genny sang was lively with late afternoon revelers, already in their clubbing costumes. Feathers, beads, sequins, and skin were abundant. The jazz was loud. The crowd didn't mind.

A woman approached me and draped a large strand of purple, green, and gold beads around my neck. "There," she said. "Now loosen your tie and dance with me."

I didn't explain that I had two left feet and hadn't danced since 1931. Instead, I spotted Genny sitting by the bar and motioned to the woman I was with her. The woman took the beads and walked away indignantly, unable to handle my rejection. I didn't care. She was gone.

Genny didn't notice me until I stood directly beside her. Her attention was on a large shrimp po-boy.

"*Laissez les bon temps rouler,*" I said. "You never have trouble with that, do you?"

She looked surprised to see me. "Oh, goodness. Look what the cat drug in. Now where's Chuck? Is he still in a snit?"

"I'm afraid so. It's my fault, however. I've been neglecting him. I think I pay more attention to Bentley."

"Bentley's better company. I wouldn't worry about ol' Chuck. Finding a dead body wasn't your fault unless you were the one who killed him."

I laughed heartily, believing she meant it as a joke. She didn't laugh, however. She was serious. When I realized that, I exclaimed, "Good gracious! Certainly not!"

"That's not the scuttlebutt on the street."

"Are you being serious, Genny? Do people really suspect me or are you playing a practical joke?"

"You know me well enough by now to know I don't laugh at bad jokes."

"Where are you hearing this?"

"It doesn't matter."

"Yes, I think it does."

"No, let's get you something to eat. Our special's Louisiana shrimp tonight. Would you like some?"

I shook my head.

"I'll get you something anyway, and then we'll talk."

"Do you perform tonight?"

"Honey, I perform even when I'm not getting paid to do so. Don't worry about that."

"But I do. Between you and Portier, it seems I've made quite a mess of your lives lately."

She told me to hush and ordered me some food. She returned with a sandwich for me that could make two meals.

"Do you always eat at the club?" I asked.

"Honey, I have to make groceries before I can eat at home."

"Make groceries?"

"Yes, don't you make groceries?"

"No, where I'm from we buy or get groceries."

She giggled. "Oh, not in New Orleans, sweetheart. Here, we make our groceries whether we buy them ourselves or have them delivered. I haven't done either in weeks. I didn't even brew coffee today. Can you believe that?"

"Why didn't you stop for some along the way?"

"I tried. I stopped at the café down the street, but decided against going in. I saw you there."

She looked at me for a reaction. I tried not to have one.

"I was talking with Angelle Lyons," I said.

"Yes, while sipping on cocktails."

"I had chicory."

"Drying her tears with the edge of that fancy, silk hanky."

"I seemed to have upset her."

"No doubt. She's the upsetting kind. I've seen her before."

"In here?"

"Sure, in here and with that seedy little man she runs around with."

"Glen Balfour. Do you know him?"

"I know of him. I don't plan to get to know him. I don't like him. Angelle Lyons must think very little of herself to be with him."

I didn't have a response to that comment. It seemed to sum up the couple's relationship on its own.

"Are you going to eat your po-boy?" she asked, eyeing my plate as she gobbled on hers.

124

I picked up my sandwich and nibbled on the end to let her know I wanted the sandwich, but I also wanted time to think.

"Trust me," she said. "I know the people in this town if that's what you're wondering. Now tell me what you've learned since I saw you last."

I told her about my experience passing out blankets and chocolate bars to those sleeping on the streets with the hopes of finding Donnie. I could see she was intrigued when I mentioned the man who climbed onto the stool next to me at the Clover Grill and gave me the lead on Miss Cora.

"Did you talk with her?"

"This morning, yes, and I also saw Donnie, but he ran away from me before I had a chance to talk with him."

"I don't understand why you need his information so bad. I think you know who this Montgomery man is without finding Donnie."

"But no one else believes Montgomery is Roger Lyons, including the Lyons family. I'm telling you I believe Donnie can get to the bottom of Mr. Montgomery's identity for me. I have to find him. He's a singer, a good one. Do you know if he's been here to sing?"

"No, he's not been here."

"How can you be so sure?"

"Because I can picture him in my head. I know everyone who sings in this club, but I haven't seen anyone like your Donnie. Surely you realize I must keep my eye out on my competition."

A waitress walked by. Genny waved her down. "Honey, get Dickie-boy here something to drink. What do you want?"

"Nothing."

"Well, we don't have chicory here." She turned her attention back to the waitress. "Get him a gimlet."

125

I didn't have time to object before a shrill voice chimed from behind our backs.

"Oh, how Moline, the Princess of Rokavia, could use a cigarette right now!"

Genny glanced at the woman then turned back to her dinner. "Not again, Moline. You said that the last time. It's old and boring. Can't you see we're eating? Where's Victorius? He's the one you should be bothering."

Moline plopped herself on a chair beside Genny.

I looked at her arms. "Victorius still has your arm cuff?" I asked.

She ignored me. "Genny, do you think your boss would ever let me sing with you on stage?"

"No."

"I could be a part of your show."

"Absolutely not," she replied, a shrimp dangling from her lips.

Moline turned her head to avoid me and whispered as if she thought I couldn't hear, "I could use some cash. I'm willing to work."

"That's fine, but not on stage with me, you won't. I have a reputation to uphold. I thought money was why you hooked up with Victorius. You said he was rich."

Moline turned again toward Genny and whispered something in her ear. This time I couldn't hear.

"What job?" Genny asked. "You have a job? Well, then, wait until you get paid."

Moline whispered something else.

Genny took another bite from her sandwich, but didn't respond.

"Do you need some cash?" I asked Moline.

She looked at me. I could see my question took her by surprise. I could also see her eyes were dilated.

"Tell me something I need to know, and it will be worth cash," I said.

"How much?"

"It depends on what you tell me. Do you know a young man around the Quarter that sings? His name is Donnie. He runs around with a woman by the name of Miss Karen or Miss Connie, something like that."

Moline's eyes widened. She looked away. "No," she said curtly. "Don't know him." Without saying another word, she rose slowly, steadied herself against a chair, and wobbled away.

Genny looked at me excitedly. "Oh, Dickie-boy, are you thinking what I'm thinking? She either doesn't need the money that bad or ..."

"The money wasn't worth divulging the answer," I said.

Chapter 10

I woke early the next morning refreshed and with a spirit of optimism I hadn't experienced since arriving in New Orleans. The sun shone through the sheers and cascaded over the top of my bed. I could feel the warmth of the rays under the covers—a welcomed sensation after some unseasonably cold nights. I sensed it was going to be a good day.

Bentley waited at my doorway to greet me. He followed me closely, wagging his tail in rhythm with each step, until I reached the doorway to the kitchen.

Portier stood at the stove with a skillet in hand and pointed to the table where three eggs over easy and a hearty portion of andouille lay, still piping hot, on a plate. To the side sat a bowl of creamy grits and four pieces of sourdough toast, lightly buttered.

I must have looked like one of the mo'ai figures on Easter Island with my stoned look and gaping mouth, staring at the feast, because Portier asked, "What are you gawking at?"

I questioned what occasion called for such a breakfast.

"Three squares a day, that's what you Hoosiers are raised on, but you haven't had a square meal since you got off the train. You don't need an occasion, Fountain. You need to sit down and eat."

I did so and devoured the breakfast gratefully.

Bentley sat by my feet. Apparently, I was more likely than Portier to drop bits of food off my fork.

"Besides, you're going to have a busy day," Portier said after he sat at the place setting across from me.

"Is that so?"

"You had a call. A Miss Cora somebody."

"Really? That's surprising. The way I left her yesterday I thought I'd never hear from her again."

"She said she had someone who was ready to talk."

"Did she say who?"

"She did not, and I didn't ask. I've become pretty good at being your personal secretary of late, Fountain, but I don't give a diddly-squat about who it is you talk with."

"What time should—oh, excuse me; please, finish your breakfast."

"No, what were you going to ask? Was it what time you should meet this mystery somebody you're so hell-bent on meeting?"

"Yes, that's it."

"Anytime you want, she said. She said it didn't make any difference. After you meet, I want you to come back. I have an idea." Portier winked at me as he popped a piece of andouille into his mouth.

"What sort of idea?"

"It's about the case."

"You mean you've been thinking about my case? I thought you were against it."

"I never said I was against it. I just don't like how you're going about it."

"Very well. Then let's hear it."

"Not now. You meet this Cora woman. I'll catch you later. Never mind about the dishes. I've got them." He winked again. "Just go."

I didn't take a chance on him changing his mind. I devoured my breakfast and immediately took a cab to the old, smoky blue shotgun in the Ninth Ward where Miss Cora lived. I wasn't surprised to see who sat on the swing, waiting for me. It wasn't Miss Cora.

Donnie sat with one foot on a seat cushion, smoking a cigarette, and rocking slowly back and forth. He didn't look at me as I approached. His focus lay down the street to nowhere in particular.

I sat in an adjacent chair.

"Want a Lucky?" he offered.

I noticed his pack of Lucky Strikes was again almost empty. I shook my head.

"Don'chu smoke?" he asked.

"Not a bit."

The boy tittered. "Everyone smokes, mister. What the hell?"

"Why do you?"

"Somethin' to do." He looked at me and added, "But you prolly don't need somethin' to do, do you?"

"I find plenty. What else do you do?"

"I dunno. Scrounge for scraps mostly. I sing tunes, bum for coins, smoke."

"Smoking helps?"

"Takes the edge off. That hard to believe?"

"No, but smoking takes the edge off of what? Life? For me, tobacco brings back memories I've worked hard to forget."

Donnie continued to look at me, but he didn't say anything.

"I don't want to bore you with my story," I said.

He took a puff and said casually, "I'll listen to anyone's story for a few coins. I'll even nod for a buck."

I got the hint. I reached into my pocket and pulled out two one dollar bills.

He reached for the money eagerly.

"I used to pick hornworms as a kid," I said.

"For fun?"

"Hardly. It was for money. My folks didn't have a lot. I was raised in a house without electricity and plumbing back in southern Indiana. I used to pick hornworms off the underside of tobacco leaves so we could eat. I can still feel the sticky goo on the leaves. Sometimes the worms would stick to the plant so tight they'd mush in my fingers as I pried them off. I'd run down to the creek at the end of the day to wash the stench of the worms and tobacco from my hands, but I couldn't. The smell wouldn't wash off. Nothing could get rid of that horrible stench from my hands. It never went away. I can still smell it to this day."

"So?"

"So I vowed I'd never chew or smoke anything with tobacco as long as I lived."

"I think you're crazy."

"Am I? Hornworms poop on those leaves, you know. You're the one smoking hornworm poop. Now, who's crazy?"

Donnie tittered again. "You used to kill 'em as a kid, and I used to keep 'em in a jar as pets. Ugly, fat, green things, weren't they? We called 'em tomato worms."

I could see his eyes drift to a place I suspected used to be called home.

"What I picked off were hornworms."

"Same difference."

"Not really. It's in the stripes. Tomato worms have white markings in a v-shape. Hornworms' markings are diagonal like a cigarette. Subtle, but different."

He blew a plume of smoke toward my face. "You're full of shit, aren't you? Worthless tidbits of shit that don't mean a thing."

"I'm trying to make a point."

"Then make it."

"There are subtle differences in everything in life. Your life is no exception."

"You got that right. My life is so subtle right now nothing is moving. At least a raindrop makes a ripple."

"But what you want out of life is bigger than a raindrop, Donnie. You can't give up. Don't let Mr. Montgomery's death be the end of you. He didn't do all he did for you so that you'd give up. He had a purpose for you. I know you'll miss his encouragement, but as long as you remember what he did for you, you'll always have that encouragement to hang onto."

Donnie dropped his cigarette on the porch and extinguished the butt with his foot. He looked into the pack of Luckies beside his leg and then leaned on the back of the swing, closing his eyes.

"What can you tell me about Mr. Montgomery?" I asked.

Donnie shrugged. "He was good, you know. He made sure we had what we needed like food and stuff to get through the night. Blankets, too. You know, things we needed.

"Do you know anything about him that could tell me who he was or where he came from?"

"Naw, man, he was pretty secret. I knew a couple of things, but they were secret."

"Secret or not, they would help, Donnie."

He shook his head. "No, they were more than secret. They were sacred."

I took a deep breath. I knew what sacred meant. It meant Donnie wasn't going to tell me what I wanted to know.

He leaned toward me, however, and said softly, "There's a couple of things I do know, however. There's this guy that used to come around and catch Mr. Montgomery off guard. Mr. Montgomery never looked too pleased to see him. He'd hand the guy a couple of bills and the guy would be off. Mr. Montgomery's mood would change real quick-like after the guy would leave. Then Mr. Montgomery would split, too. Like lightning fast."

"Who was the guy, do you know? What did he look like?"

Donnie described a man in his early to mid-thirties with dark greasy hair, handsome lines on his face and a smooth swag to his gait. He wore a nice overcoat, he said, and appeared to like being important.

"How's that?"

"Arrogant, you know, one of those cocky rich cats."

"Did he smoke?"

"Oh, yeah, the nasty ones that guys smoke down here."

"Picayunes."

"Stinks to High Heaven. I've seen the guy before in some of the clubs in the Quarter, the not so nice clubs."

"What's the other thing you know?" I asked.

"It's about a woman." Donnie described the woman, but it didn't sound like any woman I'd met in New Orleans. I caught a glimpse of his eyes, and he instinctively looked away.

"There's something you're not telling me," I said.

"I see her sometimes."

"What do you mean? Do you see her around town, around the Quarter? What?"

"No, I see her as in hooking up once in a while, like dating."

My memory recalled what Miss Cora said about a young woman taking a liking to him.

"You mean this Karen or Connie somebody?"

"Who told you that?" He looked at me, then sat back as if he could see the answer reflecting from my eyes. "If it was Miss Cora, she doesn't like her."

"Do you like her?"

"She's all right."

"What's her name?"

He shrugged. "I call her Karen."

"What does she call herself?"

"She never does. She thinks it's cute I don't know her real name. Anyway, it doesn't matter. We were at this club and someone called her Karen or something like that. Karen's what I heard. Karen's what I call her."

"But she knows Mr. Montgomery?"

"I dunno."

"But I thought you said—"

"I said I was with Karen one time when Mr. Montgomery saw us together. He looked at us funny. I thought maybe he knew her."

"Did she see him?"

"She may have. Look, I just wanted a beer, and she was buying. I didn't pay that close attention to whether they knew each other. That's all it is with me and Karen. I show her around, she buys me a beer."

"I think it's more than that, Donnie. I think you know something else about them."

"That's not true. I don't know jack."

"Do you know someone who does?"

134

I took his hesitation as a yes. "What's his or her name?" I asked. "C'mon, Donnie. This is too important to leave me hanging."

"You wouldn't know her. I doubt it's her real name."

"No one knows anyone around here by their real name."

"But she's really weird, like seriously weird. I thought her name was Memphis one time, but that wasn't it. She says she's a princess from someplace I've never heard of before."

I had met only one princess since arriving in town. "Rokavia?"

Donnie looked at me with a wondrous expression of how in the world I would know the place. His demeanor soured when I pressed him for more answers. "I'm getting tired, man," he said. "I gotta go. Thanks for the Washingtons."

I didn't argue or entice him to stay. Instead, I reached into my pocket and pulled out a five.

He stuffed it into his pocket and left.

I stood on the porch alone and took a deep breath. *Moline, Princess of Rokavia.* I should have known there was more to her than alcohol and cigarettes.

⁓

When I arrived back at the cottage, Portier met me at the door. "In the car," he ordered.

We settled in and set off towards the Garden District.

"I have an idea," he said as he drove. "There's this place on Dryades, an excellent shop. Best men's shop in town as far as I'm concerned. Not sure why I didn't think of this before. They sell fine apparel and accessories for men, including walking sticks. They may know something about that finial of yours. Do you have it with you?"

"Lucky for you I carry it everywhere I go."

"I'm not sure luck has anything to do with it, and don't tell me it's now become your lucky charm. If you ask me, that thing has been nothing but trouble. You shouldn't have taken it. Why did you do so?"

I sighed at being interrogated again. "I can't explain it, Portier, I don't know. It seemed to be the right thing to do at the time if I wanted this Montgomery fellow to receive any justice."

"I'm not sure I understand the reasoning behind what you just said, but it is what it is at this point. Maybe this men's shop is the break you need. It's a long shot, but it can't hurt."

"I'm glad to see that you've come around on this case."

"Don't get all gushy-eyed. Like I said, I've never been against you. I just haven't cared for the way you've gone about things."

"Including the finial?"

"Especially the finial and the trip to Lafayette and the traipsing out at night to pass out blankets."

"Who told you about the blankets?"

"Genevieve, of course."

"Maybe it wasn't the most productive course of action, but it did lead me to Miss Cora who led me to Donnie. I learned about a couple of people who may have known Mr. Montgomery."

"First thing first, Fountain, about this Miss Cora woman. Who led you to her?"

I took my sweet time responding. My hesitation must have raised Portier's curiosity because he turned to me with a stern expression and demanded to know.

"I don't know his name. I was having coffee at the Clover Grill when a man sat next to me. He seemed to know quite a bit about what I was doing."

136

"What does that mean?"

"I don't know exactly. It was almost as though he'd been following me as I passed out the blankets. Anyway, he told me about Miss Cora which turned out to be an accurate lead."

Portier pulled along the curb and stopped the car. His expression indicated I was in for a long, well-deserved scolding.

"I know what you're thinking," I said.

"I hope you're not. You're a man of the cloth. You shouldn't be thinking what I'm thinking right now to describe how careless and reckless your actions have been. Have you gone completely out of your mind? This man could be anyone if he's associated with Roger Lyons. He could be a detective or a mobster."

"He's not a detective. The police have all but assured me they're not interested in the case."

"Then he definitely doesn't have your best interest in mind."

"I thought that, too, until he told me about Miss Cora. That changed my opinion of him."

Portier signaled and pulled out onto the street. "I wish I hadn't suggested this jaunt," he muttered. "You never know, your mystery man could be tailing us right now."

We entered the small shop on Dryades and a middle-aged man well dressed in a double-breasted pinstripe suit, French cuffs, and 14-carat cufflinks welcomed us immediately.

Portier wasted no time explaining why we were in his shop.

I showed the gentleman the finial and asked if he recognized it.

He turned the finial in his hand to expose a smooth surface on the back. Despite the scratches and smudges, he recognized one of the engraved letters that identified his establishment. "Yes, this would be one of ours."

"Is it possible to know who bought this particular finial?"

He turned up his nose and shook his head apologetically. "We keep meticulous records of our customers and their purchases, but I wouldn't know where to begin to look. I would need a name or a date."

"Roger Lyons."

The man's congenial demeanor turned sour. "That would be impossible," he said.

"Why?" I asked. "Did he or did he not buy it here? Impossible how?"

"Impossible to divulge."

"We understand confidentiality," Portier said, "but we have reason to believe the man who owned the walking stick with this finial was Mr. Lyons."

"Then Mr. Lyons will have to come into the store, sir."

"I'm afraid that's impossible."

"Then I can't help you."

"Even if it's a life or death matter?"

"Life or death would involve the police, I assume. If that's the case, I'll be happy to answer their questions. So far the police haven't been here to question me so I can't help you, gentlemen. I'm sorry."

We left the shop without further discussion and stood on the sidewalk in the warm sun. Portier apologized for the wild goose chase.

I told him to think nothing more about it. "It wasn't a total waste. I'm certain Montgomery is Roger Lyons. The shopkeeper's evasive answers solidified what I already knew."

"If you know who he is then why do you continue to find answers to questions you know the answer to?"

"Because I don't know who killed him."

Portier took a step toward the car. I took hold of his arm and pointed to a woman walking alone on the other side of the street.

"That's Joyce Nicolet," he said.

"Yes, I know. I wonder what she's doing here in New Orleans."

"She has business ventures in the city, much like her father. It doesn't surprise me that she's here."

"She was at the theater the other night, also," I said. "I only saw her silhouette, but I know it was her."

"I don't doubt that a bit. She was there to support her brother's play."

I nodded as if I agreed, but countered, "That's true, but I can't help believe there was something more to her being there."

"What are you talking about?"

"Mr. Montgomery was at the theater, too. If he's her father, I wonder if she knew he'd be there."

"Your sleuthing skills are off on this one. You're grasping at straws."

I stood for a moment, watching Joyce Nicolet stroll down the street, window shopping as she went.

We turned toward the Golden Hawk only to have our steps blocked by two men in dark suits. The taller gentleman looked at me directly. "Reverend Fountain?"

"Yes, that's right."

He and the other man flipped identification badges in front of me.

"Detective Guy Robicheaux, NOPD. This is my partner, Oren Maison."

I stared at him, stunned.

"You found the body of a man named Montgomery?"

139

"He wasn't dead," I replied. "He was gravely injured, but yes, I'm the one who called in the emergency. He died before help could arrive. What's this about?"

"We just want to talk, following up on his death. How did you come across this guy?"

"I was taking a morning stroll, coming back from the river."

"Can you describe his wound for me?"

"Yes, as best as I can remember. He was slumped over the arm of the park bench. His head was bent down. I could see the back of his head. It was caked with blood. Some of it was still moist, but much of it was dried as if he'd been attacked a couple of hours beforehand. The medical report from the ambulance personnel probably—"

"Was that the first time you saw him?"

"What? Yes, I believe so."

The detective looked at me as if he was giving me a second chance to tell the truth. "We have a witness that saw you in the area, walking past the decedent several minutes earlier," he said.

Portier and I gave each other passing glances.

I took a moment to think. "Come to think of it, they're quite right," I admitted. "Yes, I did pass earlier. Yes, in fact, I was walking on Decatur toward Frenchmen when I first passed him. He was slumped over on the bench at that time as well. I walked to the river and circled back. It wasn't until I passed him the second time that I became alarmed and knew something was wrong."

"What did you do?"

"I ran across the street to one of the shops and had the owner call for help. Then I ran back to the man and told him to hang on, help was on the way."

"But he didn't hold on. Another witness said you killed him."

My mouth gaped before I responded, "If you're referring to the woman who stood over my shoulder as I preached the Gospel to a dying man then I'll have to protest her credibility as a witness. She had no more idea what she was seeing or hearing than the man in the moon."

"She said you took something from his satchel."

"Yes, I pulled out a playbill. I noticed the man had a playbill in his duffle bag. It so happened that the playbill was for the same play Mr. Portier and I had seen the night before. I thought it ironic we both had come from the same play less than twenty-four hours earlier."

"Would it be ironic?" Detective Robicheaux asked blandly. "Or coincidental? Maybe even calculated."

"Calculated? Do you suspect that I killed the man?"

"You were at the play. He was there. You went for a morning walk. He was there. You walked past him the first time, recognized him, bludgeoned him, continued on your way, walked to the river, and walked back to the man to act like the Good Samaritan you claim you are."

"Now see here, you said yourself there were witnesses who saw me the first time when I passed the man. Did they also tell you they saw me bludgeon him?"

"It could've happened."

"It could not have happened because I did no such thing. What motive would I have to kill a defenseless homeless man on a city street in a town where I'm a complete stranger? There is none, Detective."

"Did you know the man, Reverend? You said you saw him the night before. Surely then you knew who he was and that he might be worth murdering."

141

"I didn't know anything of the sort. Has he been identified?"

"Not formally."

"But you have your suspicions about who he is."

"Who do you believe he is?"

"I haven't the foggiest."

"Would you change your tune if I told you you've been seen asking questions about the dead man?"

"It would not. I had a life changing experience even for a pastor, Detective. A human soul is a human soul homeless or not. He deserved a name, and I intended to find out what it was."

The four of us stood in the sun staring into one another's eyes. None of us said a word until I asked, "Are you placing me under arrest, Detective?"

"Not at the moment, but I wouldn't leave town, and I'd turn over all evidence you may have in your possession concerning the case. Do you have any such evidence, Reverend?"

"I do not," I replied.

"Very well. If you did, and you didn't turn it over, such evidence could be considered tampering or an obstruction of justice."

"I understand completely."

"Do you? Well, good, because if that was the case then I would have to arrest you, wouldn't I?"

~

"You've lost your mind!" Portier said as we drove back to the Quarter. "I hope you realize you're in an absolute pickle right now."

I started to explain why I couldn't turn over the finial just yet, but he lifted his hand in front of my face.

"I don't want to hear it!" he yelled. "There's no excuse and no rationalization for lying to the police while you're holding the very evidence he suspects you have right there in your coat pocket."

"He knows no such thing."

"The hell he doesn't. Why do you think he brought it up?"

"Because I asked if I was being arrested. It was an afterthought on his part, nothing more."

"Did you not preach about arrogance on Sundays before you retired? That's exactly what you are right now. You're arrogant thinking you can outsmart the New Orleans police."

I hadn't thought of it that way. "I don't believe Montgomery was killed with his walking stick," I said timidly. "That's why I didn't turn it over."

"I thought you found it broken in the hedges near him. What broke the stick if it wasn't used to kill him?"

I couldn't explain. Of all the questions I'd asked of people, I hadn't asked about the murder weapon.

"You're not a detective," Portier scolded. "I don't care what you think of the people skills you obtained during your ministry and the issues you confronted people with to get to the bottom of their sins, but they didn't include homicide investigations . Don't you understand that? It's not your place to make a determination about the murder weapon. That's the detective's job."

"But I didn't think Detective Robicheaux was going to do it."

"Do what? His job? There you go again. Arrogance. No one will do their job quite like you, will they? So by damn you'll do it for them. Bravo! Good for you. Well, forgive me if I

143

decline to go to your citizen's award ceremony for outstanding service to our community."

I slumped into the seat of the Hawk and sulked.

Portier didn't say another word to me the rest of the trip. In fact, he was out of the car and into the cottage before I had a chance to pull on the door handle to exit.

When I entered the cottage, he was pouring himself a glass of scotch. He pointed to an empty glass in case I wanted to pour myself one, too, but I declined.

"You're absolutely right about everything, Portier," I said. "Not only have I been arrogant, but I've been stupid. I would never recommend a parishioner do the things that I have done. I'm wrong. I'll go to the police station and turn in the finial immediately."

He tipped his glass towards me in agreement, but didn't say a word. I was sure his gesture didn't mean I was forgiven, just that he was in agreement.

I left the cottage and walked the half dozen blocks to the station. Detective Robicheaux welcomed me into his small office as if he was expecting me. Getting the words of apology out of my mouth and handing the finial over to him only made the stuffy room feel that much closer.

He asked a few more questions for clarification, thanked me, then said I was free to go.

I looked at him as if I misunderstood. I expected to be interrogated half the night about the evidence I'd withheld. I expected a bright light overhead and a foul-mouthed sweaty cop spewing venomous threats into my face, ending in a coerced signed confession of my guilt. As it appeared, however, Detective Robicheaux didn't seem to believe the finial was evidence at all.

The thought crossed my mind to tell him about the woman who accused me. I wanted to emphasize that she picked up something from under the bushes that could be a clue. I opened my mouth, but closed it just as quickly. I didn't get the feeling he wanted to hear about an odd woman who picked up something from the bushes. I had already lost credibility with him. Tossing the blame onto someone else would've only incriminated me further. There was so much I wanted to ask him, however, but I didn't dare push my luck.

I left the station and decided I needed to cool my participation in Mr. Montgomery's death before I obstructed justice or, worse yet, became the target of the real murderer's desire to stop my search for the truth.

~

I invited Portier to an early dinner at Leroux's as a reconciliatory gesture. He accepted gratefully, but our conversation was lukewarm through cocktails, and even less during dinner. It wasn't until a generous slice of praline bread pudding accompanied by black coffee was placed before him did his spirits lift enough to inquire about my discussion at the police station.

"It took all of five minutes," I said. "I handed the finial to the detective and gave him a spiel about how I came across it. He laid it on his desk, asked a couple of questions, and said I was free to go."

Portier shook his head as if he was shaking cobwebs out of his ears. "I don't know what to say. I don't know whether to say 'Cheers!' or ask 'What the hell?'"

"I know. It was the oddest thing. He didn't seem to care one way or the other about the finial. He just wanted to have it."

"How did he know you had it?"

"I have no idea. I've only shown it to a couple of people in the Lyons family."

"Like who?"

"Angelle Lyons and her boyfriend, Glen Balfour."

"Maybe he didn't know you actually had something. What if he just wanted to impress upon you that he was in-charge of the investigation and not you? It might have been a matter of principle."

"That could be true, but I don't understand why. I don't get it."

"You weren't meant to *get it*. You were meant to leave the investigation to the proper authorities in the first place."

"But I did what he asked. I turned the finial over to him. He wasn't even interested. I wonder if he's followed that woman around as much as he's followed me."

"What woman?"

"The one who accused me of killing Montgomery in the first place."

"Why would Robicheaux care?"

"Because she took something. I'm almost certain of it. I don't know what it was, but she was as interested in something on the ground as she was in watching that man die."

"Don't try to find her."

"I didn't say I was going to."

"No, but I wouldn't put it past you to find out what she took."

"I don't care anymore. Detective Robicheaux's attitude this afternoon put such a bad taste in my mouth I have no desire to find out what that impertinent busybody took. It's not a bad idea, though."

"Stop it."

I placed my hands in the air as if to surrender. "I have no intention of seeking her out," I said. "You can quote me on that. In fact, let's change the subject, shall we? What are your plans for the rest of the evening? Want to take in a picture show? I hear *Carousel* is playing at the Bell."

"The cinema on Grand Route St. John?"

"Yes, I believe so. It looks like Rodgers and Hammerstein in film is the closest we're going to get to quality theater this week."

"I hate to be a stick in the mud now that you've come down from your high horse to join me, Fountain, but if you don't mind I'm rather tired this evening. I'd like to retire early. I apologize."

"No apologies needed. I've put you through the ringer today. You deserve a break."

"What about you? Do I dare leave you alone tonight?"

"Going to behave like a church mouse, Portier. In fact, if you're not feeling up to it, I think I'll go back out into the Quarter and pass out chocolate bars this evening."

"The homeless can do without chocolate for one night."

"I can't sit and do nothing."

"For my sake, I wish you'd try. Read a book, why don't you? Take Bentley for a walk. Drink scotch until you can't stand straight. Do something—anything—for crying out loud, but stay home and stay away from the homeless tonight."

I laughed and assured him I wouldn't have time for trouble. I'd bought only ten chocolate bars earlier in the afternoon at the dime store. A good twenty minute walk in the Quarter was all I needed to pass out the bars before I headed back to the cottage.

"Better yet, give the chocolates to me," he said. "I'll eat all of them if it'll keep you out of trouble."

$\mathcal{C}$hapter 11

I waited patiently for Portier to retire for the night.

Bentley watched me intently as I put the chocolate bars into a paper sack. I was pretty sure he thought I'd be kind enough to give him one. "Chocolate is bad for dogs," I said. "Besides, you've already had your tasty morsel for the evening."

He licked his chops anyway.

I bid the Lab good evening and slipped out of the front door.

Fog shrouded the Quarter off the Mississippi again. The clippity-clop of horses pulling carriages was the only sound I heard except for the occasional blast of a foghorn from a tugboat on the river. I pulled my overcoat close to me as the cold, fine mist clung to my skin and garments. The chill penetrated my bones. I pulled a tweed beret from my side pocket and covered the top of my head, wishing it also covered my ears.

I wouldn't be long, I reminded myself. Ten chocolate bars were all I had. I would then return to the cottage to a steaming cup of chicory before I called it a night.

Newspapers, old coats, and anything else the homeless could find to shield themselves from the elements covered their bodies from head to toe. Some were too drunk or stoned to be aware of their hyperthermia risk. They sprawled across the sidewalk with their head directly on the cement. I figured they wouldn't be interested in a chocolate bar.

I handed one to a young man. His face was dirty, his hands rough. He took the bar as if I had just handed him a million dollars. Another man looked at me skeptically, but took it anyway. Others refused.

"Peace be with you," I told them.

I still had two chocolate bars left in my possession when I rounded the corner from Toulousse onto Bourbon and saw a well-dressed man in front of me. He lifted his collar around his neck to ward off the misty chill, blocking a better view of his profile.

A scantily-clad woman called to him from the curb, beckoning him to enter the establishment behind her.

"Not tonight," he said and continued to walk. He turned back just enough to see me walking behind him, enough for me to see who he was. Glen Balfour.

He turned onto Bienville and walked toward the river, stopping momentarily in front of a building with faded shutters and a ruddy brick facade. He reached inside his pocket and pulled out a piece of paper. I couldn't see if it was money or a note of some kind. Glen then proceeded to the door, knocked, and was let in after a brief exchange of words. Glen handed the man the slip of paper as he entered.

I stood and stared at the door for a couple of minutes, wondering what was inside, trying to understand its intriguing draw. I didn't stay long, however. I walked toward the river in search of two more people deserving of my chocolate, but there were very few people in sight, and few cars passed on the street. I quickened my steps to be in the light of surrounding businesses. It wasn't long before I realized I wasn't alone. Another set of footsteps sounded from behind me. I stopped and reached into my pocket as if I was searching for something. I didn't have anything there to find. I just wanted to see if the footsteps came closer.

They stopped, too.

I moved on, turned at the next corner, and stopped at a well-lit building where several people were having a good time inside. I turned and waited for the person who was following me to come around the corner, but he or she never did. After several seconds, I peeked around the corner to locate the individual. No one was there, so I crossed the street and headed for Portier's cottage.

A shadow emerged from a small alley and blocked my way. My heart leapt into my throat.

"Mr. Fountain?" the man asked.

I made the sign of the cross across my chest before I acknowledged him. "Who are you?"

"Don't you recognize me?"

I shook my head as my eyes tried to adjust in the fog. "Oh, yes," I said as he lifted the brim of his hat just enough for me to see his bushy eyebrows. "Yes, you're the man from Clover Grill. Why are you following me?"

"Why are you out walking around?"

"Passing out chocolate bars if you must know. Are you a detective? Is that why you're following me?"

"I'm not following you. I'm not interested in you, but you keep crossing my path."

"You're following Glen Balfour then. You must suspect him of something." When he didn't answer, I asked, "What is that building he entered?"

"Don't interest yourself in that place. I suggest you return home."

I was about to say something else, but he shook his head. I took the hint, said nothing more, and scurried on my way.

The experience of seeing Glen Balfour and being stopped by one of Robichaeux's detectives shook me. I didn't know where I was walking, I just walked and soon passed the club where Genny entertained. I peeked through the entrance and caught a glimpse of her on stage. The scant crowd didn't dampen her performance. She sang with the same enthusiasm and gusto as if she were eating a plate of catfish.

A hostess tried to find me a seat, but I declined. Genny saw me from the stage and gestured me to come in. After her prompting, I decided to do so. I sat at a small bistro table along a wall and ordered a virgin Rickey. Genny sang a couple of show tunes that I thought were well performed, although the band was off-key and off-beat. It wasn't long before the hostess brought me my drink and passed me a note. The note said simply: *Buy a girl a drink?*

I looked toward the bar. A Rockavian princess waved to me. Her tiara and gold arm cuff sparkled from the bright stage lights.

I took a deep breath and mustered the nerve to sit next to her at the bar. She reeked of cigarettes and alcohol. "Moline," I said.

"You remember me."

"I don't forget unforgettable people."

She smiled. "Buy me a drink?"

"I don't think you need one."

"I'm a lot chattier when I drink. Does that make a difference?"

I wanted to say yes.

"Forget it," she said. "I wouldn't want you to do anything that'd ruffle those pious principles of yours. Lucky for you I don't need you to buy me a drink. This evening, I have a few extra dollars stuck into my garter."

"You must've got paid."

Moline ordered straight Petron, then lifted the hem of her dress and pulled out a five. When the bartender set the shot glass full of liqueur in front of her, she downed it without batting an eye and ordered a perfect margarita.

"What were we talking about?" she asked. "Oh, yes, the fact that you don't want to buy me a drink. I bet, though, I know four little words that'll empty your wallet for me."

"I seriously doubt it."

"Roger Lyons."

I hoped my expression didn't match my surprise. "How do you know Roger Lyons?"

"I think the question is: How do I know you're interested in Roger Lyons?"

"How do you know? Through Genny?"

"No, honey, Genny doesn't tell me anything. Contrary to what you might think, not all women stick together and look out for each other. Genny betrays me."

"I think you mistake betrayal for having a good judge of character. Roger Lyons are only two words, by the way."

"I have much more than Roger Lyons to tell you about. I'm pretty sure Connie and Donnie are worth some cigarettes, don't you think? Oh, wait, Connie and Donnie make five words. Oops, now you know I'm not very good at math." She laughed heartily at what she thought was a very clever quip. "So what about it? Are they worth some cigarettes?"

"Cigarettes'll kill you."

She smiled sensuously as she licked her upper lip. "So will Carmen Nicolet."

Again, I hoped my surprise was well hidden. "I don't know anything about Carmen."

"Really? But I thought you knew that sweet little boy named Donnie."

The mention of Donnie's name suddenly made me anxious. It was quite clear to me that this princess friend of Genny's knew a lot more about people than Genny gave her credit.

"I know a young man named Donnie, but not in regards to Carmen Nicolet," I said.

"That's the Donnie I'm talking about."

"I thought he was seeing a woman named Karen."

Moline laughed. "Karen, Carmen, Connie, Donnie. What's the difference, Reverend?"

"Are you saying Carmen Nicolet is this Karen?"

"Or Connie. I call Carmen Connie. Donnie calls her Karen. We all know who we're talking about."

I leaned on the back of the stool while my head spun.

"She's here in the club, in fact," she added.

I took a quick glance around the room but didn't see her. A large man in a black toga approached, suddenly blocking my view. I noticed his strong, solid forearms.

"I gotta go home, Moline," Victorius said. "Look at my sandal, broke beyond repair."

"Well, come back. I'm not walking home alone. You gonna come back?"

He said he was, but lamented about his loss. "This is cheap stuff you buy me, Moline."

"Then buy it yourself, sweetheart. Do me a favor before you go. Tell Connie to come over here. The reverend wants to talk with her."

Victorius gave me the once over before agreeing. He limped toward an open doorway.

"What's through the doorway?" I asked.

"Some rooms."

"Is Carmen through there?"

She nodded unconvincingly.

"I don't believe you."

"Then bug off. You won't buy me a drink or a pack of cigarettes. You insult me. You sit there all hoity-toity like some arrogant ass and have the gall to say you don't believe me. I've done nothing to you to deserve that."

"You've lied to me, that's what you've done. You can't be trusted."

"I haven't lied to you one bit."

"You're wearing just one arm cuff. When Genny asked what happened to the other one you said Victorius broke his and you gave him yours to wear. He's a large man, and he has large, strong arms. Your arms are thin and frail. Whatever the cuffs are made out of doesn't stretch, Moline. He could never have put one of your cuffs on his arm. You lied to Genny. It makes me wonder why you lied. It also makes me wonder what else you've lied about."

Moline finished the backwash in her drink and climbed down from her stool. "Tell Genny she never has to speak to me again—ever."

I watched Moline walk to the entrance and wait for Victorius to emerge from the open doorway. He soon limped out, and they were gone. I turned around on my stool and finished my drink.

"Want another?" I heard a voice say.

I looked up to see if the male bartender had been replaced by a female. The voice, however, didn't come from the bartender.

Carmen Nicolet sashayed around me and sat on the stool that Moline had vacated. The sweet smell of her expensive perfume permeated the air. She wore an ivory dress, diamond tennis bracelet, and matching necklace.

"You look very nice, Miss Nicolet," I said.

She looked at her outfit and smiled. "Thank you. The dress is mine, but the jewels are my mother's."

I raised an eyebrow. "Does she know you have them?"

She chuckled. "You're funny. You don't mind what you say to people, do you? My family isn't used to listening to people tell us things we don't want to hear."

"That must come with money."

She smiled coyly. "Speaking of money—or someone who is usually asking for money—where did Moline go?"

"I think I said something she didn't want to hear."

"Victorius said you wanted to speak to me. Is it because you have something I don't want to hear?"

"Not in particular, but it might be something you don't want to answer."

She lifted her finger, and the bartender responded immediately. "What's your pleasure, Reverend?"

"I was drinking a virgin Rickey."

"Well, that certainly isn't a word we hear very often in this town."

"You mean Rickey?"

She laughed again. "Oh, I like you, Reverend. Tomas, will you make him a virgin Rickey? Oh, I can hardly say it without laughing. And a Tom Collins for me. You're a peach, Tomas, thank you. So, Reverend, did you ever tell me what happened to Moline?"

"I think she went with Victorius back to their house to get new sandals."

"I wonder if she'll be back."

"Probably not. ... What do you know about her?"

"She's harmless, a bit needy, but who isn't nowadays, you know? I got to know her when I started coming to this club. I didn't know you were a clubber yourself, Reverend."

"I'm not. I'm an acquaintance of Genny Duval."

"Genny? Are you really? She's fabulous, isn't she? Genny is absolutely the tops."

"I'm also an acquaintance of a young man named Donnie."

The bartender set our drinks in front of us. Carmen told him to put the drinks on her tab. She lifted her glass to toast. Although cordial, she no longer smiled. "Donnie's a sweet boy, Reverend Fountain," she said. "Are you here to tell me not to see him anymore?"

"That wasn't my intent."

"Good because I would have ignored your order. I have a good time with Donnie. I buy him beer, he makes me laugh."

"So he says."

"Is there something wrong with that?"

"Not if your motive for being with him is honorable. You see, Donnie has some issues that he's working through. You know he has issues. I don't believe for a second that laughter's the only reason you're with him?"

She smiled.

"Let me ask another question," I said. "Did you know a Mr. Montgomery?"

Carmen placed her index finger on her chin and pretended to think. "Montgomery. Montgomery. Yes, I believe Donnie has mentioned a Mr. Montgomery to me before."

"I didn't ask that. I asked if *you* knew a Mr. Montgomery."

"Oh, I myself? No, I can't say that I did. Are you talking about the man that died you believe is my grandfather?"

"Step-grandfather if I understand correctly."

"Yes, of course. No, Reverend, I'm sorry. I didn't know him. Have you found out if he's my grandfather?"

"Not entirely."

"That's too bad because my grandfather's here in New Orleans, you know."

"You've seen him?"

"Oh, yes. Does that surprise you? It shouldn't. He's hiding from me. That's why he's here. He has the means to take care of me, Reverend, but he doesn't. He absolutely refuses to do so."

"Perhaps that's because you're not entitled to his care."

"I'm his granddaughter."

"No, you're his step-granddaughter. If you want to be cared for by your grandfather then ask your biological father to get in touch with his biological father. That's the family tree you should be barking up. That's how it works. Besides, you're very young. Why do you need financial assistance above what's being provided to you?"

"I have a lifestyle. Surely you can see that."

"I can see your pupils are dilated much too wide for your own good."

"I paint, you know, and sculpt."

"What does that have to do with whatever drug you're on?"

"Creativity. I need my creativity to paint and sculpt, and I need money to buy the creativity it takes for me to paint and sculpt well. So, you see, my request for my grandfather's assistance isn't selfish. It's professional."

"But to create through drugs isn't really your creation now, is it? It's the drugs' creation. I remember reading once that Lewis Carroll was accused of using drugs to write *Through the Looking-Glass.*"

"Carroll refuted the use of drugs."

"Nevertheless, he lost some credibility as a result of the allegations. The point I'm trying to make is that you need keen senses to create well so that you can claim your own irrefutable brilliance as an artist."

Carmen Nicolet yawned as if she was ready for the conversation to end.

But I wasn't through. "What I don't want, Miss Nicolet, is for you to lead Donnie to the same senseless use of drugs that you've allowed yourself. Is that understood?"

"What's it to you?" she asked with a vehement glare.

I glared back. Toby Markle came to mind, but my guilt over Toby wasn't any of her business. I repeated, "Is that understood?"

She finished her drink and climbed down from the stool. "What I understand is why Moline left you sitting by yourself. You're a terrible bore. You want to find Donnie? Fine, then go to Lake Pontchartrain where the two of you can jump into the lake together. Good evening, Rev."

Chapter 12

The next morning I woke to warm sunshine, penetrating through the sheers. For once, it wasn't Portier exhibiting a poor disposition. It was me. I was in a terrible spirit. Even Bentley had the good sense to stay out of my way as I stumbled toward the kitchen and reached for the percolator.

"Chicory's in the cupboard," Portier said as he pointed.

"I don't want chicory. I need something stronger."

The telephone rang in the next room.

Portier didn't budge. I glared at him, hoping he'd take the hint that I was in no mood to answer the telephone.

"You might as well answer it," he said. "It's never for me in the morning."

I set my coffee cup on the table and gave him another dirty look as I proceeded to the phone. "Portier residence, Fountain speaking."

"Reverend Fountain? Detective Robicheaux, New Orleans Police Department."

"Yes, Detective, what can I do for you? If it can wait until later, I'd be very much obliged."

"Manfred Lyons called. The family wants to identify the body of Mr. Montgomery in the morgue. I suppose you had something to do with that."

"I encouraged the family to do so, yes, but they're coming on their own free will."

"Nevertheless, they'd like for you to be in attendance."

"What good would my presence be?"

"Spiritual, I believe."

"I can arrange for a priest."

"No, they want you. They specifically asked for you to be there."

I assured the detective I would accompany the Lyons family precisely at ten o'clock.

By the time all the parties arrived, which was closer to ten twenty, I felt thoroughly out of sorts. The Lyons entourage included Manfred Lyons, his brother, Andre, and Manfred's business colleague, Reed Alemand.

Manfred must have noticed the surprise on my face to see Reed Alemand with the gentlemen. "He was kind enough to offer to come," Manfred explained. "Just as you were. Thank you very much."

Detective Robicheaux led the men into the morgue.

I sat quietly on a wooden bench outside and waited. It didn't make sense for me to be in the room, especially if Detective Robicheaux had questions for them.

A woman typed on an Underwood behind a counter. I wondered if she was in charge of the records of who went in and out of the morgue.

"Excuse me," I said. "I'm Reverend Richard Fountain here with the Lyons family and Detective Robicheaux. May I ask if anyone else has been in to identify the body?"

"Yes, a woman came in yesterday as a matter of fact," she said.

"Would it be possible to get her name?"

She shook her head. "No, sir, I can't divulge that, but I can tell you I don't believe she was a relative. She saw the deceased, but said she was mistaken."

"Did she seem distraught?"

"What does that matter? She wasn't a relative."

"Yes, I understand, but it could be important."

"She left composed, very relieved. That's why she didn't seem to be a relative."

I thanked the clerk and returned to the bench. The three men and the detective soon emerged from the morgue. I could tell from their faces that the man I knew as Mr. Montgomery had been identified as Manfred and Andre's father, Roger Lyons.

Manfred appeared somber and deep in thought, as if all the years of his life had suddenly flashed before him. His eyes were dry, but he was unsteady on his feet, as if he couldn't see where he was stepping.

Andre broke down into tears. He covered his eyes and blew his nose into a handkerchief.

Reed Alemand wrapped his arm around Andre's back for support and led him to a chair.

I walked to the men, placed my hand on Andre's shoulder and said a prayer for the group.

Detective Robicheaux walked towards us and said, "We'll be releasing the body to you soon so that you can make proper arrangements in Lafayette. We're not done with our investigation, but we have all we need right now."

Before leaving, he reached into his pocket and pulled out the finial I had turned over to him the day before. He handed it to Manfred Lyons. "I thought you might like to have this," he said. "Reverend Fountain turned it over as possible evidence, but it isn't needed."

"Isn't needed?" I asked. "I don't see how that's possible."

Robicheaux looked at me but didn't respond.

After several long seconds, it seemed as if nothing further was going to be discussed. I suggested that we leave the morgue and find a place nearby to refresh.

Alemand agreed and recommended a restaurant.

"You gentlemen go on. I'll meet you there," I said. "I have something I want to ask Detective Robicheaux."

When they left, I turned and walked to the detective who stood at the counter, finishing some paperwork. "May I have a word?" I asked.

He looked at me with indifference.

"The finial. I have no trouble with you giving the finial back to the Lyons family, Detective, but to say it has no significance to the investigation, well, I find that rather hard to believe."

"What's so hard to believe, Reverend?"

"The fact that Mr. Lyons was bludgeoned to death, and his broken walking stick was found near the body. It was obviously the murder weapon."

"I don't know how the walking stick got broken, Reverend, but it wasn't the murder weapon."

"What? How do you know? Did you find a different weapon used?"

"We didn't have to. He wasn't bludgeoned."

I stared at him in disbelief.

"I wouldn't normally reveal such information in an ongoing investigation," the detective added, "but if it will keep your meddling hands out of the situation, I will tell you this. It's true that Mr. Lyons hit his head. He had a large gash wound on the back of his head as if he had been bludgeoned, but he actually fell. Whether he was pushed or tripped accidentally against the iron railing edging the commons area, I don't know at this point, but there's blood on the railing

162

consistent with a fall against it with his head. I'm sure you didn't check the iron railing while you were nurturing the dying man, Reverend, but we did."

"Are you considering his death an accident or a homicide, Detective?"

"Oh, it's a homicide, but the cause of death wasn't due to what happened to the back of his head."

"Then what, may I ask?"

"He was strangled."

I gasped and started to say something, but I couldn't spit out the words.

"You didn't see any strangulation marks. Is that what you're trying to say?" the detective asked. "No, of course, you didn't. Mr. Lyons was bent over on the bench and his head was contorted downward, hiding the ligature marks around his neck. The perpetrator wasn't able to apply the pressure on his throat long enough to kill him immediately. He must have been interrupted. So much was going on, I'm pretty sure you missed the ligature marks. You missed a lot of things that morning."

"I didn't miss the actions of that woman standing behind me, accusing me of killing him, Detective. Do you know who she is?"

"We have a name."

"I didn't ask if you had a name. We all know that no one uses their given name in this town. I asked if you knew who she was, what her background was, if she used an alias, that sort of thing. I think it's very important. I'm telling you she picked something off the pavement that could be significant. There's something very suspicious about her and her actions."

"I could say the same about you and the finial, Reverend. Now if you don't mind." Robicheaux returned to his paperwork.

I left without further argument.

~

I entered the café where the Lyons brothers and Reed Alemand sipped cocktails. A second-line parade marched past the building led by a brass band with two dozen revelers in costumes, spinning parasols, and dancing free-style down the middle of the street. We sat somberly in stark contrast to the spectacle and the patrons inside the café who laughed and danced as the small, late morning parade passed.

I sat down and thanked the men for making the trip to New Orleans. "Who had the change of heart about identifying your father if I may ask?"

Manfred twisted the swizzle stick with his finger and said, "It was Joyce's idea."

"When was this?"

"Last evening. She had returned from New Orleans and said the drive gave her time to think. She thought it would be in our best interest to contact the police department."

"Was she at the morgue?" I asked.

The men looked at me with astonished expressions.

"I'm sorry. I saw her yesterday on Dryades," I added.

Manfred shrugged. "She likes to shop. What can I say?"

"I thought you'd say she stopped by to see your father's body for herself while she was in town."

No one spoke until Andre changed the subject by saying, "What are we going to do now?"

"We're going to continue our lives just as we did the day he disappeared," Manfred replied.

"But we have no money."

"No, brother, that isn't true. *You* don't have any money. The rest of us are doing fine because we didn't squander our income on theater ventures that went belly up."

"You won't be fine if that audit of yours turns up something."

I looked at Manfred, hoping he would give a response.

"The audit is going fine," he said.

"An IRS audit?" I asked.

"Yes," Andre said, then abruptly turned to Alemand. "Are you okay, Reed?"

Alemand looked pale, but I suspected the question to him was not about his physical or emotional health, but his financial standing.

Alemand appeared relieved when the waitress stopped by our table to ask if we were hungry.

"He doesn't have a drink yet," Manfred said, pointing to me, "and I wouldn't mind an oyster po-boy. Too bad it isn't Monday. I'd really like some red beans and rice. Gentlemen?"

We each ordered and the waitress left. It appeared everyone had forgotten or lost interest in the question posed to Reed Alemand by Andre—everyone except me.

"I understand you have some money invested in Andre's plays," I said.

"You're hearing that from Charles Portier," he responded curtly, "and I would like to remind him that sharing confidential information about his clients' accounts is unethical and may be criminal in some cases."

"Oh, I assure you my friend wouldn't break professional confidence."

"Then how did you know of my investment?"

I looked at Andre for assistance.

"I'm afraid it was me, Reed. I apologize. Reverend Fountain was at the house in Lafayette, and I came home in a very bad way. I was worried about *Dickies* and I said too much. I apologize."

"Your investments aren't a secret, Reed," Manfred replied. "I'm not sure why you're getting so bent out of shape over something everyone already knows about."

Alemand took a deep breath. "You're right. I apologize, Reverend. Everyone does know. Why shouldn't you? The truth is: I'm as antsy about the prospects of Andre's plays as he is."

"So I ask again, Manny, what are we going to do now?" Andre asked.

"I guess you'll have to wait until the will is read."

"I thought father was going to change the will."

Manfred told his brother to relax. "You know how father was. He used his fortune as extortion to make us behave as he pleased. I doubt he meant a word of it."

"But do we know for sure?"

It must have been the look on my face that made the three stare at me curiously.

"What's on your mind, Reverend?" Manfred asked.

I shook my head. It wasn't the time or place to tell them what I was thinking—that knowing who benefited or who was cut from their father's will was probably the answer to who killed their father.

"Right after lunch I must be getting back to Lafayette," Alemand said. "Much to do."

"I'll be in the office as well," Manfred replied.

"You'll do no such thing," Alemand insisted. "We just identified your dead father. You should be with your family, including your sisters."

Manfred lowered his head. "You're right. Forgive me, I should. Then you'll come, too, won't you, Reverend? We could use someone accustomed to handling grief. You're welcome in our home."

I accepted Manfred's heartfelt invitation. His acknowledgement that I was welcome sounded genuine, although I wasn't so sure Joyce and her stepdaughter, Carmen, would feel the same way.

Chapter 13

Portier drove me to the Lyons' home in Lafayette later that day. He squawked about doing so, but I believed his curiosity was getting the better of him. Halfway through Terrebonne Parish, however, he wished he hadn't volunteered. The drive was tedious and monotonous through the bayou. It didn't help his disposition.

I, on the other hand, found the bald cypress and tupelo trees, rising majestically from the murky depths of the swamps, full of intrigue. I imagined watery eye balls of alligators sunning in the reeds, peering menacingly as we passed. I heard black-bellied ducks whistling through the air. Snowy egrets glided effortlessly from one water hole to the next while a Mississippi Kite flew above, scouring the wetland for dragonflies on the wing.

I was about to mention how wonderful nature was when I looked at my friend and saw his disgruntled expression. "We're making good time," I said. "Why the glum face?"

He gave me a side glance and responded, "You don't get it, do you? This trip has nothing to do with making good time. I've been thinking. Why in the world did Manny invite you to come to the house? You've been nothing but a thorn in the family's side until now."

"I think it came from Manny's perspective of the situation. He's made himself out to be an outcast within the family, keeping an arm's length away from all emotion and involvement. I'm not sure I'm a welcomed guest as much as I'm a safe buffer between him and the other family members."

"I suppose having a preacher around will calm any mischief."

"Oh, I hope not," I said. "I should probably wish that to be true, but I hope just the opposite occurs."

"Is that why you're going, to stir some trouble within the family to root out a murderer?"

"Not at all. If trouble is brewing, one doesn't have to stir the pot to smell the aroma. I might pry the lid open a little, but nothing more, I assure you."

Portier tried to appear disgusted, but he couldn't help but grin just a bit from the corners of his mouth. I believed he was glad he came along.

~

Angelle Lyons greeted us with her usual youthful flair, donned in a pastel taffeta dress and white cardigan sweater. She led us to a large room in the back of the house with floor-to-ceiling windows on two walls overlooking a vast garden.

"I apologize that nothing is in bloom yet," she said. "It really is beautiful in the spring."

"Dies out in summer?" Portier asked.

I was shocked he asked such a thing. To ask Angelle Lyons if her garden dies in summer was as tasteless as me asking if one of her siblings was a murderer.

"A little," she said with a courteous smile, "but father pays good money to see that it doesn't happen. New plants come into bloom when others fade away. Are you Mr. Portier?"

He bowed.

"Mr. Allemand hoped you would come."

"Oh, he did? He wasn't expecting me to do business, was he? I didn't bring his files."

"I wouldn't know about that, but I don't think so. I think he just wanted to talk. May I offer you something to drink?"

Portier accepted a gimlet. I said I was fine.

"Is your brother Manny with Mr. Alemand right now?" I asked.

"Yes," she responded. "They'll be here shortly. I'm so glad they took your advice and identified my father."

"How have you been with the news?"

"His death was something I expected ever since you first inquired. Still, though, when Manny phoned and gave us the news, I have to say I took it rather hard. It was quite a shock, but I'm doing better now."

"You seem to be."

"Yes," Portier added. "I'd say you've composed yourself rather well."

She smiled timidly and looked away.

"But then I think you knew it was him all along," I said.

She sat on the edge of a nearby chair and looked at me, her expression hard and defensive.

"Didn't you?" I repeated. "You've made many trips to New Orleans in recent months."

"Glen has business in New Orleans. I go with him."

"I'd venture to say it's the other way around. He accompanies *you*." I waited for a reaction but didn't receive one. She didn't even blink as she glared at me. "I believe he comes along so that you can do *your* business while he gambles and goes to the clubs."

"What Glen does on his own time is none of your concern. Furthermore, what business would I have in New Orleans?"

"None since your father died."

Angelle continued to glare at me. She started to speak then appeared to have second thoughts about doing so. Eventually she said, "You know, Reverend, at first, I thought your inquiries into my father's death were nothing more than a genuine interest to see that his life had proper closure. I'm beginning to believe, however, they're much more than that. You suspect—you actually suspect—that one of us deliberately killed him, including me. That pushes your questions beyond an interest to something personal and impertinent."

"It was just an observation on my part."

"An observation better left to the police, don't you think? After all, your question about me being in New Orleans implies that I knew my father was in the city, living in deplorable conditions. If I was truly a suspect in the minds of the police, I'd think they'd have been to see me by now."

"I would've hoped so, too, Angelle, but since they haven't, I need to ask on my own behalf."

Angelle laughed. "On your own behalf? What gives you the right?"

"The very fact that the police consider me to be a suspect. I have a personal interest to get to the truth so I must ask you again: Did you often come to New Orleans to see your father?"

"Why would I?"

"You found out he was playing the part of a recluse. Did you hire a detective to find that out? Did the detective try to convince your father to return to Lafayette?"

She settled back into her seat. "How do you know this?"

"A man's been following me around. He knows quite a bit about my helping the homeless in the Quarter and Bywater. One time I was on Bienville Street. I saw your boyfriend there. This man who I thought was following me was there, too, but I was wrong. He wasn't following *me*. He was following your boyfriend. I just happen to be around. I believe the man was a private detective. At first, when I thought I was the only person he was following, I didn't know who he was or what he wanted. When I realized he was following Glen, I had to ask myself who would be so interested in Glen's whereabouts to have him followed. That person would be you. This detective is also how you learned about your father being a part of Labreville. The detective found out where your father was, he told you, and you went to see your father. I have sources, too, Miss Lyons, and my sources say a certain woman had been around to see Roger Lyons. I put two and two together. The woman was you."

Angelle's eyes widened with alarm. I was certain she was taken by surprise by my conclusion. Her eyes darted about the room before she took a deep breath and relented to the fact that I knew the truth. "I did go see my father," she confessed. "I went to see him after I found out what he was doing and how much he was spending on his homeless camp."

"How did you find out?"

"Just as you said. I hired a friend of mine who works part-time as a private detective. He found out for me. But I only visited my father once or twice."

"Why at all?"

"I've explained that to you before. Money. My father's absence created a financial strain for me. The other times my father took these absences, he continued to provide me with a substantial allowance. This time, however, the allowances suddenly stopped."

"I can venture a guess as to why they stopped."

"You don't have to guess. Father found out that a substantial portion of the allowance he was sending me was being confiscated by my boyfriend to subsidize his boozing,

172

gambling, and other business operations—monkey business to be exact. Father didn't like it, and he cut me off. I went to New Orleans to reason with him. When that didn't work, I asked my friend the detective to follow Glen. When I learned Glen wasn't being honest with me from the detective, I told my father I'd get rid of Glen if he would resume the payments."

"Did he agree to that?"

"Glen's still my boyfriend, isn't he?"

"Then he said no."

"It's my own stupid fault. I did something very, very foolish. I'm embarrassed to tell you what I did. You'll think I'm childish and pathetic."

"I'm pretty sure I've heard worse, Angelle."

She glanced at Portier and then to me, but said nothing.

Portier suddenly sat erect as if he had a revelation. "You tried to extort him!" he blurted.

The accusation startled me as much as it did her.

"It's true, isn't it, Miss Lyons?" Portier contended. "When your father refused to pay, you tried to extort him. In return, you promised you'd keep his anonymity secret. It's not hard to follow what was going on."

I didn't object to Portier's line of questioning. Instead, I turned to Angelle to give her a chance to refute his allegation and to set the record straight.

She didn't. Instead, she reached for a hanky from a side pocket of her cardigan and dabbed at her nose. "If you knew my father, gentlemen, you would know that threatening to reveal his whereabouts and what he was doing in exchange for money would not only be fruitless, but it would backfire. It backfired. He became angry and said for me to go ahead and tell. Once the truth was out, he would instruct his lawyers to disinherit me immediately from any and all benefits from his trust."

"Wouldn't it have been simpler to have gotten rid of Glen Balfour?" I asked. "Surely your life would have been simpler as well."

"It's very complicated. I really do like being around him. He makes me laugh."

"I hardly consider boozing, gambling, and womanizing as a laughing matter."

"You know what I mean."

"No, I really don't. So how did you leave it with your father?"

"I think that's rather complicated. I stopped receiving an allowance just as he said then out of the blue before his death, an allowance appeared. No note, nothing about why he had a change of heart, just a substantial check. I was shocked to receive it. I was so cruel to him."

"Perhaps he knew you didn't mean it."

"I really didn't mean it," she said remorsefully. "You have to believe me. I don't know why or how it came out of my mouth. I love my father, but it happened just the same. I couldn't take back what I said. When I received the money, I was more grateful that he had forgiven me than I was at getting the money."

I gave the young woman time to compose herself before I continued. "Forgive me, Angelle," I finally said, "but I must ask where you were in the early hours the morning your father died."

"I was at a club."

"In New Orleans?"

"Yes, on Frenchmen Street."

"Who were you with?"

"Glen, of course."

"The entire night?"

"Yes, for the most part."

"What does 'for the most part' mean?"

She didn't answer.

"Did you kill your father?"

She placed her hands to the sides of her face. "No! Why would you think such a thing?"

"Was Glen with you the whole time?"

Her eyes fixated on the floor.

"Angelle, it's important."

Sounds from the front of the house, including the voices of several men, startled Angelle. She lifted her head and her eyes darted between Portier and me. "Please, gentleman, not a word in front of my brothers. I beg you."

I nodded as the Lyons brothers and Reed Alemand entered the room, making solemn small talk and noticing our presence.

"I thought that was your car, Charles," Alemand said. "See, gentlemen? Charles did accompany the reverend to Lafayette."

"Sharp little Hawk you have out there, Mr. Portier," Manfred said. "Fun to drive?"

"Not only fun, it's exhilarating. I trust you two completed everything at the office you needed to accomplish."

Manfred and Reed looked at each other and nodded reluctantly.

Angelle stood. "Gentlemen, if you'll excuse me. I haven't asked Henri to get your drink yet, Mr. Portier. May I have him bring something for the rest of you?"

"That would be very kind," Manfred said. "What are you gentlemen drinking? Gimlet, Portier? Very good. How about French 75s for the rest of us? If it's not too much trouble."

Angelle left quickly, and the three men took their seats.

175

"Had she been crying?" Andre asked.

I shook my head. "No, why do you ask?"

"Her eyes. They looked a bit red, and she had that hanky in her hand. She never carries a hanky with her, does she, Manny?"

"I wouldn't know. My wife does. I thought all women did, but I don't pay attention to things like that normally."

"Is she upset?"

"She was reminiscing a bit," I replied. "I think memories brought some tears, but nothing terribly disheartening."

"That's why I asked you to come," Manfred said. "It's better to have someone here who is used to dealing with grief and unsettling news."

"If it makes any difference, I could cry," Alemand said abruptly, rubbing his face vigorously with his hands and leaning back against the seat cushion.

Everyone in the room turned their heads.

"Really?" Portier asked. "What have you got to cry about?"

"That play for one," Manfred said.

Andre lifted his hand for the men to stop. "We're beating a dead horse, you two. We went over this at the office. Must we bring it up again?"

I turned to Manfred for insight.

"I shouldn't have said anything," he responded. "Andre's right. We've already discussed the disappointment of the play's performance."

"Failure, not disappointment, Manny," Alemand countered. "Don't sugar-coat it."

"My brother invested a lot of money toward its success," Manfred explained to me. "He was counting on that success to pay some debts and to invest in additional plays."

"You're forgetting about me," Alemand said. "I invested a chunk of change on the damn thing, too."

"You haven't been forgotten at all," Andre replied. "How can you be forgotten? You keep throwing it in my face!"

Manfred tried to quell the tension by saying, "Perhaps we should defer this conversation to another time. The reverend and Mr. Portier came here to console our hearts, not our pocketbooks."

"On the contrary," Alemand spouted, "I think I'd like the reverend to hear what you have to say, Manny. Having an independent third party listen to how this venture is going to be resolved isn't something I'd object to."

"Then all I'll say is that Andre's right. No one's been forgotten. There's just not enough funds to provide a return."

Alemand leaned forward in his chair and said somberly, "I don't mean to be morbid, but I must ask: Now that the old man is gone, perhaps the floodgates will open soon so we can recover our losses."

Manfred and Andre glanced at each other without saying anything.

Alemand noticed the exchange and sat upright. "What?" he asked. "There are enough funds in Roger Lyons' trust for his heirs, isn't there?"

"Yes, there is plenty of money, Reed."

"Then why the long faces?"

"We'll have to wait until the reading of the will to find out what's in his last wishes."

Alemand turned ashen. "That can't be. Surely, Roger's own flesh and blood are benefactors; surely, you'll receive an inheritance, Andre, and make good on the investments."

The brothers didn't respond.

Alemand rose and began to pace. "Where the hell are those drinks?"

Manfred stood. "Let me inquire. Reverend Fountain, would you mind assisting?"

Half-way down the hall, Manfred and I ran into Henri, carrying a tray of cocktails.

"Thank you, Henri," Manfred said. "We'll take two of them right here."

"I don't want anything," I said.

"Then be sure to give the extra one to Mr. Alemand. I think he could use it. Thank you, Henri. Reverend, will you follow me?"

Manfred led me into a room and gestured for me to take a seat. He closed the door behind him. I sensed by his demeanor our conversation was going to be direct and unpleasant. He sat across from me and crossed his legs, staring deeply into his drink as he swirled the ice with his index finger.

"What's on your mind, Manfred?" I asked after sitting patiently for several seconds. "You can be frank with me. After all, I've been candid with you and your family."

"Yes, you have," he replied. "Perhaps a bit too candid. I asked you to the house this afternoon on very congenial terms, Reverend. A man of your experience and stature could have been a stabilizing presence to my family."

"Are you saying you'd like to rescind the invitation?" I asked when he paused and didn't continue.

"Quite frankly, I didn't care for how my sister looked when we arrived at the house. I know Angelle. I know and care for her very much. I don't believe she was reminiscing over my father's death as you said she was. Her expression wasn't sentimental. It wasn't sentimental at all. I believe you said something very incriminating that upset her."

"An interesting word choice, Manny. I don't know what to say."

He lifted the finger that was swirling ice for me to be quiet. "I don't want you to say anything. In fact, I don't want to hear anything anymore out of you. Do I make myself clear? We shouldn't have been discussing our financial affairs in front of you. It was a private matter, and I regret it, but I also apologize to you for doing so. Now that it's done, however, I think it's best that you leave and not come back."

I nodded somberly. "I'll respect your wishes, but I can't apologize for my inquiries given the circumstances."

"What circumstances? There are no circumstances, Reverend. You ask your questions as if you're investigating a homicide. The detective in New Orleans said my father's death was not suspicious so why are you probing as such?"

"If that's what you believe then there seems to be some inconsistency between what the detective told you and what he's told me."

"Then I'd leave it up to the detective to determine what he wants us to know."

I took a deep breath to hold back opinions that would upset my host even further. "You're probably right. I know my friend Mr. Portier would agree with you. But isn't there something in the back of your mind that nags at you as being a little suspicious about your father's death—even just a little?"

"No, sir, I don't, and out of respect for the privacy of my family, I must request that you stop delving into matters related to my father, living or otherwise. We're very grateful you brought the possibility of his death to our attention, but now that it's been confirmed we consider the matter closed and wish to bury him peacefully and with dignity."

179

I nodded, acknowledging his request to cease my investigation into the matter.

"Now if you'll excuse me," he said, "I'd like to be with the other gentlemen. I'm not going to be rude. You're welcome to join me, but we'll be limiting our conversation to social pleasantries and nothing more."

I declined the invitation, saying I had intruded on the family's time long enough. "If you'd be kind enough to tell Mr. Portier that I'm ready to leave, I would appreciate it."

Manfred seemed relieved that I wasn't going to stay. "Certainly. Then I think you'd be more comfortable waiting in the other library. I'll take you there. Please make yourself comfortable while I send for Charles."

Manfred left, and I crossed the hall.

I love a good library rich in solid wood tones with contemporary and classic books. Joyce Nicolet's library was all that and more. Her selection in fiction and nonfiction material was diverse and voluminous. I perused the shelves and noticed immediately several historical and political texts. Early twentieth-century books on business, finance, economics, and conservative presidential memoirs were segregated from current political satires and biographies. I assumed the older, conservative works belonged to Roger Lyons. The newer, more controversial books which presumably belonged to Joyce Nicolet sat on the more visible and convenient shelves in the room.

Several authors caught my attention. I pulled their books to briefly review their contents and still held one when Portier entered the library.

"There you are, Fountain. I say, what did you say to Manny?"

I turned and presented a look as if I had no idea what he was talking about.

"Don't deny it," he said. "I hadn't finished my drink with Reed and Andre when he stormed in and said you were ready to leave. It was quite apparent he was ready for me to leave as well."

"I'm not sure I know what you're talking about. Manny and I had a very pleasant conversation."

"I doubt that seriously. Manny didn't look at all pleasant."

"It's an upsetting time for the entire family. Their issues can't be blamed on me."

"Can't they? I wonder, Fountain. You've upset people everywhere you've been this trip. And now, you've invaded Mrs. Nicolet's private collection. I would put that book back on the shelf if I were you."

"And why is that?" a voice announced from the doorway. We turned and saw Joyce Nicolet, standing perfectly poised and apparently pleased that I was taken in by her array of political texts. "Private or not, books are meant to be opened to allow our minds to open with them."

I smiled and thanked her for being so gracious.

"What have you there in your hand, Reverend?" she asked. "Ah, yes, Eugene Debs, a fellow Hoosier. You're from Indiana, aren't you, if I remember correctly?"

"That's right."

"Then you agree with Mr. Debs that this country needs to change."

"I agree that improvements are needed, but I'm not so sure Mr. Debs has the answers correct."

"Doesn't he?" she asked, walking to the center of the room.

I glanced at Portier who gave me a pleading expression not to upset another member of the Lyons family.

181

"I'm not sure I remember anything about Eugene Debs," he said to Joyce.

"Political activist from Terre Haute," she replied. "Progressive thinker. Five time presidential candidate."

"The last time from prison," I interjected.

"His civil liberties were violated during a strike, Reverend. That's why he was in prison. He was arrested unfairly, a man for common people, founding member of the Industrial Workers of the World."

"And Socialist, Portier. Founding member of the Social Democratic Party," I added.

I received another pleading expression.

"You're beginning to sound like my father," Joyce said. "My father enjoyed his material wealth and the ability to increase that wealth more than he cared about those who helped him achieve it." She laughed. "My father certainly disagreed with the writings of Eugene Debs and others, but I find it ironic that it was him who introduced me to socialism."

"He did?" I asked.

"Indirectly, yes. He knew Huey P. Long before Long became governor. I was in my late twenties when Long was assassinated at the state house, but by then I was keenly aware of his *Share Our Wealth* program to help the poor. I was drawn to it. Do you remember the program, Mr. Portier?"

"Yes, I'm afraid I do, and I have to admit that I'm surprised you were taken in by it. You realize that Governor Long proposed limiting the amount of wealth any one person could accumulate."

"What's wrong with that? The way I see it is the wealthy get wealthier while the poor get poorer."

"True," Portier said, "but that stymies research and development, it stymies productivity within this nation, and

182

it creates a passive society where people wait for other people's good fortune to fall upon them. And let's not forget that would affect your wealth tremendously, Mrs. Nicolet."

She waved Portier's comment off with her hand. "That's my father talking through and through. I disagree with you totally. I have enough as it is, and there's no precedent that people would respond as you say."

"But it only stands to reason."

Joyce Nicolet suddenly beamed and walked briskly to the bookshelf behind her desk. "Not if done in the way prescribed in this marvelous book, gentlemen." She rubbed her index finger along the spine of several books. "Ah! Here it is. Wallace Wattles, *The Science of Getting Rich*. Oh, I forgot. He's also a Hoosier from a place called Elwood. How interesting. You may take the book along with you if you like. He writes that the hidden key to wealth is overcoming psychological barriers through a form of mental healing if you will."

I frowned. "I don't follow you, Mrs. Nicolet."

"What I'm trying to say is that financial healing and stability for the poor can be spiritual in much the same way that physical healing is spiritual, but we must first conquer the mind. It's a form of mind training. That's all we need to do, gentlemen. We need to do a better job of reaching out to individuals with mental healing and positive thinking. We do so little of that in our society."

I didn't know how to respond so I said, "I apologize, but I'm not familiar with Wallace Wattles or his work."

"You should, Reverend. He was a Methodist, not that you're a Methodist, but he was influenced very heavily by the church to develop his theories."

"Interesting," I said. "Then perhaps I should read what he has to say and compare it to the book I use."

"Yes, by all means, see for yourself how the two compare. What book are you referring? Who is the author?"

"The Bible. I think you can figure out the author."

Any semblance of interest by Mrs. Nicolet dissipated quickly.

"What's the matter?" I asked.

"I'd go with Debs or Wattles first. The book you use is full of inconsistencies, inaccuracies, and patriarchal propaganda."

"Then you're reading it wrong."

"Am I? I thought it was the Word of God."

"It is the Word of God, do not get me wrong, but it's meant to be read allegorically as much as it is literally if you are to obtain any spiritual understanding of the human experience. That is, if you have the emotional and spiritual capacity to engage in the human existence."

Joyce gave me a dry, cynical look. "I get it, Reverend. You're no longer speaking about the Bible, are you? You're referring to my relationship with my father, and I'm aware of what you're trying to say."

"Then I stand corrected. Apparently, you do have the ability to see things allegorically."

"I want to make something very clear to you. I loathed my father. I'm not sorry he's dead. I'm glad to be free of his money and the burden of living as a daughter in his shadow. I loathed his capitalistic ideals and his materialistic aspirations. I always have."

"But from what I've seen, you've benefited from his success quite abundantly."

"On the surface, yes. Deep down, however, I'm ashamed of who I am and who I've become. I'm ashamed to be his daughter."

"Then give it away. Give it all away. There's time to become the woman you've always wanted to be. Your father was trying to do just that when he died. He became homeless to help the homeless. That's not something to be ashamed of."

Instead of an agreement in the spirit of Eugene Debs or Wallace Wattles, I received an icy stare.

"Right," I said. "That's what I thought. You're a hypocrite of the worst kind. You speak of sharing wealth and being in solidarity with the poor, but the closest you want is to pay taxes to a government to let them to sort it out. I should remind you that government is a very poor steward of your money in case you don't remember your history lessons well. It's also not a smart business move. I know your kind, Mrs. Nicolet. You feel better about yourself when you write a check here and there to charities while you spout venomous accusations of a father you wrote off twenty years ago as a political adversary. That's what you should be ashamed of. You should be ashamed you never took the time to understand your father. You didn't know him at all."

"And you didn't, either, I should remind you. Not really. You spent, what, five to ten minutes with him while he was dying and that qualifies you to lecture me on my beliefs and my emotions? How dare you. You're nothing but a pompous cleric." She glared at me before saying, "Get out. Allow me to have Henri escort you to the door."

"We can find our own way, thank you."

I turned to Portier who stood with astonishment. He glared at me as I passed, but he followed me to the Golden Hawk in silence.

I didn't speak until we were on a main thoroughfare, then I said, "Do you mind if we not take the Terrebonne route back to New Orleans?"

185

"Then how do you want me to go?"

"Through Baton Rouge. I'd like to stop by the State House."

"The State House will be closed by the time we get there. Why do you want to go there?"

"I was thinking of visiting the Secretary of State's office. I'd like to research all of for-profit and not-for-profit corporations the Lyons family have recorded with the Secretary—especially those of Joyce Nicolet."

Portier sighed. "You have no business doing that. You don't know the first thing about corporations and the information recorded with the Secretary."

"Where else am I to get the information I want? I can't imagine you'd break your clients' confidence by giving me such information."

"The Lyons aren't my clients."

"I know, but Manny is Alemand's associate. That's close enough. You wouldn't tell me what you knew about them even if you knew it."

"That's not the point."

"I think it's a very good point. Even if you were willing to tell me what you knew of the Lyons' affairs, it might not be complete. I think the Secretary of State would have the most current and accurate information about their businesses."

"You're assuming the Lyons recorded everything properly and legally."

"I'll soon find out, won't I? Will you take me tomorrow?"

Portier focused on the road while he considered my request. "Better yet, I'll go in your place," he said. "I wasn't planning to go to Baton Rouge until next week, but I can move things around and stop at the State House in between clients."

"Thank you. The information will complement nicely what we learned this afternoon."

Portier's demeanor turned sour. "What we learned? Are you kidding me? What did we learn, Fountain? No, wait, I can tell you what we learned. The only thing we learned was how to piss off every member of the most influential family in the state of Louisiana. I dare say, you picked a very poor time to express your political and religious opinions with Joyce Nicolet."

"Is that what you think I was doing?"

"I have no idea what you were doing. All I know is you need her cooperation. You could use an ally with the family right now. Expressing your views on socialism and Christianity polarized her into the opposite corner."

"On the contrary, I achieved exactly what I was hoping to learn. You forget that Detective Robicheaux thinks of me as a suspect. I need another plausible suspect to detract him. People like Joyce Nicolet are highly devoted, outspoken, and vigilant in their political and financial beliefs whether they say it as such or not. I was merely trying to determine if she had a motive for wanting her father killed."

"You're telling me you encouraged that antagonistic conversation just to see how badly she wanted her father dead?"

"Precisely, and I thought I was quite successful. Not only that, but we can add Manny, Andre, Angelle, Glen Balfour, and Reed Alemand to our list of suspects. We learned that each of them had a plausible motive as well."

Portier thought about what I said and agreed solemnly whether he wanted to admit it or not. "Still, I wish you'd be more careful," he said thoughtfully. "By the looks on their faces, they each have a motive for killing you as well."

187

Chapter 14

"Would you join me for dinner?" I asked Portier after he'd made a drink at his cottage and sat comfortably with Bentley by his side.

"We'll have to go out. I haven't made groceries, and what we have needs to be pitched. Where are you thinking? Want to hit Leroux's again?"

"No, let's do something different. I was thinking about going into the Central Business District. I haven't been to Mother's yet."

Portier's tired eyes suddenly lit up. "The blackened ham does sound rather good, doesn't it?"

Bentley licked his chops.

"Not on your life, boy," Portier scolded. "Ham isn't good for a dog, and I don't plan to spend the rest of the evening in Cabrini Playground waiting for it to exit your system. When would you like to go, Fountain? I'm ready whenever you are."

"Finish your drink. I'll get better walking shoes."

"No, no," Portier insisted as he rose from his chair. "I'll drive. Mother's is too far."

"Says who? You just put the car in the garage from our trip to Lafayette. The walk will do us good. Besides, I want to clear my mind of a few things."

"As long as you promise the walk will be uneventful."

188

I couldn't promise him that so he refreshed his drink and placed it in a Dixie cup. "Wish there was a lid for these damn things," he said. "I hate sloshing good liquor out onto the streets."

"In most cities that wouldn't be a problem, you know. They wouldn't allow you to have an open cup of hard liquor on the street in the first place."

"I don't want to hear of places outside of Paradise, Fountain. I suppose Bentley will be okay. We won't be gone long, will we?"

"I have my fingers crossed and a rabbit's foot in my pocket," I said, leaving the room to slip into my walking shoes.

"Left hind foot?" he asked when I returned.

We stepped outside onto the cottage's stoop.

"Shot with a silver bullet," I replied as he locked the front door.

"In a cemetery?"

"On a rainy night."

"Full moon?" I asked teasingly.

"New moon, even better."

"Ah, but on a Friday?"

"The thirteenth, in fact."

"I guess we're ready then. Can't be too careful in New Orleans."

"Never taken for granted. Are you able to talk, walk, and drink at the same time?"

"I'm not a child, Fountain."

"Good because I have something I want to ask you," I said as we walked toward Bourbon Street. "Do you know anything aside from your business with Reed Alemand about the various businesses in which the Lyons family are involved? I'm not interested in what they own necessarily, just other businesses interests."

"Goodness, that's a loaded one. I'm not sure I can answer that until I visit the Secretary of State's office. Why are you asking?"

"I'm very curious. Why do you think the IRS is so interested in Manny Lyons right now?"

"I don't think they are."

"But he's being audited."

"No, he acts like he's being audited, but he's not the target. Some other business is being audited. Manny has information that the agents need to complete their audit of this other business."

"What business is that?"

"Couldn't tell you. I haven't had a reason to know. It doesn't affect Alemand so I don't ask, and Manny is very private as you know."

"A bit too private, don't you think?"

Portier disagreed. "He lives in a glass house. Everything he does, every investment, every donation is scrutinized by the public. He's in the society pages of Lafayette, Baton Rouge, and New Orleans constantly. It's a natural coping mechanism for him to be private."

"I suppose you're right. Just the same, I hope your visit to the Secretary of State's office will be helpful."

"I still don't know what you're looking for."

"I'm pretty sure we'll know it when you find it. I forget what street Mother's is on."

"We'll need to cross over a block or two to Peters. It's on Poydras at Tchoupitoulas."

I remembered, and by the time we crossed palm-lined Canal Street, my steps became second nature towards the café.

Portier talked very little as we made our way between the office buildings of the CBD. We talked nothing more of Roger Lyons, the Lyons family, Mr. Montgomery, Genny Duval, or Detective Robicheaux. In fact, our fast pace was exhilarating and exactly what I needed to clear my head. That was until I looked across the street and saw two men in front of a bank.

I stopped suddenly.

Portier walked ahead, but turned around to see what was holding me up.

"Isn't that Reed Alemand?" I asked, pointing.

Portier looked. He didn't say anything, but I could tell by his expression that he recognized his client.

"Who's he talking to?" I asked.

Portier shook his head as he walked towards me. "The man's employed with the bank, but I can't place him. Let's move on, Fountain. It's best Alemand doesn't see us."

"I don't care about Alemand," I said. "I don't like the mannerisms of the guy he's talking to."

Portier looked more closely. "Yes, I see what you mean. They appear to be arguing."

"That's putting it mildly. I can't hear what they're saying, but it looks like it could turn into a full-blown row."

"Wait," Portier said, motioning me to stand still. "It looks like Alemand's leaving."

He was right. It appeared as if Alemand had said what he wanted to say. He adjusted his fedora and straightened the collar on his suit coat before making what seemed to be a final demand.

The man ignored him and turned to enter the bank.

Alemand walked down the street with a determined gait.

"I'm going to follow him," I said as I stepped off the curb.

"The hell you will!" Portier demanded. "Let Alemand be. It'll bad for both of us if he spots you."

"No, not Alemand. The other man. I want to know who he is. I'll be right back. You stay here."

Portier took a deep breath, but gestured for me to go as if he was too tired to argue.

I ran across the street and entered the building. The entrance opened into a large hall with marble floors and elevators at the end. Teller stations to the right of the lobby were in the process of closing for the day.

The man stood in front of one of the elevators until the car reached the main floor. I walked up behind him quietly and acted as if I, too, was interested in going up.

The door to one of cars opened and the man stepped in first, greeting the woman who manually operated the elevator from within the car. She closed the outer door then latched the inner accordion gate before asking what floor we wanted. I waited until he announced his destination first. She looked at me, and I nodded.

"That's fine," I said.

We went up four floors before the elevator clanged to a jolting stop. She opened the accordion gate then opened the outer door. I motioned for the man to exit before me. He nodded politely to the woman, and then turned to the right and walked down the hall. I stepped out of the car and watched where he walked. He must've heard that I wasn't following and stopped suddenly to turn my way.

"May I help you find a department?" he asked in an amicable tone.

"Thank you," I said. "No, I'm on the wrong floor. I can see that now. I'll just wait for another car."

The answer appeared to satisfy him, and he walked to the next office, opened the door and walked in.

I hurried toward the door he'd entered. Frosted glass covered the upper half of the solid wood door, and the words *Reginald Falgout, Office of the Auditor* was stenciled in bold, prominent lettering on the surface of the glass.

That's all I wanted to know.

I returned to the elevator, and the attendant took me down to the main floor where an impatient Portier was pacing on the marble floor inside the building.

"I thought I told you to wait outside," I said sternly.

"And I thought I told you to stop this nonsense. I listen about as well as you do."

We continued our walk to the café.

Portier could hardly stand our silence after we sat and perused the menus placed in front of us. We ordered coffee and blackened ham before I spoke:

"Is your client being investigated?" I asked. "Please be honest with me."

"I have no idea what you're talking about."

"Reed Alemand. Is he being investigated?"

"By whom?"

"Anyone—the IRS, an outside accounting firm ... the bank perhaps?"

"I'm not going to play a guessing game, Fountain."

"That man Alemand was talking to is named Reginald Fall-gow You know him?"

"You mean Fowl-goo?" he replied, correcting my French. "Reginald Falgout? Yes, I know him. Was that him? By gum, he looked familiar, yes. Older, though. Much older than I remember. Must not be aging well. A bit of the booze, I'd say."

193

"I don't care about his booze. Why would your client have anything to do with the bank's Office of the Auditor?"

"I couldn't tell you. I honestly have no idea. His accounts aren't out of order. I reconcile them every month. I tally his cash register almost daily. Why, the man is Scrooge in the flesh when it comes to his pennies. Nervous as a twit, he is. He allows nothing out of order."

"That was clearly an argument he was having with Mr. Falgout outside of the bank."

"So it was, but it doesn't mean it has anything to do with him or with me."

I sat back in my chair, my mouth gaping. "That's the most ridiculous thing I've ever heard you say," I replied. "You're burying your head in the sand if you believe their conversation is immaterial. What I saw were two angry men about to go at it with each other. Two professional men don't do that on a city street unless they're both involved in something. There's been enough going on that I believe it's worth looking into."

The waitress came to our table and refreshed our coffee. Portier looked up and asked if our meals were almost ready. She smiled and said she'd check. He sipped his coffee and ignored me.

"I don't expect you to help me on this," I said. "He's your client. You do what you think is best. Me? I'm not going to let what I saw slide. I'm going to find out what that argument was about because I know an argument when I see one. I know a murder when I see one, and I know a family who's hiding something when I see one, too. You forget I was a minister once. You forget that when it comes to the dark side of human existence, especially in families, I've walked through valleys with them many times. The Lyons family is no different."

Portier continued to sip his coffee. Even though the pattern on our tablecloth drew his eyes, his ears focused on every word I said.

"And I have no doubt," I added, pressing my index finger squarely on the table in front of him, "that right now we're walking through the valley of the shadow of death with these people."

Chapter 15

Portier and I walked in silence toward the French Quarter from the restaurant. Even though my belly felt satisfied, a gnawing pang grew inside my gut the farther we walked.

"I think I'll run over to the police station if you think you'll be okay going back to the cottage alone," I said.

"At this hour?"

"It's not that late. I'm pretty sure detectives work overtime in this city."

Portier didn't argue.

I entered the police station as if it were my second home and approached the front counter. "Detective Robicheaux, please. Reverend Fountain here."

The officer gave me a doubting look as he picked up the receiver. I couldn't hear what was discussed. The officer's syllables were soft, short, and selective. "He's about to leave," he said.

"It'll only be a minute."

"Better be a hot minute."

The officer rose from his seat and opened the door to a stark, but clean, hallway. Detective Robicheaux stood in the hall in front of his office and escorted me to a dark, wooden chair in front of his desk. A lazy, golden hue shrouded the room from the evening sun, highlighting mounds of uncompleted paperwork.

"To what do I owe this pleasure, Reverend?" he asked in an amicable tone of voice, but his expression exposed it as insincere.

"I shouldn't be long. A couple of questions, a few comments are all. I trust your day went well."

"What can I do for you?"

"Corporate dealings of the Lyons family. What can you tell me of them? Have you looked into them?"

"First of all, Reverend, this is an active investigation. I'm not privy to divulge our facts, especially not to you."

"I'm not here to be adversarial."

"It doesn't matter."

"Why? Because I'm still a suspect?"

"Because it's an active investigation."

"Then I'll turn my question into a comment. I'd look into the ownership interests of their investments if I were you, Detective. I have a feeling there are more than we can imagine. Some may even be tied together in a way that conflicts with each other."

"And you know this how?"

"From conversations with the Lyons family and a hunch I have that they aren't being totally transparent with me."

"Why should they be? You aren't as important to them as you make yourself out to be."

"Good point, Detective; however, they talk and say things in front of me that I can't help but overhear."

"What I don't understand," he said, "is why you continue to surround yourself with these people in the first place."

"I'm usually invited. I've gained their trust."

Robicheaux sat back in his chair and smirked. "I find that hard to believe."

"Nevertheless, I've a strong feeling that almost every member of the family knew their father was in town long before I discovered his body. They didn't divulge that information to each other because they had their individual motives for keeping his location a secret."

"Financial motives, I imagine."

"Of course. That's why I asked if you've looked into their corporate holdings in greater detail."

"Thank you for the information. I'll look into it."

"And the will?"

"Pardon me?"

"Roger Lyons' Last Will and Testament. I'm sure you've looked into it as well. There's scuttlebutt amongst the family that he was going to change it. I wonder if he did, and if he did, who loses and who benefits by the change."

"Who told you this?"

"Again, I'm merely a trusted bystander in the room as comments are being made."

"Yes, of course," he said with apprehension. "Well, now, if that's it, I thank you for coming in, and—"

"The woman," I said abruptly.

He stopped and looked at me as if he had no idea to whom I referred. "The woman at the scene when Mr. Lyons died. Have you interviewed her any further?"

"Reverend, I do appreciate the information you've shared, but I must remind you again that what I've done or what I've not done, who I've interviewed or who I've not interviewed are not points for open discussion."

"I understand, but she was at the scene. I was at the scene. I distrust her answers to you. I was hoping you would've re-interviewed her."

"I can tell you that I tried to go to her place of residence, but she wasn't there."

"Wasn't there? You mean as in gone to the grocery? Went for a walk? Skipped town?"

"The address she gave us was invalid. It was a transient community. No one had ever heard of her there."

"Was this transient community out by St. Roch, by any chance? Does it go by the name of Labreville?"

"Yes, but how do you know about that?"

"It's one of the communities Roger Lyons established when he went by the alias Mr. Montgomery."

"Well, she wasn't there."

"Odd, isn't it, that she would give you an address of a community developed by the same man she claims I murdered in front of her very eyes."

Detective Robicheaux's expression hardened.

I waited for a response, but none came, so I prompted, "Don't you think that's odd?"

He sat upright and placed his elbows on his desk, interlocking his fingers and gritting his teeth. "No," he said, "I don't find that odd. I don't find it odd in the least. What I find odd is your overwhelming interest in a case you have no business investigating."

"I want to clear my name."

"Or cast suspicion in another direction. There's a point when someone's involvement in a case goes beyond being helpful. It becomes intrusive, and you're rapidly approaching that point, Reverend. I suggest you let us do our job, and you back away."

"That's preposterous, Detective. I'm not trying to cast suspicion onto anyone but the murderer."

"What would you say if I told you we found a gold nylon cord in your possession?"

I frowned and didn't answer. I didn't know what he was talking about.

"A judge issued us a search warrant to go through your things in Mr. Portier's cottage while you were away this evening."

"That can't be, and how did you know I was away?"

"We found several items of interest to us, one being a gold-threaded nylon cord we believe was used to strangle Mr. Lyons on the park bench after he was pushed and fell against the wrought iron fence near the bench. What do you have to say to that?"

"It isn't mine and never belonged to me. I don't know how it could've gotten there. I don't know who would've had access to Portier's cottage to plant it there, and I had no idea that a nylon cord even existed."

"What if I told you we also have a witness who's willing to testify that he or she saw you with the cord in your possession before and after the incident?"

"I would say your witness is a bold-face liar."

"The cord is in the lab as we speak, being analyzed. We should find bits of tissue or hairs from Lyons' beard within the fibers where you tightened it securely around his neck."

"You can analyze all you like. You'll find nothing that links me to the murder weapon."

"Then you deny categorically that you killed Rogers Lyons with a nylon cord after bashing his head against a wrought-iron fence?"

"I most certainly do, Detective, and I must protest this line of questioning. I can't believe you're making these accusations against me."

"Then you can believe this, Reverend. Stop your meddling. Stop your investigative meddling into a case that's being actively conducted by the New Orleans Police Department. Do you understand? I hope I've made it very clear that this is a very serious matter, and I'm adamant that I want you to stop. Your intrusion is only making matters worse for you right now."

"Are you saying I'm still a suspect?"

"No, Reverend, I'm saying you're my only suspect, and I'm telling you to butt the hell out."

I nearly choked from the cotton-like feeling in my mouth. My head began to spin. I asked if I was free to go. When he waved me out of his office, I took my leave and stumbled into the hallway. My knees felt weak from the shock of Robicheaux's accusation.

I was in trouble. For the first time, I understood the serious consequence of being involved with the death of Roger Lyons. I thought the detective's prior attempts to scare me were just that—to put the fear of God into me to change my investigative behavior, but now his investigation was escalating into a nightmare beyond comprehension.

Portier!

Suddenly, I remembered that my friend walked ahead of me to the cottage. What a nightmare he faced, coming upon a swarm of officers and detectives converging upon his home, helplessly watching them ransack his house, finding evidence that had been purposely planted.

I wasn't a good runner. Too much time had passed since the last time I'd run. My knees snapped and cracked, and my ankles ached with the pounding of my feet upon the pavement. I heaved large amounts of air into my lungs to no avail. The burning sensation was too much to bear, and I stopped to rest alongside a shotgun's front cement wall.

I took a moment to pray as I composed myself and caught my breath, but I felt too exasperated with fear and uncertainty to think clearly, to put two cohesive words together for my Lord to understand. Tears began to stream down my face.

I looked up, realizing that I didn't have to be composed. The Lord understood my fear, saw all things as they happened, and knew my heart. All I had to do was trust that the truth would be revealed in His perfect time.

I took a deep breath and started towards the cottage again. I didn't run. I walked briskly, but I didn't feel the need to run anymore. I rounded the corner onto Ursulines; darkness loomed on the front of Portier's drab little cottage. All was quiet. The cottage stood undisturbed. Light from a small lamp in a front window illumined through the sheers—the only sign of activity.

No one was on the street. I expected to see neighbors conversing on their stoops about the invasion they witnessed near their homes. None of that occurred. No pedestrians walked on the sidewalks. No cars passed in the street.

I approached Portier's stoop and reached for the doorknob. It turned easily. I opened the door cautiously and peaked into the dimly lit room. Seeing nothing of interest, I opened the door wider. Bentley lay curled beside his master's chair, sleeping soundly. Portier sat in the chair slumped to one side, his mouth open. His nostrils flared with each snort from the depths of his throat.

I swung the door open to enter. Bentley woke immediately, popping up his head and rising clumsily to meet me at the doorway.

"Shhh, boy, don't wake him now. Shhh. Did you have some excitement?" I rubbed his ears and patted his coat, wishing he could talk and tell me all about the police's search before I heard it from Portier with both barrels blazing.

Portier didn't wake until I closed the door tightly. He snorted a couple of times then looked at me with groggy eyes, smacking his lips to get the saliva flowing in his mouth again. "What did you do? Go drinking with the whole police department?" he asked me, sitting upright in his chair.

"I wasn't gone that long."

"I must've fallen asleep. It sure seemed like a long time. Damn, I spilled my drink, too."

"You must've been tired."

"Yes, I'm tired. I'm exhausted. You exhaust me, Fountain. You're absolutely exhausting."

"Nothing else?"

He glared at me as if asking what else could be more exhausting than my arguments with him.

"Did you have any visitors?" I asked.

"Genevieve stopped by. She wanted to give me some crayfish tails she ordered from the club."

"Did you take them? I wouldn't mind having some tomorrow."

Portier tried to get out of his chair, shaking a foot that had gone to sleep. "Oh, hell, no," he said. "I'm not putting any of those critters in my refrigerator. You want crayfish tails we'll go to a good place, but I'm not taking any crayfish from a seedy club. Who knows where it came from?"

"No one else?"

"What do you mean 'no one else?'"

I sat in a nearby chair. Bentley followed and sat beside me, panting and looking up with the hope that I would pet him some more. "Did you not have the police here? Did they not serve you with a search warrant?"

Portier's eyes widened with alarm. "A search warrant?"

"They didn't find a gold nylon cord or take anything out of the house?"

"What are you talking about? Here? Tonight?"

"Yes, while I was at the police station."

"What did you say to those people anyway?"

"Never mind that. You mean the police were never here?"

Portier walked towards the kitchen. "Fountain, you've put me through hell and back these past few days, but nothing as horrific as a police raid occurred upon my home this evening, thank God."

"Yes, yes, thank God," I said, making the sign of the cross across my chest. I wondered why Robicheaux would play such a cruel trick on me.

"You want something?" Portier asked. "I'm going to refresh my drink."

I declined. "No, I think I'm going to step out again."

"It's going to rain."

"Didn't feel like it."

"Wasn't it overcast?"

"Yes, but—"

"It's going to rain. It's coming in from the Gulf. You should stay indoors."

I didn't want to stay indoors.

"Where are you going?" he asked.

"I thought about seeing if Genny would go to her club with me."

"What the hell for?"

"I want to talk."

"Bentley's a good listener. I talk to him all of the time, and he never gets me into any trouble. I'll leave you two alone. You can talk to him. You don't need to go out." Portier left the room.

Bentley's panting mouth looked as if he was smiling at me.

"I'm sure that's very true, Ben-buddy, but you can't help me this time. Don't tell your master, but I want to see if that Donnie kid is around. I need to talk with him to see what more he can tell me about people who hung around with Mr. Montgomery, er, I mean, Mr. Lyons. You don't care, though, do you, boy? You just want a treat. You want a tasty morsel, Ben?"

His tail began wagged fiercely.

I walked into the kitchen to get a slice of bologna from the refrigerator. Upon entry, I saw Portier standing over his half-made drink with his head down as if he was going to be ill.

"Are you okay?" I asked. "You should sit down. Here, let me make that for you."

"No, I'm fine."

"You don't look well at all. Are you sure?"

"Yes, I was just thinking," he said, standing erect. "Sometimes when I think I start to vomit because of what I have to think about."

"Gracious, then let's make your drink and go back into the parlor and finish our discussion."

"No, the last thing I want to do is have another discussion with you. I was thinking about what you said to me at Mother's before we had our blackened ham. You're absolutely correct. I'm burying my head in the sand. Something's not right with Alemand. I can't put my finger on it, but it's not right. That argument he had on the street with Falgout was out of character."

"What do you mean? There's something you're not telling me, Portier, or you don't want to tell me. What is it?"

"Falgout's not only the head of auditing at the bank, he's much, much more." Portier looked at me so that I could see the grave expression on his face. "I neglected to tell you an important point about Falgout. He's a fraud examiner. He investigates all kinds of schemes that employees and customers pull that involve the institution. He does even more than that. He also assists law enforcement in helping them understand how criminals use the bank to facilitate illegal transactions. He can trace transactions from one account to another account or from his bank to other financial institutions. He's a great asset to the local police, sheriff departments, FBI, and IRS agents."

"Then it might not be something he's working on for the bank, but something he's working on for law enforcement. Do you think there's a possibility that Alemand is involved with something illegal or did something illegal to fund his venture with Andre Lyons?" I asked.

"It sure looks that way. It bothers me, but what bothers me even more is why I haven't spotted anything in the books that would be a red flag. Red flags can crop up anywhere. Why haven't I seen any? Alemand is a smart man, don't get me wrong, but he doesn't know accounting from a sack of beans, and he wouldn't be good enough to hide something from me."

"What do you think his discussion with Falgout was all about?"

"I don't know. Maybe Falgout was tantalizing him about something. Maybe Falgout saw something from his end in the bank that he asked Alemand about. You've heard Alemand bellyache about the investment he made in *Dickies, Stocks, and Jabots*. He laments over his finances even when there's nothing to lament about. He overreacts. Maybe Falgout gave him a call, and Alemand got defensive and let him have it. I don't know. I can't figure it out."

"Why wouldn't Alemand talk to you first, though, before approaching Falgout?"

"That's what's bothering me. He normally would. Why he didn't this time has me a bit spooked."

"I see, yes, it could be he wants it hid from you as long as possible."

"It could be worse than that. What if there's something in the books I overlooked that could implicate me as well in whatever he's doing. Ignorance is no defense. I'm not a fly by night accountant. I'm a CPA, and I've been a damn good one for years. I know what I'm doing."

"Don't start thinking like that. I know what I'm talking about, too. I had a bit of paranoia set in this evening myself. I talked myself out of it with good reason. It wasn't true. Don't fret over Alemand's problems that may not be your problems. What might appear on the surface isn't what might be going on underneath. It'll all straighten itself out soon enough."

Portier finished preparing his drink. "You still going out?"

"Yes, and I need to get going." I turned to exit, but was stopped abruptly by a Golden Labrador in my path. His eyes were fixated on my every move since entering the kitchen. "Ah! Bologna! I promised you a treat. I say, Bentley, you have the patience of a saint and the memory of an elephant."

I broke the slice of bologna into three equal pieces and tossed them at Bentley. He caught each one of the slimy rewards with precision, then gulped them without them hitting a taste bud. It did my heart good to see him enjoy his treat as he did, although I wasn't quite sure if he knew what he ate.

I'd only seen such skill one other time—watching Genny Duval eat Mississippi catfish at the club.

Chapter 16

I knocked on Genny's door to see if she'd like to accompany me to her club. I was hoping we could talk along the way to see if she'd observed anything unusual from the clubs' cast of characters such as Princess Moline, Victorius Caesar, Carmen Nicolet, Glen Balfour, and Donnie …

I realized I didn't know his last name.

It didn't matter. Genny would know who I was talking about. To my dismay, however, she didn't answer the door to her cottage.

I walked swiftly to the smoke-filled club where she sang with the hopes of finding her there. The club was brimming with music, laughter, and dancing, and the cabaret energized with people in costume, some without. It seemed much too early for such revelry, but I looked at my watch. The time was almost ten o'clock. Not early at all for New Orleans. The evening's festivities were well underway.

I took a seat at a table along the wall so I could get a panoramic view of the venue.

Genny finished a sensual rendition of *Whatever Lola Wants* from *Damn Yankees*. The audience—even those not paying attention—raised their glasses and shouted crude remarks as she stepped from the stage. She took it all in, batting her eyes and swishing the feather boa around her neck as if she were stripping it off. Genny winked as she walked towards me, strutting in character with the number. Her derriere moved in rhythm with the beat of a base drum that stopped only when she sat on a bistro chair beside me.

"Oh, that was fun!" she exclaimed, fanning her face with her boa. "It's a warm evening tonight, isn't it?"

"Warmer on stage based upon what I just saw."

She crinkled her nose. "No, honey, it's not warm; it's hot on stage, sizzling hot. They love me, don't they?"

I couldn't disagree.

"So what brings you to the shady side of town, sweetheart? May I have Tomas bring you a drink? I want one. Liquor this time, I promise." She lifted her finger and caught the attention of a passing attendant then ordered a drink for each of us.

"I just came in for a moment, Genny," I said.

"That's what they all tell their wives," she giggled.

"No, seriously, I came to see if that Donnie kid was here."

"Then you'll be disappointed."

"Seriously? He's not here?"

"See for yourself. Ask his girlfriend. She's sitting over there."

I looked to where she pointed and saw Carmen Nicolet sipping on a tall drink and laughing coyly with a gentleman leaning against the bar.

"Who's she sitting with?" I asked.

"No idea. A new beau, I suspect. Whatever you said to her about Donnie the other night must've worked. She's onto a new sugar daddy."

"Donnie was hardly a daddy, and he had very little sugar."

"I know, but he had what she wanted. Same difference."

I watched carefully as Carmen ordered another round of drinks and reached for her sequined handbag. She undid the clasp and pulled out a bill to place on the counter. The bill must've been a large one based upon the look in the man's eyes and the smile on his face. She rubbed her hand along her bare thigh to change his focus.

"That dress leaves little to the imagination," Genny said, glancing at me for a reaction.

I didn't have one. Another person had drawn my attention. Glen Balfour was making his own moves on a blonde who was giving him equal attention.

Genny followed my gaze. "Your other favorite person."

I frowned as our waitress brought drinks to our table. The waitress saw my expression and thought it was about the drinks.

Genny laughed, "Oh, no, sweetheart, the drinks are fine. My friend doesn't like some of our customers."

The waitress turned to see who was at the table I watched. "Oh, him. Yeah, me neither. Big money, cheap tipper. All blow, no go. You know the kind, Genny."

"Hey, do something for me, will you?" Genny said. "See that woman in the short, white dress, talking to that handsome nobody at the bar?"

"Yeah, you mean Connie?"

"Connie, Karen, Carmen, whoever, yeah. Ask her to come over here, will ya?"

"Sure," she said and walked away.

"No!" I exclaimed.

Genny patted my hand. "It'll be fun. Trust me."

"I don't want fun. I don't want to talk with her."

"You don't have to say a word. I'll do the talking. I just gotta find out something. Those two characters, that Connie somebody and that …"

"Glen Balfour."

210

"Glen Bal-nobody have oodles of money. They drip in the stuff, but here they are, dancing and schmoozing with critters that ain't got a pot to piss in. It doesn't make sense."

"It makes perfect sense," I said. "They have low self-esteem. They feel better about themselves being with people they believe are inferior to them."

"Speaking of which," Genny said, pointing to the door.

I turned to watch Moline of Rokavia and Victorius Caesar enter the club.

"Isn't that something?" Genny added. "Moline's usually never this late to the club. I wonder where she's been. The little traitor better not be hitting another club first."

I watched them walk to the bar. They stood beside Carmen and her date but didn't acknowledge them. Moline turned toward the dance floor with her back against the bar and surveyed the crowd. Genny waved. Moline saw her, but ignored her.

"She's got her cuff back," I said.

"So she has. It's her trademark, you know."

"I figured as much. That's why I called her on it when she said she gave it to Victorius to wear."

"Oh, I remember." Genny chuckled under her breath. "She must've found it. It's the only thing that looks nice on her. The rest of her is a mess. She looks like Victorius had to drag her down the street to get her here."

I looked closer. Genny was right. Moline's costume appeared unkempt, and her hair was tangled and bushy. Her disposition was out of sorts, too. She looked drawn and tired. She turned to Victorius and spouted what appeared to be a couple of insults to him. He tried to ignore but couldn't. They began to argue.

"She looks like she's in a bit of a Katzenjammer," I said.

211

Genny looked at me as if she wondered at my sanity.

"Katzenjammer," I repeated.

"Yeah, I have no idea what that means."

"Sure you do. It's that feeling you get with a hangover or a bad headache."

"Katzenjammer?"

"It's a German term. It translates to cat wailing. That's exactly what she appears to be doing to poor Victorius over there."

"We French have another term. It's *avoir mal aux cheveaux.*"

"Which means?"

"Hairache."

I laughed and shook my head. "The German language isn't as pretty as French, but I dare say it's more accurate. Moline's hair is hurting, that's true, but she's definitely acting more like a wailing cat."

We watched as the waitress who gave us our drinks approached Carmen at the bar and said something in her ear. Carmen gestured to the gentleman that she had to leave, but would be only a second.

She walked toward our table cautiously. "I thought I made myself clear last time that I didn't want to talk with you again," she said to me when I was within earshot.

"He feels the same way," Genny replied. "I've seen you in here before."

"So? What of it? You're the singer, aren't you?"

"Very observant since I was just up there."

"Yes, well, who couldn't miss those doorknobs you're wearing as earrings." Carmen looked down at Genny's costume. "I didn't know they made bedspreads in material like that."

"Why so hateful, Carmen?" I asked. "You had nothing but praise for Genny the last time I saw you."

"Yeah, well, that was before I knew she was your friend."

Genny smiled and sweetened her tone. "I didn't call you over to spit insults back and forth. As someone who works in this club, I wanted to thank you for coming in and spending money with Tomas at the bar. I've noticed a lot of bread coming out of your purse. I'm sure he appreciates it."

"If I have it, why not enjoy it? I'll be coming into a lot more money very soon—a lot more than you'll ever make with that voice of yours."

"And where's the money coming from? The man you murdered?"

I gave Genny a sharp look of disapproval.

"My grandfather wasn't murdered. He had an accident. Reverend Fountain can tell you as much."

"It doesn't matter," I said. "I doubt you'll ever see a dime from him."

"Oh, you don't think so?"

"He's not your grandfather as you claim. He has no legal obligation to give you a thing."

"I think the courts in Lafayette Parish will disagree with you if I have to contest the will. They'll surely take pity upon me and award me something from his estate once they hear of the horrific emotional abuse I suffered as a child in his house."

"You have a very naïve view of the world, Miss Nicolet."

"No, I know how the world works. I believe it's a kind and forgiving world, especially in the courts. I would've thought you believed it, too."

"Be it as it may, I've lived long enough to know the world isn't always kind, nor is it forgiving."

"As a man of the cloth it's your job to make it such."

213

"I may be a man of God, Miss Nicolet, but where there's no kindness or forgiveness I seek justice."

Carmen smiled as if she had me backed into a corner. "I thought justice and judgment were up to God. I didn't realize how highly you thought of yourself."

"You're quite correct, but we're His hands and feet on this earth and we're called to do His work. My calling is justice."

She smirked again and started to turn away before I called her back. "Are you no longer keeping Donnie's company?" I asked.

"I don't find that any of your business."

"Do you know where I can find him? Is he at Labreville?"

She laughed. "There's no solace in that dump. You should know that, Reverend. What comfort is there? Donnie's nothing, but he's a singer, and he takes his singing seriously. He needs space to create. Labreville isn't a place to create, so he goes where he can be inspired."

"Where's that?"

"Why don't you ask your God? You're so high and mighty about him. If he's as you say he is, let him tell you where Donnie is. Now if you'll excuse me."

"You're too late," Genny said to Carmen before she could turn around to leave. "You'll not find your new boyfriend at the bar anymore. When you left to come see us, he absconded with the large bill you placed on the counter and went out that side door. I'm pretty sure he's onto the next shiny object."

Carmen turned abruptly towards the bar. Her face blazed with a deep-red hue. Her nostrils flared. She gave us a look that could kill before she bolted for the exit.

"Good riddance," Genny said. She looked at me to see if I felt the same, but she must have seen the dejected look on my face. "What's the matter?"

I shook my head. "I'm very ashamed."

"Of what? Of her? Of what you said to her? Oh, no, you should be damn proud to put a woman like that in her place."

"I'm not called to be 'damn proud,' Genny. I'm called to lead people to a greater place. That was very poor judgment on my part. It was poor judgment to have come here."

"Don't say that. Don't go. It was my fault what happened with Carmen, not yours. Sometimes my idea of a fun time is at the expense of others. I'm sorry."

I patted her hand to let her know she hadn't offended me. We sat in silence for several minutes. I caught her looking at me from the corner of her eye with a look I'd seen many times before in parishioners who had a spiritual question for me but hesitated to ask it at the expense of sounding silly or trite.

"It wouldn't be a dumb question whatever the question you have," I said.

Genny blushed. Even the heavy coating of rouge couldn't hide her embarrassment. "Very well. Did you mean what you said?"

"Yes, I meant every word to Carmen. I just wished I hadn't said it."

"No, no, not that. She deserved all you said. I meant what you said about being kind in an unkind world."

"There is kindness in the world, don't get me wrong. There's kindness all around us, but it's still a very hard world to survive for some people. If you're a person like Donnie who struggles to make it through each day, you'll find it even harder. For people like Donnie, the world isn't kind. Our role should be to make it kinder."

"Maybe we need more things in this world to help remind us; more symbols, expectations, rules, guidance, that sort of thing."

"Another law?"

"Oh, I don't know. Maybe, if it'll help."

"Does another law make you want to be more lawful? Does having another Bible help you pray more? How about another hymn? Does singing one more hymn encourage you to forgive your brother or sister? Does it compel us to apologize to Carmen Nicolet? No, of course not. We don't need more things in this world to remind us we should be better people. What we need is self-awareness about our faith and a soul that yearns to change, a soul that wants to do what's right without having things to remind us to do them. It's getting to the point where we worship the things that represent God more than we do our relationship with God."

Genny let my words sink in a second before she said, "So tell me something about this Roger Lyons fellow. What do you really think of him? I know very little of him, but he seems to have led a very material and self-serving life, yet you're taking the call to find justice for him very seriously."

I took a deep breath and thought back to the day I saw Roger Lyons slumped over the park bench. The image haunted me. I cringed. I sipped my drink then stared into my icy glass.

"If you'd rather not answer, I understand," she said.

"No, it's all right. You asked about Roger Lyons. What I think of Roger Lyons is as complicated as what I think of the rest of his family. I regret some things I said to Roger as he was dying. I saw him as a homeless destitute with no hope and no future. I should've encouraged that life no matter what it appeared to me at the time. Life isn't always as it appears. Much to my surprise, I found out he was a very wealthy and materialistic man who became destitute to better serve those he had neglected all his life. He was now doing something more meaningful than he'd ever done before."

"Is that why you look after Donnie; because you see something different in him?"

"That's complicated, too. I don't believe running into him on Royal Street the first night I came into town was a coincidence. How was I to know that some kid on the street, singing a song, would be tied to a man I found murdered the next morning? Not only that, but I discover he's seeing the step-granddaughter of the very man I find murdered. It has to tie together somehow."

"I wouldn't know. I believe in coincidences, but they don't happen to me."

"I don't believe that."

"It's true. I see it happening with other people all the time but not to me."

"Then you're not paying attention. Life is full of coincidences and twists of fate that enhance our human experience. You're not grasping the full opportunity of your life by not paying attention to the coincidences of people and experiences that cross your path."

"So you believe Carmen and Donnie are an opportunity?"

"I'm not sure I would characterize them as an opportunity, but I can't ignore they've crossed my path. Carmen is boasting too much about her step-grandfather and what she's going to get from him. She's also spending a lot of his money before she has it. She feels entitled. I believe she used Donnie to get to her step-grandfather who Donnie knew as Mr. Montgomery."

"Their connection is a bit eerie, isn't it? Her eyes have nothing in them. I don't like her."

"And I don't trust her."

"Then Donnie could be in danger."

"That's why I have to find him. He's not only in danger from Carmen Nicolet, but he's in danger from himself.

217

Carmen has no more use for him. When I told her to stay away from him because I didn't want her around him, she didn't find it very difficult to let him go. She was off to another sap immediately."

"Then the danger from her should be over."

"Not if she needs to get rid of him because of what he knows about Roger Lyons' death. Donnie could come back to haunt her."

"I see, but what do you mean by Donnie being a danger from himself?"

"This town is a fun town, Genny, but it's hard to survive, especially for a guy like Donnie. Word is already around the Quarter that he's a thief. The future is bleak for him. There are only three places in this country for men with mental issues: the sanitarium, jail, or the morgue."

"Do you know where he is?"

"No. Carmen mentioned a place where he can create and be inspired. I have no idea where that is." A lull in our conversation gave me time to think. "Wait. Maybe I do. I remembered she told me once to jump in the lake with him. It may not have been a simple figure of speech. Does Lake Pontchartrain have an area where locals hang out?"

"Yes, there's a place along the lakeshore."

"How can I get there?"

"Let me see if there's someone getting off shift that has a car."

"If they'll drive me there, I can get a cab back," I said.

She walked to the bar, asked a few questions then went to a table in the corner of the room. She came back to me quickly. "If you don't mind how he's dressed, that guy over there is heading out to Gentilly. He can drop you off."

"The one with no pants?"

"Yeah, but he knows where the locals hang out along the lakeshore."

"Has he been drinking?"

"I don't ask that."

I shook my head. "Is there a payphone here?"

Genny pointed to the opposite corner of the room. "You gotta dime?"

I nodded and hurried to the phone and called the only person I knew who I thought would help.

Jeffrey listened to my request and replied immediately, "You don't mind riding in my half-ton, do you? It ain't no Golden Hawk."

"I don't care about your truck," I said. "I'd ride in a rickshaw if that's all you had."

Chapter 17

"You sure you oughta be out on a night like this?" Jeffrey asked as he pulled into a graveled parking spot along Lake Pontchartrain. A light mist started to cover the truck's windshield.

"I won't melt."

"I'm not talking about the rain."

"It won't take me long. I just want to see if he's here."

"I don't like it."

I patted his shoulder. "Portier would be proud of the way you're talking to me. You're spending too much time with him, you know."

"Yeah, yeah, just make it quick, Reverend F. I told you this ain't the Hawk. If we have to make a quick get-away, your ass better be faster than this truck."

I slid out of the cab and onto the gritty lot. Jeffrey pointed me towards where young people hung out. I bundled my overcoat around my waist and tightened the fedora on my head as I made my way toward the lake.

Breezes picked up the closer I got to the shore. Lamp posts scattered along the walkway illuminated very little through the misty fog. Drops of rain splattered around me; enough to keep late-night goers from the lake. If this was a hangout for young people as Jeffrey said, it was void of anyone tonight—except for a lone silhouette, sitting on a cement wall along the lakeshore, feet dangling off the edge.

Donnie didn't look up when I approached.

I didn't say anything at first. I watched him as the brackish waves of lake water splashed against the concrete and rolled along the ledge. For a moment, I considered sitting beside him, but the damp chill in my knees begged me not to do so, and the thought of a soggy bottom when I rose compelled me to remain standing.

"I saw Carmen tonight," I finally said. I have no idea why I started off with a hurtful comment like that, but I did, and I couldn't take it back.

"Was she with a new guy?" When I didn't answer, he added, "I suppose I have you to thank for that and for getting me nudged out of the way."

"I didn't nudge you out of the way. I did talk to her. I won't lie about that. I told her not to hurt you. She'd have to answer to me if she did. It was a matter of time before she moved on, Donnie."

"That wasn't your call to make."

"That's true, it wasn't. I'm sorry about that, but that's the only thing I'm sorry about."

"You've no idea how she made me feel when I was with her. She was the only person who didn't judge me, who didn't think twice about being with me. She never once acted as if I'd take something from her."

"That's because *she* was hoping to take something from *you*, Donnie. She used you to get to Mr. Montgomery."

"You're full of shit. You always have been."

"I know it's hard to—"

"Shut up. I don't want to listen to you anymore. You hear me? I only had one thing going for me in my life and now she's gone, so just shut up and go away."

221

More raindrops fell into the lake. It wouldn't be long before we'd be caught in a deluge.

"Come on, let's go," I said. "I won't talk, and you don't have to listen. Let's get you someplace dry."

"I'm good."

"But it's raining harder."

"I said I'm good. I want to stay. I'm one of them."

Light from the park lamp reflected off streams of rain flowing from his cheekbone. His gaze didn't leave the shroud of darkness that loomed across the lake.

"One of what?" I asked.

"Raindrops. I'm just like one of them. I fall. I make a tiny ripple that disappears, and no one thinks anymore about it—ever."

"That's not true. You're different, Donnie. I've told you that before. You can make something of yourself."

He didn't budge.

I tried again. "Come on. I have a ride. Let's get something to eat then I'll take you to Labreville or to the Marigny, wherever you want to go. Just come with me."

Donnie looked up. "No, you go," he said without expression. "I mean it. Just go."

The rain fell harder. For the first time since meeting Donnie, I felt as if I wasn't going to break through to him. He appeared to be caught in a cycle of despair that he couldn't overcome, and now, I was at a loss for words that would give him the hope and strength he needed to keep fighting.

I turned and walked along the levee to the path that led to where Jeffrey had parked the truck. The farther I walked away from the lake, the fewer lamps illuminated the way. It didn't seem to matter to me, though. The darkness I walked through wasn't even close to the darkness I imagined Donnie was experiencing.

Raindrops hit the ground with timely precision. The live oaks swayed with the slap of the drops upon their leaves. The water slid off the brim of my fedora, hitting my pant legs as I walked. The cold wetness stuck to my skin, but didn't make me quicken my gait. I didn't care about being wet. I couldn't feel the cold. One foot went before the other, but I didn't hear my shoes hit the footpath.

I was so immersed in thought and sorrow that I didn't hear the rustling of the bushes lining the walk. I didn't hear the footsteps coming rapidly from behind until I felt the blade of the intruder's knife cut a swatch out of the sleeve of my coat. It didn't hurt. Not at first. I knew something had cut my arm and tore my clothing, but what happened didn't dawn on me until I turned and saw his arm extended above his head to deliver another, more accurate, blow. I instinctively reached for his arm to stop his forward thrust. Adrenaline gave me the strength I needed to fend off the strike, but he came at me again just as fierce.

I stepped back as quickly as I could, but tripped on the uneven path and fell against the shrubs. He lunged, and I rolled to the right. His torso landed partially upon me. I tried to move him off of me so that I could stand, but I was unable to do so.

He lifted himself more easily than I was able, but he didn't come at me. Instead, he reached into the bushes and appeared to search for something he'd dropped. I gained momentum and hit him on the side of his covered face. I pounded him again and tried to leverage myself against his body to pull myself on my feet, but he batted me away and grabbed my throat. I rolled to the ground. His hands pressed hard upon my pharynx. I tried to gasp, but couldn't. Confused and exhausted, I couldn't get my arms in a position to lift him off me. Energy drained quickly from the muscles in my arms.

Without warning, the attacker suddenly fell upon me and ceased moving. The pressure upon my throat released. I coughed a few times, then pushed his body off me. Another figure stood above the two of us. He tossed a branch from his hands onto the footpath.

"You okay?" the man asked.

I recognized Jeffrey's voice, but I didn't answer. I wanted up from the muddy path. I wanted to stand and be ready for any additional onslaught from the attacker.

"What the hell happened?" Jeffrey asked.

I rubbed my throat. "You tell me."

"Who is he?"

I shook my head and realized my fedora was no longer protecting my head from the rain. Raindrops pelted my forehead and dripped into my eyes. I couldn't see. I searched and found my hat on top of one of the shrubs. I retrieved it and put it on my head.

"Forget the damn hat, will ya? Who is this guy?"

Jeffrey bent down and lifted the mask from the attacker's head.

I rubbed the rain from my eyes and looked upon his face. To my surprise, he wasn't a man.

"What the hell? Who is she?" Jeffrey asked. The tone of his voice indicated he was as shocked as I was.

I looked at her for a moment unable to comprehend what she was doing at the lake, why she'd followed me to this location, and why she'd tried to kill me.

Jeffrey looked at me. "Well? Do you know who she is?"

224

I nodded. "She's a princess," I said in disbelief. "She's a Rokavian princess from Illinois."

Chapter 18

Bentley watched Portier pace the floor of the living room the next morning. If he was hoping his master would detour towards the kitchen to get him a tasty morsel, he was going to be disappointed.

"It does no good to pace," Genny said, tending to my arm.

"This is a nasty business," he replied. "Someone has to pace. The three of you haven't got a lick of apprehension in your body. You especially," he said, pointing his finger at Jeffrey. "You had no business taking Fountain to the lake."

"Come now, Portier," I scolded. "Jeffrey warned me not to go, but I didn't listen. If it weren't for him I wouldn't be alive right now. If you must be angry, be angry at me."

"Oh, I am. I'm mad as all get-out, but I'm not just angry. I'm worried. I didn't sleep a wink after we got home from the hospital. I heard every noise on Ursulines. I worried about who was out there and who was going to burst through our front door. Gracious, Fountain, you have no sense of danger or consideration for those around you."

"That's not true. I have a great deal of consideration for people, just not you. You can take care of yourself. Besides, I wouldn't have gotten into this mess if Genny would've let me do what I wanted in the first place."

She frowned. "How is this suddenly my fault?"

"I'll tell you how," I said. "I wanted to talk with Moline the first night I met her. Do you remember that? You said no, she wasn't someone who'd have pertinent information because, oh, what did you say? You said she wasn't ..."

"Down and out."

"Yes! That's it. She was down, but she wasn't out, and I needed to find someone who was both. Apparently, you were wrong."

"I'm not the one with a stab wound, though, am I?"

"I could've learned something from her that night, I'm sure of it."

"Hold still," Genny said. "If you want me to take care of these cuts from the bushes and this stab wound, you're going to have to hold still and stop blaming me for something that wasn't my fault. You're a mess, and the dressing on your arm should be changed, too." She wrinkled her nose. "Blood is starting to seep through. Moline cut you pretty good."

"Can you change it?"

"I'm not a nurse."

I watched her unwrap the dressing. She took three rounds of bandages off my arm before she had to stop and take a deep breath.

"That's okay," I said. "You don't have to do this. I'll head back to the hospital. I can't even look myself."

"Then turn your head."

I closed my eyes and did so.

"It's not as bad as it looks," she said after the dressing was completely unwrapped.

I felt relieved and opened my eyes, but I still couldn't look. I made sure my eyes focused on the end table beside me. "What's this?" I asked, perusing the items on the table.

Portier turned towards me. "*Jazz* magazine."

"I can see that. No, the envelope."

Portier turned away.

"Looks like an invitation," Genny replied. "You got some new friends, Chuck? Is it a party?"

"If you must know, it's an invitation to none of your business."

Genny scoffed when I reached with my good arm to turn the envelope to an angle so I could read the return address.

"Manny Lyons?" I asked Portier.

"Just something he's having."

"Like what, an open house to his new business?"

"It's none of your concern because you won't be going. You're in no shape to be doing anything until your arm heals, and I'll not have you dripping blood on the floor of a Lyons family business after you've practically accused them of spilling the blood of their own father."

The telephone rang. "Discussion over," he said as he answered it. "Hello? Yes, this is Charles Portier. Why, good morning, Miss Lyons." He cupped his hand over the receiver and whispered, "It's Angelle Lyons. Yes, Miss Lyons. What? Yes, he's doing well, thank you. Word travels rather quickly. How did you hear about his incident? Oh, yes, yes, I'm sure he would've been the first to know." He cupped his hand again. "Glen Balfour," he whispered to me. "Why, yes, we're going to be in this afternoon. That would be very kind."

"Is she coming here?" I asked impatiently.

Portier shooed me away with his hand and continued to talk on the phone.

"I want to speak with her," I implored.

"Excuse me one second, Miss Lyons." He placed his hand over the receiver and said, "No, Fountain, I think you've done and said enough."

"But I want her to bring me something."

He handed the phone to me indignantly.

I greeted Angelle and told her how much I appreciated her thoughtfulness. After telling me how sorry she was to hear of my accident she said she would be in New Orleans and asked if she could stop by to see how I was doing. "I'm one who has to see for myself if you're doing well," she said. "We've had our differences recently, but human kindness isn't one of them."

I said I would be delighted if she would visit. "Could you do me one small favor, however?" I asked, then told her what it was.

She said it was a small request, and she'd be happy to do it.

I handed the phone back to Portier who said good-bye to her and hung up. "I don't see why she'd drive all the way from Lafayette to see you," he said.

"She's not," I replied. "Andre is driving. He has business in town. She's coming along for the ride."

"To check on that scoundrel she calls a boyfriend, no doubt."

Fortunately, several raps on the door interrupted his cynicism.

Bentley reached the door first, wagging his tail as if a large slice of bologna was on the other side.

Portier opened the door and stood in the doorway without greeting the visitor.

"Mr. Portier, is it?" the man said. "Detective Robicheaux, New Orleans Police Department. May I come in?"

Portier motioned for the detective to enter. Another man who I didn't recognize entered as well.

"This is Detective Warren Malois," Robicheaux said. "I came to see how Reverend Fountain was doing. Ah! And I see the young man who saved him from certain death is here, too. Very good. I have a few more questions I'd like to ask if I could."

"I believe we've answered everything last night and early this morning, Detective," I replied. "I thought we were very thorough."

"That you did and you were. Much appreciated. One other thing, however." He turned to Jeffrey. "I want to be sure I have my facts straight. Tell me again what you saw last night."

"From the beginning? Yes, sir, well, as I told you earlier, I was sittin' in my truck waitin' for the reverend to come back from talkin' to this Donnie kid we told you about. It started to rain. I got kinda worried. Outta the corner of my eye, I saw a person walkin' in the grass just off the foot path leading from the levee. Suddenly, rain started comin' down harder so I got out of my truck to get the reverend so we could go. I didn't like it out there, and I didn't like seein' that person out there, either. The person made me nervous. There was this tree limb not far from my truck so I picked it up for protection and headed towards the footpath. That's when I saw the reverend walkin' towards me and this person come out of the bushes. In a split second I saw the reverend gettin' attacked. I didn't think. I just ran, and the next thing I knew I had broken a limb across the back of the person's head. The person dropped, and the reverend rolled the body off him so he could get up."

"Lucky for her the limb broke."

"Is she still alive?"

Robicheaux nodded. "But she has a brain bleed. The hospital's seen worse, but it's touch and go. She's still unconscious. I think the docs are keeping her that way. She's not talking, as you can imagine. That's why I need to know if you saw anyone else in the area before you spotted her near the path."

Jeffrey shook his head.

"Then how'd she get there? Were there any other cars in the area?"

"Not that I could see. We were pretty much the only ones there. That's why I didn't like being out there in the first place. I urged Reverend Fountain not to stay."

"We're looking for an accomplice," Robicheaux replied, "someone else who may have been involved in the attack."

"Oh, there's an accomplice all right," I said bluntly. "I don't see why this Moline woman would have reason to attack me unless she was paid or provoked to do so."

Detective Malois turned to me and asked, "Were you the one who provoked her?"

"I beg your pardon?"

"Why would she have reason to attack you?"

"Any conversation I had with that woman wouldn't be considered a provocation, I assure you. I've had conversations with her in the past, and I did call her out on something once, but that's all. It was just one time. It's not a Christian thing for me to say, but she's a dreadful woman. She lied to me once, and I couldn't let her lie and get away with it. I called her out on it. I couldn't let her think I was more stupid than she is."

"And what was that? The lie, I mean."

"Her arm cuff."

Genny let out an expletive and leaned backward, hands in the air.

We all looked at her, surprised by her sudden reaction.

"Those serpent arm cuffs she wears," Genny said. "They're her signature, a part of her Princess of Rokavia costume. She wears them all the time."

"Except once," I explained. "We noticed she had only one cuff for a while. When asked about it, she said something about Victorius misplacing his."

"So she gave him hers," Genny added.

"Which was absurd, Detective. If you noticed Moline's arms and compared them to Victorius's arms you'd see immediately there was no way Victorius could wear one of Moline's arm cuffs. His arms are much too big. I called her out on it."

"I did see her arms," Robicheaux said. "She was wearing nothing on her arms."

"That can't be," Genny replied. "She's never without them. Did the hospital staff take them off to treat her?"

"They weren't among her possessions. I asked to take a look."

"That's very odd. Don't you think that's odd, Reverend?" Genny asked.

"I wouldn't know. I only know she's a liar," I said.

"And an attempted murderess, too," Portier added.

"Yes, that's right, Detective." I leaned forward which aggravated my arm. I grimaced in pain. "Portier's right. Surely her attack upon me last night is reason to exonerate me as a suspect. You've been barking up the wrong tree for a very long time. Your lack of attention to the real suspects in Roger Lyons's death has put me in grave danger."

"Now hold on, Reverend. Our investigation didn't do anything of the kind. You purposely violated my warnings not to get involved, and you put yourself in the danger you were in last night. You were never a suspect, not a viable one anyway. I said what I said to you to impress upon you the danger you could get yourself into, but that didn't do any good, did it?"

"Then who's on your suspect list?"

"I'm not at liberty to say. The investigation is still ongoing."

"Did you look into Roger Lyons' will?"

"I did, but, again, I'm not at liberty to say."

"Then I must tell you my probing into the facts of this case will continue to be ongoing as well."

"I advise against that, Reverend. It's obvious to us that this Moline woman didn't work alone. There's someone out there pulling the strings, someone less stupid than she is as you would put it. Your life could still be in jeopardy." The detective stopped to collect his thoughts. "No, I'll go further than that. Your life *is* in jeopardy, and unless you stop your amateur sleuthing into the lives of people you don't know or understand the next time I see you will most likely be in the crypt next to Roger Lyons in the city morgue. Have I made myself clear—again?"

I nodded.

"In words, Reverend."

"I understand."

"Are your fingers crossed?" Portier asked.

"No fingers are crossed," I said, waving them in front of my face. "I completely understand."

Detective Robicheaux took a deep breath and sighed. "Yes, well, we'll see if your actions follow your words."

Chapter 19

Andre and Angelle Lyons arrived in the early afternoon just as clouds dispersed and the sun poked through the sheers of the front window. Jeffrey and Genny left before lunch. Just the three of us remained when the Lyons siblings tapped on the door: Portier, Bentley, and me.

Angelle was as feminine and beautiful as I'd ever seen her with her porcelain skin and soft, wavy hair, under an airy bonnet of pastel blues and yellows. Her dress flowed gracefully around her as she stepped into the parlor.

Of course, Bentley greeted her first, wagging his tail, hoping for as much attention from her as I did. She tried to be polite, but crinkled her nose when she lifted her white-gloved hand for him to stop. She greeted us warmly, however, and asked how I was doing. I'd no sooner finished describing my condition when she asked suddenly, "Is Glen not here?"

"You were expecting him?"

"Yes, he said he'd meet us, didn't he, Andre?"

Andre acknowledged that he did.

"I wonder if I could use your telephone, Mr. Portier," Angelle asked.

"Of course, my dear. Please use the phone in my den. It'll give you more privacy." Portier led her out of the room.

Andre stepped forward to shake my hand, but Bentley growled, and Andre stopped abruptly in his tracks.

I scolded the Labrador. "Bentley, sit!"

The dog did so.

"I'm sorry, Andre," I said.

He took a step forward again.

Again Bentley growled.

"What's going on?" Portier asked, entering the room. "I heard growling. Come here, boy. Out you go. I'll not have any of this." Portier took the Lab out the back and entered again with sincere apologies to our guest. "I don't know what's got into him, Andre. I'm very sorry."

"Please don't blame the dog. I'm not very keen on animals. He could probably sense it."

"Nevertheless, it was very kind of you to bring Miss Lyons to New Orleans."

"That's quite all right. I have much to do here today. I hope to revive *Dickies, Stocks & Jabots*. I came into town to drum up some interest."

"Additional investors?"

"Yes, as a matter of fact."

"I'm terribly sorry to hear about your father, Andre," Portier said, "but surely there is something there for you in his will."

I glared at my friend for bringing up the issue of the will again.

Andre saw it. "No, it's all right, Reverend. We'll know soon enough about the will, but I'm not counting on anything. My father and I had a strained relationship. I shouldn't depend upon him."

"What about Mr. Alemand?" I asked.

Andre's demeanor changed. He looked at me indignantly. "What about him?"

"He's an investor, isn't he? Wouldn't he like the play to continue so that he could recoup some of his investment?"

"I'm afraid Alemand and I aren't seeing eye to eye at the moment."

"Oh dear; what about?"

"I'd prefer not to say."

"Of course. I beg your pardon." I wondered if it had anything to do with Reed Alemand's conversation with the forensic auditor in front of the bank that Portier and I saw, but I didn't dare delve any further.

An uncomfortable silence passed before Andre said, "Besides, I'm in town for other reasons than the play. I'm helping my brother prepare for the open house of his new company. It's tomorrow."

"Yes, I know," I said. "Mr. Portier and I were invited."

Portier started to object, but Andre did it for him. "I hope you can't make it."

Angelle entered the parlor. "Can't make what?" Her red eyes appeared as if she'd been crying.

"Nothing, darling," Andre said. "Manny's open house. What's the matter, dear?"

She shook her head.

"Isn't he coming?"

"He has business," she replied.

I tried not to show an expression, but my lips automatically curled in disgust.

Angelle turned to me, effectively ending the conversation with her brother. "Are you talking about the open house? You'll be coming, won't you? Both of you?"

"I'm afraid we can't," Portier replied.

"We'll be delighted to," I countered.

She looked from one of us to the other in confusion.

I gave Portier a dirty look.

She changed the subject. "I'm glad you're feeling better, Reverend. I tried to bring what you wanted, but I'm sorry to say I couldn't find it."

"Couldn't find it? Are you sure? That's very odd."

"I should say so. It was on the fireplace mantel when you were at the house that one time, but now it's gone."

"What are we talking about?" Andre asked.

"That picture of all of us at the Krewe of Acadia Mardi Gras ball. You know the one. It's the one with Mother in it. We were all in costume. Several photographs were taken. I had the best one framed, and I placed it on a shelf in the library Joyce uses. Reverend Fountain asked to see it when I telephoned this morning, but it wasn't there."

"I wonder if Henri or one of the maids took it down."

"Why would they do that? They usually leave our things as they are."

"Let's forget about it, Angelle," I said. "It was just a thought I had. I remembered seeing it the first time I visited the house, but it dawned on me recently that I didn't see it last time. I was hoping the picture would joggle something in my memory."

"Not to despair," she said. Angelle reached inside her purse and pulled out an envelope. "The framed photograph you saw on the shelf was one of several photos taken at the ball. We had a local photographer develop the roll of film. I found the others. I hope they'll help."

I smiled at the stroke of luck and reached for the packet without hesitation. After withdrawing the black and white photographs from the envelope, I scanned each of them, and then counted their number. "Strange," I said, "there are only twelve pictures here, Angelle. The packet from the photographer indicates that the film was a roll of sixteen."

"Are you sure?" She took the pictures to look. "I know the one we framed wouldn't be in here, but the others should."

"There's none of you," I pointed out.

She looked at me curiously before going through the pictures once again. "There isn't, is there?"

"Angelle, look at the negatives that came with the prints," I said. "Are they all there?"

She pulled the negatives from the envelope. I noticed almost immediately that the roll had been clipped in several places, meaning that some of the individual negatives were missing.

"How many are there?" I asked.

"There's only twelve," she replied. "How odd; four are missing."

Andre took the envelope from his sister and also looked through the photos and negatives.

"I don't understand why they wouldn't be there," Angelle said. "I'm so very sorry, Reverend. Andre, you didn't take any of the pictures out, did you?"

Andre perused the stack and handed them back to her. "Now why would I do that? They meant nothing to me. Besides, Mother was in most of them. She was drunk throughout the evening, hanging on every man under the age of thirty-five. I was embarrassed that photographs were even being taken."

"Andre!"

"It's true, Angelle. You know it's true. I make no bones about it."

"Did you feel the same way about your father?" I asked.

"I've answered all the questions I'm going to answer from you today, Reverend—about my father, about my business, about Manny's reception, about Reed Alemand, and about the photographs. Your line of questioning has been inappropriate and intrusive."

"He's only trying to help," Angelle said, touching her brother's arm. The gesture seemed to calm him.

"If you ask me," Portier interjected, "someone deliberately wanted those pictures removed. You said it wasn't on the mantel any longer?"

"That's right. Nowhere in sight. It wasn't placed in another location within the room, either. There's a small desk along the wall. I looked in its drawers, but no photographs were in them."

"You remember what you wore that night, don't you?" I said.

"Oh, absolutely! I loved my costume. It was one of the best ever. Mother gave me the dress. It was an old formal she had— light blue, elegant. Joyce gave me the sash. I wore it over my shoulder. She also lent me the wig and her jewelry."

"Jewelry?" Andre asked. "I can't believe she'd part with it."

"It was paste. I knew it was. I know jewelry like I know my sister. Oh, and Manny gave me a scepter to hold. I forget where I got the hat. I wore a hat, didn't I, Andre, a feathery white, mystical thing. It was gorgeous. That's about it. I don't know if that was any help to you, Reverend."

"Actually, it was. Thank you. Everyone is very good to you, aren't they?"

Angelle smiled. "Yes, they are. They all are. My brothers are dear. My mother is bothersome and father is, well, you know my father, but Joyce and my brothers are precious to me. They do so much for me, they really do." She reached for Andre's hand.

He took it and raised it to his lips for a gentle kiss.

"They'd do almost anything, wouldn't they?"

Angelle lost her smile. "What are you implying?"

"Nothing. Just making a general comment. It's very noble, especially of your brothers to watch over you as they do."

"We should be going," she said abruptly. "I'm so very sorry I didn't have the photograph for you, and it's too bad you can't attend Manny's open house."

"I didn't say that," I replied.

"But I thought Mr. Portier said you couldn't."

"I've changed my mind," Portier said.

I looked at him to see the expression on his face. It appeared sincere.

"Yes," he added. "I gave it some thought. There's no reason why we shouldn't attend."

Angelle nodded but said no more. Andre turned to go. They said their good-byes and left quietly.

I looked at Portier for further comment to his change of heart, but he didn't acknowledge me, so I asked, "Did you notice something almost immediately, Portier?"

"What? That Bentley disliked Andre Lyons?"

"A good judge of character, I'd say."

"If Bentley had been here for the entire conversation, he may have even growled at Angelle. I believe you ruffled her feathers with that bit about her brothers' help. Where did that come from?"

"I have no idea. It just came to my mind. I must've been thinking it subconsciously. Apparently, I wasn't far off the mark."

"And what do you make of that Glen Balfour?"

"I'm pretty sure I've written scores of sermons on his kind over the years."

"I'm sure you have. What about Andre? I've changed my tune on that man. I dislike Alemand doing any more business with him."

"I'm beginning to believe Mr. Alemand feels the same," I said.

"What do you mean?"

"I've wondered what he was doing talking to that forensic bank auditor. I thought he was in trouble and being investigated. I don't think he was talking to that auditor about himself at all. What if he was there to talk about Andre Lyons? What if he suspects fraud related to The Landalia, and what if Andre is trying to cover it up and Alemand found out?"

Portier sat in a nearby chair and gave it some thought. "I hate to think like that, Fountain," he said eventually, "but I see where you're coming from. I'd feel much better about my professional relationship with Alemand if that was the case. Tell me something, though. It's about that photograph you wanted to see. Nothing struck me odd about your conversation with Angelle and the photograph except for one thing, the mother."

"Yes, I know. I don't know what to think about her appearance. It's odd the mother suddenly popped into Lafayette to attend the ball. I'm not sure, though, if that's what's really bothering me about the picture. After all, many people return home to Louisiana at Mardi Gras time. That's not unusual."

"There's one thing that is very unusual, however," Portier said.

"What's that?"

"Why you haven't asked about my trip to the Secretary of State's office in Baton Rouge. There's plenty of time to talk about it, and if you're feeling up to it, I think it's best explained if we make a visit to the bank. It'll become clear when we talk with Reginald Falgout."

I sat up in my chair so fast I nearly tore open the stitches in my arm.

Chapter 20

I led Portier to Reginald Falgout's office. I knew exactly where it was located because I'd followed Falgout to his office not long ago. His secretary greeted us professionally, but she pulled her bifocals from her nose and reserved comment until Portier told her the reason for our presence. I followed her focus when she glanced down at her phone. A small light glowed under the number of an extension.

"He's on the phone, but I'm sure it won't be long. Would you have a seat, please?"

We sat, but it wasn't comfortable. Chairs in an auditor's office weren't meant to be comfortable, I suspected.

Portier fidgeted and tapped his foot on the carpeted floor.

"You're not nervous, are you?" I whispered.

"No, I'm angry," he replied.

"Angry? What are you angry about?"

"My client. What did I miss in Alemand's books? What was hidden in them that could've shed some light on this damn case of yours that I overlooked—or worse yet, I ignored."

"I doubt you ignored anything, and if anything was missed it doesn't mean you were careless or incompetent. Individuals who are bound and determined to misrepresent their books are going to find a way to do it."

"Don't you think I know that? But there's one thing I've learned over the years; it's that no matter how diligent people

243

are in their fraudulent scheme, they always slip up once or twice somewhere. No one can keep all of their ducks in a row at all times. The last thing I want is my reputation and integrity questioned because I overlooked something."

"I doubt if Reed pulled the wool over your eyes."

"If he did then he's a smarter man than I give him credit."

"So what are you going to ask this Mr. Falgout?"

"I don't know just yet. I'm hoping divine intervention will blurt the questions right out of my mouth."

I chuckled. "Yes, well, if that's what you're relying on, I think it's prudent to have a Plan B. God does answer prayer, but sometimes the answer is no."

"Okay, then I'll revert to my good judgment, but you have to promise me you'll sit and say nothing. That's hard for you to do, I know, but you must. I may say some things that aren't quite true, and I'll not have you falling on your knees, praying for my soul because of it. It's either that or you can sit out here with Miss Eagle Eyes, peering over her glasses at you."

"Not on your life. I wouldn't miss your rain dance for anything."

Suddenly, the door opened. Mr. Falgout stood in the doorway with a half-smoked Camel between his lips. His tie was loose and the top button of his shirt was undone. He rubbed his slick, black hair out of his eyes with the palm of his hand and said, "Gentleman, I'm not sure how I can help you, but I have a few minutes now. Lillian, please hold my calls for me. Thank you. Right this way."

He stepped aside as we entered and closed the door.

I'd never met an auditor with the demeanor of this gentleman. He shook our hands, but didn't look us in the eye. Instead, he focused his attention on some papers faced up in a folder on his desk, then he strode behind his desk, closed the folder, and concealed it in a drawer before speaking. "I was just on the phone with Mr. Alemand, a respected customer of ours," he began. "He said I could expect your visit. I remember you, I think, Mr. Portier. We've worked together before, haven't we?"

"Yes, sir, years ago. It was a money laundering situation."

"Ah, I remember now, down in Lafourche Parish, the case of a couple of doctors. Cousins, I think. We should probably leave it at that. Confidentiality and all. What can I do for you regarding Mr. Alemand? Surely you don't suspect foul play with his accounts here at the bank? I've looked at his ledger, and it appears to be in order."

"Was there a reason other than my visit for you to review his account?"

"No, but on occasion we do review accounts like Mr. Alemand's on a cyclical basis. Our director of depositor services is diligent in having an objective review performed on high profile accounts."

"You consider my client to be high profile?"

"I consider Manfred Lyons to be. Mr. Alemand is his partner."

"Then your review of Mr. Alemand's accounts isn't to protect my client's interest; it's to protect Mr. Lyons' interest *from* my client."

"I didn't say that."

"It doesn't matter because in a sense that's why I'm here. This is my good friend and colleague Mr. Fountain. Whatever we have to say can be said in his presence. Mr. Alemand gave us his authorization to speak to you, so I'll cut to the chase. I've noticed some irregular transactions in his books the past few months. I haven't contacted you before now because Mr.

Alemand always had an explanation for the entries, but I've reached a point where I need an independent opinion."

"You don't suspect wrongdoing, do you? Is money being transferred between your client and other bank account holders?"

"That's what it looks like. Did you notice any such activity in his account as you reviewed his ledger?"

Mr. Falgout shook his head and looked off to one side. Whether he was seriously trying to think or was just biding time, I couldn't tell.

"I was particularly curious about transfers with Manfred Lyons," Portier added.

Falgout shook his head again. "None comes to mind."

"I see. What about Andre Lyons and a theater group called The Landalia located in the Quarter?"

"Oh, yes, I've seen money being transferred from Mr. Alemand's account to Andre's. There was a large amount that he authorized us to transfer while Andre was renovating the building."

"That sounds about right. Anything unusual in the amount or frequency?"

"Nothing that Mr. Alemand didn't inform us about in advance. Anything else?"

"No, not regarding Andre, but what about Manfred's business accounts?"

"I thought you just asked about Manfred a moment ago. I already answered you."

"Yes, but when I mentioned Manfred Lyons, I meant both his personal and business accounts. I got the feeling you only answered my question related to his personal accounts. I'm asking about his business."

Mr. Falgout glared at Portier.

My friend didn't waiver. He didn't blink or give any indication he would allow the question to pass. I leaned forward so I wouldn't miss the response.

At first, none came. Eventually, Mr. Falgout said, "I'll have to look into that further for you."

"Please do, if you wouldn't mind," Portier said. "Oh, and Manfred is having an open house for his tool-and-die company tomorrow. I hope you're invited. I was curious if my client had invested in this company of Manfred's."

"I wouldn't know. I'll look into that as well."

"Thank you. One other thing: I was at the Secretary of State's office in Baton Rouge the other day, looking into the officers of some companies my client has been working with. Are you familiar with The Atchafalaya Preservation Foundation? I believe they're interested in the preservation of the wetlands and wildlife in the Atchafalaya Basin."

Falgout sat erect to give an air of confidence, but it was short-lived, collapsing when he looked off to the side and failed to make eye contact. "Yes, that's true. That's their mission."

"I believe it has charity status, doesn't it? Meaning there are certain federal and state regulations over the use and transfer of the organization's funds."

Falgout shook his head. "I wouldn't know about the particulars of the foundation, I'm sorry."

"That's all right. I just thought I'd ask. Roger Lyons was chairman of another foundation—The Lyons Foundation. He was recently found murdered as you probably know."

"Yes, I'm familiar with The Lyons Foundation and his unfortunate death." Falgout's demeanor didn't change. "They are bank customers of ours, but I don't recall any transactions that appeared inappropriate between your client and The Lyons Foundation. In fact, I don't believe your client is even on the board of directors, so I'm not sure why your line of questioning is relevant."

"But you say you've reviewed the foundation's accounts."

"Yes, most definitely."

"Recently?"

"Well, no, not recently, but I can assure you we take great care of our business accounts, especially those that are as high profile as Roger Lyons."

"That's interesting," Portier said.

At that, my friend took a pen from his suit coat pocket and began to write some notes. I looked at the page. The words were gibberish, not making sense. In fact, some of the scribblings weren't even words. I looked at Falgout who had as much interest in what my friend was writing as I did. Of course, I assumed he couldn't see the notes, or he'd have told us to leave his office immediately.

Portier finished his scribbling, placed his pen back in his pocket, and smiled.

An uncomfortable moment of silence persisted before Falgout asked, "Is that all? Did I answer your questions sufficiently?"

My friend nodded confidently and thanked Mr. Falgout for his time and patience. "I do hope we'll see you tomorrow at Manfred's open house," he added.

Falgout shook his hand, but made no promises.

We left the office quietly, and I remained silent until we left the building. Once on the street, I stated, "If you ask me, you didn't go into that meeting flying by the seat of your pants. You knew exactly what you were going to ask because you knew exactly what you were doing. You didn't need divine intervention at all."

Portier beamed. "I surprised even myself. In fact, I do believe I'm a better forensic auditor than he is. I gave him a good dose of his own medicine, didn't I? What glorious fun that was. Wait. Do you mind if we go to that lounge across the street? Do you see it? I'd like to get a booth along the window, facing the bank. We can have a drink or two while we wait."

"Wait for what?"

"The fur to fly. I'd bet my bottom dollar Falgout is high-tailing it to the bank's depositor services department to pull The Lyons Foundation account ledger. When he sees the balance in the account, we're going to see him bolting out of the front doors and running down the street like his pants are on fire."

My eye brows rose. "Who will he be after?"

"I suspect as many of the Lyons siblings as he can herd together."

"What for?"

"Patience, Fountain. The answer will become clear soon enough. We have to hurry."

Fortunately, we found an open booth by the window. An afternoon crowd trickled into the small lounge. Some of the patrons wore ties and suits, probably from the bank. Portier said he hoped they'd get as big of kick at seeing Falgout running down the street as he.

Portier downed his gimlet, and I was three-quarters through my ginger ale when the bank's door opened and Falgout stepped out onto the sidewalk. He was in such a hurry to exit that he didn't bother to look to see if anyone stood in his path. By his fast gait, it appeared he would've knocked down anyone in his way.

"Thar she blows." Portier laughed out loud, delighted that his prediction came true. "We can head home now."

"What? Don't you want to see where he goes? Who he meets?"

"Oh, I know who he's going to meet, but I don't give a flying rats end where he meets them. He called the Lyons family together, mark my words. Let's go." Portier pulled some bills from his money clip and placed them on the table.

~

We arrived back at the cottage promptly. Portier opened the back door to the garden and let Bentley into the parlor while I slumped wearily into a chair.

"Not now, Ben," I said to the panting pup who wanted me to scratch behind his ears. "I'm tired. Go lie down."

Portier stood by the phone and looked at me. "Are you going out?"

"Do I look like I'm going out?" I replied, cradling my arm. "No, I'm pooped. I need to rest. I overdid it. This arm hurts more than I thought it would."

"Are you able to answer the phone? I need to run an errand and make some groceries, but I'm expecting a phone call. I can't do it all."

"I'll take a message. Shouldn't be beyond my capabilities."

"We'll see." He patted Bentley on the head and left the cottage.

I soon found out what he meant by "we'll see." The phone rang not more than five to ten minutes after he left. An angry Reed Alemand was on the other end of the line.

"What the hell did you two tell Reginald Falgout?" he demanded.

"I can have Portier call you, Mr. Alemand."

"No, you tell me. You were there in his office. Not sure why you were there, but since you were, tell me what the hell you two said to him."

"I assure you Portier limited his questions to address your accounts only."

"The hell you did. I seriously doubt that. My accounts don't include inquiries to The Lyons Foundation or that other foundation you were asking about."

"Atchafalaya Preservation."

"Even more irrelevant to my accounts."

"May I ask what this is about?" I asked.

"About? You know damn well what this is about. Manfred called me. He was furious and panic stricken about your meeting with Falgout. I couldn't believe it myself. It makes me wonder about Roger Lyons's personal accounts if this is what happened to the family's foundation account. More importantly, how did you and Portier find out?"

"I beg your pardon. Find out what? What happened with the family's foundation?"

"Don't give me that."

"Mr. Alemand, please. I'm telling you the truth. I don't know what you're talking about."

"The Lyons Foundation is defunct, gone, kaput, no longer. The money has been redistributed."

"What? I don't understand."

"I bet you don't."

"Distributed where?"

"You tell me, and then you tell Portier I want to talk to him right away. You hear me? I want full disclosure on what he knows. I don't care about the damn foundation, but if Roger Lyons's personal accounts have also been closed and the funds withdrawn, I need to know about it. I invested a lot of my own money into The Landalia, and, by damn, I need to know if Andre Lyons will be able to make good on my investment."

"As soon as Portier returns, I'll have him call you. In the meantime—"

"There will be no 'in the meantime', Mr. Fountain. Nothing can be done in the meantime, and I don't want the two of you to do anything further. Have him call me immediately."

It was a good thing I had nothing more to say. Reed Alemand slammed the receiver down so hard my ear drum throbbed. I took a deep breath and returned to my chair. I'd been sitting no more than five minutes when the phone rang again.

This time, it was an angry Joyce Nicolet on the line. She wasted no time getting to the point. "How dare you meddle into my father's financial affairs," she complained. "You had no right to access his accounts."

"We did no such thing, Mrs. Nicolet. We were inquiring into transactions related to the accounts of Mr. Portier's client Reed Alemand."

"Mr. Alemand has no business with my father so I hardly believe that's the truth. No, you knew something before ever going to see Mr. Falgout at the bank."

"How do you know we went to see Mr. Falgout? Our conversation with him was no business of yours and didn't include you."

"But it included The Lyons Foundation."

"Your father's foundation and all state and federal not-for-profit foundations are public knowledge. Did you not know what your father was doing with the organization? Aren't you on the board of directors?"

Mrs. Nicolet hesitated before replying, "My father didn't have any family members on the board. Despite the name of the foundation, there hasn't been a family member on the board for years. My father wanted it that way for independence and objectivity. I don't make a point of meddling into my father's affairs even on the foundation level."

"Don't you?"

"And what is that supposed to mean?"

"I assumed you'd made it your point to keep on top of your father's financial affairs. I don't mean that in a bad or offensive way. You're an astute businesswoman. Keeping on top of a foundation with your family's namesake would seem to be prudent. If that's not the case then the news of the organization's dissolution must have shocked you."

"It wasn't just the dissolution. It was who he designated as the beneficiary of the foundation's assets that was the most disturbing news to us, and clearly unacceptable. You had a hand in that decision, I'm sure of it."

"I don't know what you're talking about. I didn't find out about the foundation's status until twenty minutes ago. What your father did was done on his own accord. It had nothing to do with me. I didn't know your father until ten minutes before he died. I don't even know who benefits from his Last Will and Testament."

"And if I were you, I wouldn't concern myself with it because it's none of your business. Good day, Reverend Fountain. I do hope this is the last our family will hear of you."

"On the contrary, we received an invitation to Manfred's open house tomorrow."

Silence.

"Mrs. Nicolet?"

She hung up.

I took a deep breath and sat down. Not only did my arm hurt worse, but my head pounded fiercely and acid churned in my stomach. "I want some milk, Bentley," I said. "Would you like a tasty morsel?"

The Lab's ears shot upright. He licked his jowls and darted for the kitchen.

The phone rang again as soon as I stood. I debated whether to answer.

Bentley's furry head peeked around the doorway. His sad, hopeful eyes beckoned me to the refrigerator.

"I can't," I told him. "I have to get this. Your master is my master when it comes to the phone. I promised him." I reached for the phone and identified myself, but I heard only silence on the other end. "Hello?" I repeated.

A soft, grave, feminine voice said, "It's Angelle Lyons. I'm sorry to bother you this afternoon, but it's important."

"What is it, Miss Lyons?"

"It's something my family learned today. I don't know what to make of it."

"It's quite all right, Miss Lyons," I said. "I've already heard the news of your father's foundation. I'm as surprised as you."

"What? Oh, yes, I'm sure you are. Everyone is it seems." Her voice didn't sound convincing.

"Aren't you?"

"I don't really care. Father's foundation affected me very little. The news of its dissolution doesn't matter one way or the other to me."

"Then what's troubling you?"

"It's the matter of my father's will. After the meeting with the bank auditor, my family and I met with father's attorney. He was very forthcoming about the terms of the will."

"So you found out who was excluded from the will when your father changed it?"

"That's just it, Reverend. No one was excluded. He left all of his personal fortune to us—his children. All of it."

"Then your father was bluffing. Even though he dissolved the family foundation, he left his personal estate intact."

"Yes. It's a horrible thing to bluff about, but the attorney said my father never had any intention of changing his will to exclude us. I assume father teased us to make us appreciate the fortune more when he died. Maybe it was to appreciate him more, too."

"Then all is right with the world, I should think."

"Not exactly. In fact, it's worse. That's what has me so upset. If he was murdered before he changed his will, but he never had any intention of changing his will, then his murder was for nothing. We lost our father for nothing."

Chapter 21

I was sitting in my chair, nursing my arm, sulking over Angelle Lyons's last words to me when Portier entered the cottage with a sack full of groceries. I didn't get up to help him, but he must've thought I would because he told me to sit still.

"Did I get a phone call after I left?" he asked after putting the groceries away.

"Not one, but three."

He grinned. "So Falgout's impromptu meeting with the family ruffled the feathers of more than one bird, eh? Manny Lyons. Was he the first caller?"

"He wasn't any of the callers. No, the first caller was your client Reed Alemand. The second was Manny's sister Joyce."

Hearing the two names pleased my friend even more. "And the third call?"

"Angelle Lyons. The family learned their father hadn't changed his will after all. Not only that, but he had no intention of changing his will."

"So everyone inherits."

"Apparently. It seems he died for nothing. It has Angelle very upset."

"Is that what you think? That he died for nothing?"

"No, it only confirms to me that he wasn't killed for his money. There was a different motive. I'm sure of it."

"Good."

"Good? I hardly see anything good about it."

"I meant good, I'm glad you feel that way, because that's what I believe also."

"Does your belief have anything to do with what you learned at the Statehouse regarding the dissolution of The Lyons Foundation?"

"Every bit of it. I learned that the board of directors of The Lyons Foundation voted to dissolve six months ago. I had no idea the assets of the foundation had already been distributed, however, until we saw Reginald Falgout run out of the bank to meet members of the Lyons family. I suppose Reed told you there was no money in the foundation account."

"Yes, that's why he called. He's concerned it means there's no money available from his personal estate."

"Oh, the poor sap. Let him wonder. He should've known the finances of the foundation were separate from Roger Lyons' personal fortune."

"But he's concerned Roger liquidated his personal fortune as well."

"Then what you're telling me is he doesn't know what the family found out about his will. Well, good. It'll do him good to think he won't be receiving any money from Andre. Maybe he'll think twice before he makes hasty investments into worthless ventures like The Landalia. Tell me something, though. Does Angelle's phone call bother you at all?"

"Yes, it bothers me very much."

"It's a curious call, isn't it?"

"I can't put my finger on why it is."

"Can't you, or are you trying to deny it's a possibility?"

I looked at him as if I didn't know what he was talking about.

257

"She may be guilty," he explained. "Her tears may be of guilt, not loss."

"Oh, I see. Yes, I do realize that. I'm not in denial. I'd rather not think about it, though."

"Have you realized other things, too? Do you have other suspicions?"

"I do, but they haven't been thought out completely. I believe I know who killed Roger Lyons, but I don't have a motive with these latest developments. On the other hand, it sounds like you know the motive, but you don't have a suspect."

Portier laughed heartily. "Yes, we're both on the right track. Soon our tracks will come together, I'm sure. I think we deserve a nice meal at Leroux's to discuss our theories."

"Let's do something better," I said. "After dinner, let's swing by Genny's club to see who's celebrating their windfall."

Portier and I had a nice dinner at Leroux's, barely speaking of the meeting Reginald Falgout had with the Lyons family. He encouraged me to order the tenderloin tips, but I refused. I was partial to pork raised in the Midwest, and didn't want to be disappointed in the flavor and quality.

"When in New Orleans I want seafood, rice, and gumbo with a side of potato salad," I explained. "I can have all the tenderloin, ham, bacon, and chops I want when I get back home."

"But it's very good here," he replied. "You should go out on a limb and give it a try."

"I've done nothing but spend my entire time in New Orleans out on a limb."

Portier laughed. "And you make a lousy Tarzan, by the way. You mentioned something about swinging by the club where

Genevieve sings after this. I recommend you swing home, instead."

"I'd rather go to the club. I want to see who's there, but I also want to listen to Genny sing. She's quite entertaining. She knows her audience."

"I'm going to pass, but you go ahead."

"Retiring early?"

"Reading first. I'm just now getting around to reading James Salter's novel *The Hunters.*"

"Oh, it's excellent."

"So I've heard. I must be the only male in America who hasn't read it yet. It's more stimulating to me than listening to another one of Genevieve's renditions of *Mairzy Doats* with adults dressed as children. I don't want you drinking tonight. Do you hear me?"

"I hadn't planned on it," I said, hoping the tone of my voice indicated that I didn't appreciate being talked to as if I were a teenager.

"See that you don't. I want your wits about you. None of this getting stabbed in the dark and clubbing princesses again."

"I won't be long. My arm still hurts."

"Then why are you going?"

"My curiosity is greater than my pain."

"I can't tell you who'll be there, but I can save you a trip about Genevieve," he said. "She'll be singing *Boom Boom Boomerang.* I'm fairly certain of it."

~

Portier was wrong.

When I arrived at the smoky club, Genny was in the middle of a rousing chorus of *Shinnamarink.* The crowd joined in and loved it. Glen Balfour sang near the stage. Carmen

Nicolet tapped her foot against a rung of her barstool. They applauded when Genny finished her last *boop boop de doop*.

Men blew her kisses as she crossed the room towards me. A young man dressed as Peter Pan tossed glittered fairy dust. Victorius bowed in front of her.

She sat next to me and dabbed the nape of her neck with a paper napkin. "It's a surprise to see you here," she said. "Is your arm better?"

"Not really, but I wanted to come. You brighten my day, and what a day it was. It was quite active, counting the Lyons family. I had to see who was here." I told Genny what had transpired at the bank and the meeting called by Reginald Falgout.

"You know how to stir a pot," she said. "I'm so glad you came to visit, though. I wake each morning, looking forward to hearing what you'll do next."

"Today's activities weren't my doing. You have Chuck to thank for that."

She laughed loudly. "I knew all along half of his heart was into this case of yours. He likes to give everyone a hard time. Oh, look. Glen Balfour is going over to your favorite person who thinks she's a granddaughter. See that? I wonder what's brewing."

"Not much," I said. "It looks like Carmen is giving him the brush off. I'm glad Angelle isn't here to watch his behavior."

Genny tapped my arm then pointed to a table in the corner of the room. "Angelle's sitting with her own friends. She looks rather glum."

"She is glum. She found out her father didn't cut anyone from his will."

Genny laughed. "Well, that's the damnedest thing I ever heard. She's upset because her father left her a fortune?"

260

"She believes whoever killed him for that fortune did so needlessly."

"Poor baby. Maybe she can dry her tears on her daddy's stock and bond certificates."

I gave Genny a dirty look.

"And why is Carmen such a sourpuss this evening?" she asked. "Look at her. She has a face as long as a horse."

"I should've clarified. Roger Lyons didn't leave a cent to his step-grandchildren, only his wife and children. Carmen got a dose of reality today. She got nothing. I see Glen is all alone now. I'm going to talk with him. I'll be back."

"I won't be here. I have to prepare for my next set, sweetheart. Be careful. Talk to you later."

Balfour grinned when he saw me approach. "Reverend Fountain! *Laissez les bon temps rouler!* I suppose even a stuffy old preacher from the Midwest needs to go clubbing once in a while to sow his oats."

"I can assure you I'm not here to sow any oats."

"Then you're here to tease us."

"There's very little to tease about tonight."

"Come now. I have to disagree. You may not admit it, but you're a bit of a tease when it comes to your questions, insinuations, and accusations."

"I have accused no one, Glen, but when I do you'll be the first to know."

"What makes me so special?"

"Ex-felons are always the first to be accused. You should know that."

Balfour lost his grin.

"Your past wasn't hard to look into," I said. "Angelle's problem is that she's not a good judge of character. She didn't look into your past. Her father on the other hand ..." I paused

261

and waited for a response, but I didn't get one. "Her father wasn't as trusting, was he? I suppose he looked into your criminal history and discovered your questionable past. I also suspect he knew you were dating his daughter solely to get at her money, and he confronted you about it."

"That's ridiculous. He had disappeared by the time I started dating Angelle. He's been gone for six months. There's no way he knew of my involvement with Angelle."

"On the contrary, he'd been meeting with Angelle. He knew about you from the beginning. He knew who she was dating. He looked into you."

"How could he have done that?"

"Please, Mr. Balfour. The Lyons family hires private detectives as often as I used to pass around collection plates. You confronted him about what he learned. Before you deny it, there's a witness who saw you with him on at least one occasion."

"I assume this witness is one of these private dicks you speak of. Well, in that case he's either a liar or a fabrication of your imagination. I wouldn't put it past you to make something like that up to see how I'd react, but as you can see, I'm not fazed a bit. Sorry to disappoint you."

"And I wouldn't put it past you to murder Roger Lyons to swindle Angelle out of her inheritance," I said.

"Why would I do that?"

"Oh, goodness, where do I start? To pay for your mounting gambling debts for one. To continue your boozing and womanizing lifestyle for another. Your improprieties are enough to convict you on circumstantial evidence alone. This is in addition to what I know of your contact with Roger Lyons before he died. I suggest you talk to the police before I get to them. It'll go easier on you."

Balfour's face grew ashen before he looked towards the bar.

I looked also. "Did Carmen have something to do with the murder, too?"

He spun towards me. "Not 'too', Reverend. Carmen had every bit of motive to kill him herself. She and that group of losers she hangs with—the ones who live in their Roman fantasy world."

"Are you implicating her because she refused your sexual advances? I saw you talking to her at the bar. You can't deny she pushed you away."

"Are you out of your mind? I wouldn't go near that walking cesspool. Not even me. I didn't make any sexual advances to her. What are you talking about?"

"I saw you lean in to her and say something. She pushed you away. What did you say to her if it wasn't sexual?"

"I said, 'Nice try, doll', for trying to play the part of the poor, neglected step-granddaughter who was wrongfully left out of the old man's will. She reacted as I suspected. The spoiled brat batted me away. That's the truth, Reverend. Make out of it what you want, but that's the truth."

"Are you saying she killed him to hasten her inheritance?"

"I'm saying it was either that or she knew in advance she wasn't in the will and killed him out of spite. I don't know how she found out if that's what you're going to ask. Maybe she slept with the attorney, maybe she hired her own private dick, I don't know. A woman like Carmen Nicolet has her ways. She certainly has the temperament to follow through with something like murder."

I studied Balfour, assessing his words in terms of sincerity and probability.

"Ask her," he said, noticing my skepticism. "She's still at the bar. You better talk to her before she's off to her next victim."

I didn't bother wishing him well. As I walked towards the bar, Carmen turned and saw me. She quickly turned back around and sucked on the ice cubes in her glass. "What sordid lies did the bastard tell you that you believe, Reverend?" she asked when I reached her.

"Nothing relevant. It wasn't important. No, wait, that isn't true. He did mention that you killed your step-grandfather for snubbing you out of his will, but other than that he didn't have much to say."

My reply drew a smile from her face. "He's such a disillusioned ass," she said. "Surely you realize that. So I'm a killer, am I? How did he say I went about finding and killing the mysterious Roger Lyons?"

"You have a network of Roman friends who are familiar with the area and the people in it. I assume he believed it was the same way these friends introduced you to Donnie who introduced you to Mr. Montgomery who you realized was your step-grandfather in disguise."

She laughed. "That's very far-fetched. Cute and ingenious, mind you, but very far-fetched."

"Is it? I don't believe it's far-fetched to believe that Moline hunted down Mr. Montgomery that morning and killed him for you. After all, you told Moline you were going to be rich. She believed you were going to share your wealth with her."

"Moline's an idiot, but she wouldn't hurt a fly."

I nearly burst out laughing. "Talk about being disillusioned. She didn't accidentally bump into me at the lake, you know."

Carmen frowned. "Yeah, I forgot about that."

264

"But you didn't forget to tell her I was going to be there, did you?"

"First of all, I didn't tell her you were at the lake. Second of all, I didn't even tell you Donnie was at the lake. Thirdly, even if I did, how would I know you two would actually go there? No, whatever you did that night you did on your own accord. And I didn't talk to Moline. She was impossible to talk to that night. The girl was stoned and drunk. Whatever she did was on her own accord as well. I had nothing to do with the attack on you, and I had nothing to do with Moline. I still don't."

"Not even while she lies in the hospital?"

"Oh, is she in the hospital?"

"Don't play dumb. I thought you might be concerned."

"I don't give a shit."

"Nice friend you are."

"She's not my friend. None of these people are my friends. When are you going to get that through your head? Do you think I'd waste my time getting to know these peasants?"

"That's my point. No, I don't believe you'd waste your time unless you had a good motive for doing so. Finding your step-grandfather for his money was a good motive."

"There are plenty of people in the Lyons family with the same motive. You can't use that line on me. I mean really. Think about it. Unless, of course, you're so completely enamored by Angelle Lyons' charm and beauty that it's jaded your common sense."

"Before you go down the Angelle rabbit path, I already know about her father stopping her monthly allowance because of who she was dating," I said.

"But did it stop her? She didn't want to give up her dreamboat. She had no alternative but to do what she did."

265

"Are you implying she knocked off her own father?" I asked astonished.

"You say that as if no one has ever killed a parent before. We're talking about a great sum of money. It would be worth it."

I shook my head and gave her a solemn look. "Taking a human life is never worth it, especially if you're caught."

"Caught? Are you kidding?" Carmen belted out a menacing laugh. "Who would dare challenge a member of the Lyons family? You don't understand our Southern ways."

"But he wasn't killed in Lafayette. The family wouldn't have the same clout in Orleans Parish."

"You're naïve, Reverend. You're either naïve or simply daft. New Orleans is governed by money. Don't you think the family has spread enough money around New Orleans and Baton Rouge to have as much clout on the city and state level as in Lafayette?"

For once, Carmen made a good point.

"Not to mention my step-grandmother," she added coyly. "Don't you think it's a coincidence Alexandra's back in town?"

"Her husband just died. Her presence isn't a coincidence."

Carmen grinned. "Yeah, right, because she was always there for him in life."

"I don't believe either one of them was there for each other."

"It doesn't matter. She's not here for the funeral if that's what you're thinking. That gold digger is here for the reading of the will."

I remembered back to my conversation with Angelle. "And she wasn't disappointed, I hear."

Carmen ordered another drink then looked at me sharply. "Why should she be? There's one thing you need to know

266

before you go any further. No one disappoints my step-grandmother at any time. She doesn't allow it. Not even Roger Lyons." She turned towards the bar to watch Tomas finish making her drink.

I walked away. It was time not only to leave Carmen, but to head back to Portier's cottage. I scanned the room to say good-bye to Genny. Instead, I saw Angelle Lyons walking towards me.

"Reverend Fountain," she said, "before you go, I think you should know that all of my siblings will be at the open house if you're planning to go."

"I assumed they would. Why is that news?"

"It won't be pleasant for you if you're there. They'll have no intentions of being cordial even at this social event. I wouldn't go if I were you."

"I would've thought knowing they weren't excluded from your father's will would have appeased them."

"On the contrary, they believe you're going to see it as a motive for murder."

"Wasn't it?"

"No, Reverend," she said sharply. "In fact, when the will was read, my siblings appeared neither elated nor relieved. The attorney might as well have told them about the weather."

"Even Andre?"

"Oh, well, now, Andre, yes. Of course, he was both interested and relieved. He wasn't elated, but he was definitely relieved."

"I'm surprised there was so little reaction out of your brothers and sister."

"I'm not," she said. "Not really. Very little surprises me about my family anymore. When you've had the parents we've had, you learn early that being surprised is a character flaw. We've become a strong lot."

"Is it strength?"

She considered the question thoughtfully before saying, "It's helped in other aspects of our lives. From that perspective it's strength, but from a family perspective, you're probably right. It isn't strength. It's a coping mechanism." She looked towards the bar and stared at her step-niece with contempt. "I saw you talking to Carmen. I'm sure she had hateful things to say. Carmen has to realize someday that she's a Nicolet, not a Lyons. She hates me."

"I wouldn't take it personally. I don't think Carmen is capable of loving anyone but herself."

"But I do take it personally. She hates me for being a Lyons. There's nothing I can do about that, but she's bound and determined to ruin my life over it. She's practically accused me to my face of my father's death. Don't tell me she didn't try to convince you of it, too."

"I won't lie to you. She did, but I take everything she says with a grain of salt."

"I didn't kill my father. I've told you before that I loved him. He's hurt me, that's true, but he's my father, and I love what he's done for me and the things he's given me. It was his way of showing how much he loved me."

"Then I wonder if you'll do one more thing for me, Angelle."

"Why should I?"

"To resolve who actually did kill your father. If you didn't do it then you won't mind. You were kind enough to bring me those Mardi Gras pictures of you and your siblings' costumes. Will you bring me something else?"

She agreed after I told her what I wanted.

"It'll take some doing," she warned.

"That's okay, it's important."

"Then I'll see what I can do."

"Good. Tell me something else, Angelle. When the board of directors of The Lyons Foundation voted to dissolve the organization, they were required by law to give the remaining assets to another not-for-profit organization. By any chance, do you know to what organization the assets were transferred? Was it Labreville by any chance?" When she nodded, I asked, "How did your family react to Labreville being the recipient?"

"We weren't shocked by Labreville. What took us by surprise was the person he placed in charge of the community who'd be responsible for its management. We'd never heard the name before. I remember because Manny, Joyce, and Andre had plenty to say about father giving the assets to such an obscure individual."

"Do you remember the person's name?"

"Of course. It was odd because there was only a first name. It was a Miss Cora or something like that."

Chapter 22

I went home immediately after talking to Angelle at Genny's club, but I found the house quiet. The light was out in Portier's bedroom, and I assumed Bentley was snuggled at his master's bedside. As much as I wanted to wake my friend and ask how much he knew of Miss Cora from the records he reviewed at the Secretary of State's office, I let him sleep.

I turned on an end-table lamp to relax in a chair next to it before retiring. Portier's novel *The Hunters* lay on the cushion. I moved the book to the table and plopped down. I was tired. My arm hurt. I laid my head against the chair's high back and closed my eyes.

The image of Miss Cora, rocking contentedly on her front-porch swing, came to my mind. Although learning that she was the beneficiary to The Lyons' Foundation's fund through Labreville surprised me, it didn't disturb me. I could almost hear the squeaking of the swing's chains as she hummed in the gentle breeze.

I must've dozed a bit because I twitched just as I started to fall asleep.

I yawned and tried to pull myself out of the chair but stopped when I heard a lone set of footsteps on the sidewalk outside. I sat back and listened. It wasn't unusual to hear footsteps, since the cottage's foundation was adjacent to the walk. What was unusual was hearing only one set of footsteps at this time of night. I couldn't distinguish whether the steps belonged to a man or to a woman because they slowed as they neared the cottage. Underneath the parlor window, they stopped.

I held my breath.

The parlor window was too high to see into the cottage from the outside even for a tall person, so I wasn't troubled by someone looking in. I was troubled by the silence. The person seemed to be standing stationary in front of the cottage. I had half a mind to turn out the light and tiptoe to the window to peek outside, but any movement of the sheers or extinguishment of the light would surely cause the person to move away.

My heartbeat sped up, causing the throbbing in my arm to increase.

The person took a few steps to the front stoop, opened the metal letterbox, dropped something into it, and closed the lid. The sound of the footsteps soon resumed, going back the way they came. They faded quickly.

I sat for two or three minutes without moving a muscle. Finally, I gathered the nerve to rise from the chair and walk to the front door. I unlocked the deadbolt and opened the door carefully, hoping I hadn't been tricked by the footsteps walking away. The last thing I wanted was another shadowy figure attacking me in the night. But I saw no one.

I opened the letterbox and retrieved a square envelope addressed to me made from formal paper of good quality. After closing and locking the door, I retreated back to the chair next to the end table, peeled the flap of the envelope open, and pulled out the note. It contained only two sentences on one line, crisply typed:

Make her give it back. The money's not hers.

The author obviously referred to Miss Cora who was now in charge of the Labreville community, recipient of The Lyons Foundation's assets. How the person knew I was acquainted with her was a mystery in itself. How the person knew I would understand what the few words meant was an even greater mystery. I replaced the note inside the envelope and set it on the table, no longer unnerved by the episode. The pounding of my heart diminished, and the fight or flight sensation in my chest retreated. I wasn't scared. I was angry.

What a coward, I thought, *to send me a mysterious message in the middle of the night rather than to confront me face to face in the morning.*

Yes, that angered me very much. Whoever sent the note was a spineless coward!

⁓

"I wish you hadn't contacted Detective Robicheaux without consulting me first," I said to Portier the next morning as I brought my second cup of coffee into the parlor.

Portier was looking out of the window onto Ursulines when I walked in. "I had to," he said, releasing the sheers. "It was in our best interest. That note was a direct, ominous threat against us."

"Against me. It was addressed to me."

"But if they had known that I was the one who went to the Secretary of State's office for the information, they would've put my name on it for sure."

"It wasn't a threat. It was just two lines of cowardly ignorance."

"Ignorance is the worst kind of threat," he said.

272

The conversation ended because I couldn't disagree. "I'm going to call the detective just the same and tell him not to come. I can talk to him by phone. I want to talk to him anyway."

Portier walked away from the window, and filtered sunlight brightened the room. "You haven't said much to me about this Miss Cora," he said, sitting in a settee.

"Not much to tell. She's a delightful woman, spiritual and reserved, passionate about the unfortunate in the Ninth Ward."

"But what about her?"

"I just told you."

"No, you told me what she's like, not who she is."

"What she's like is who she is, Portier. What do you want to know? Her profession? Her address? Her family lineage? I assume you want to know if she's capable and responsible enough to manage a foundation with the size of investment portfolio she's been given."

"Don't cop that attitude with me. It was a fair question under the circumstances. You don't know her any better than I do. You met her once, but you don't know her."

"Roger Lyons knew her. That's good enough for me," I said.

It must've been good enough for Portier, too, because he got up from the settee and asked if my coffee needed warmed.

"She does wonder how she'll manage without him," I said, ignoring his offer for coffee.

Portier sat back down. "There. That tells me more about her than passion, profession, or address. I want to know if she has the capacity to know what she doesn't know."

"I understand your concern. I'll speak with her after I speak with Detective Robicheaux and let you know."

"Please do, and when you speak to her, offer my services free of charge. It'll be my donation to the cause." He rose again. "Are you sure you don't need your cup warmed up?"

"No." I smiled. "If I need it heated I'll simply place it against my chest where your offer to help her has warmed my heart."

Portier told me to fly a kite (in so many words) and walked into the kitchen.

I reached for the phone book on a shelf under the end table. The French Quarter station's number was highlighted in bold on the front cover. I lifted the phone receiver and dialed the number, requesting the detective when the operator answered. It wasn't long before Robicheaux was on the other line.

"There's no need to make a special trip to Portier's cottage about last night's event, Detective. I apologize for his hasty decision to call you. The incident was harmless. The only crime committed was placing an unstamped envelope into a United States letterbox. Hardly something to file a police report over."

"What did the note say?"

"It said: *Make her give it back. The money's not hers.*"

"What does that mean? Her who?"

I explained Labreville to him and how Miss Cora fit into the scenario. Robicheaux tried to sound interested, but I could tell he was no longer concerned about what Portier described as a threatening note.

"Did I hear there's some sort of business ribbon-cutting ceremony today?" he asked.

"Yes, sir. Manfred Lyons is opening a new company. Mr. Portier and I plan to attend the reception."

"Do you think that's wise?"

"I think it'll be enlightening. If you're able to attend, I'd appreciate your presence. Also, if you'd be so kind as to bring along the officer who did the original questioning of me on Decatur Street where I found Mr. Lyons, it would be very helpful."

"What do you have planned, Reverend? I'm not in the habit of taking an officer from his duties to attend a reception without good reason."

"I thought the good reason was self-evident, Detective. It's to resolve this issue of Roger Lyons's murder once and for all."

"Which, of course, you were able to resolve by staying completely clear of the investigation as I requested."

"Not entirely," I admitted humbly.

"I didn't think so."

I ended the conversation with the detective dismissing my invitation to the open house. I entered the kitchen where Portier was dividing a slice of bologna into small pieces and throwing them into Bentley's mouth.

"I'll be going out when you take Bentley for a walk," I said.

"Who said I was taking him for a walk?"

"You always do this time of day unless you want to go with me to meet Miss Cora."

"I suppose you want to take the Hawk if I don't go."

"You don't have to go, but, yes, the Hawk would be nice. I know my way this time."

"The bridge over the Industrial Canal is a tricky one to maneuver."

"I've crossed bridges before without hitting them. I'm sure I can do it again. Are you coming is the bigger question."

I watched Bentley gulp the last piece of lunchmeat down his throat and wait for more. Portier patted his head and told him he was a good boy, but that was it. He then looked at me and said, "Keys are in the drawer there. I'll see you when you return."

The drive to the Lower Ninth Ward passed without incident. Traffic was light. Although I knew the vicinity where Cora lived, the exact street and address had escaped my mind. I found it eventually, backtracking often, and parked in front of the familiar smoky blue shotgun.

Miss Cora swung casually on the porch. She wore the same loose frock she'd worn during my last visit. Her dingy white apron was tied loosely around her waist. She wiped her hands on it and patted the vacant cushion next to her on the swing, beckoning me to sit down as I approached.

"I wondered when you'd be back," she said softly.

"It took me awhile."

"So you didn't know about The Lyons Foundation being dissolved and given to Labreville when you came to see me the first time?"

"No, I didn't. I didn't learn for sure until last night. Why didn't you tell me? You could've said something when we talked about whether the community would be able to sustain itself after his death."

"I figured the less anyone knew the better. Mr. Lyons operated Labreville quasi-anonymous. There wasn't any reason to tell you that information. Besides, I didn't know you."

I nodded to let her know I understood, then I took a couple of deep breaths.

"What is it?" she asked.

"The Lyons family wants you to give the money back, you know."

"Of course they do. That's because they don't understand what Labreville meant to their father. They don't understand their father was trying to change his life. He wasn't there yet,

276

but he knew where he was going and where he wanted to end up. That's more than I can say for them."

"You don't have to give the money back. The Lyons Foundation was lawfully dissolved by the board of directors and given to Labreville, a bona fide organization."

"Oh, I know. I don't intend to give the money back. Our directors may not be as savvy or as mighty or as rich as them folks, but they're equally committed to their cause. I'm committed to the cause, too, Reverend. It's what Mr. Lyons wanted. Or should I call him Mr. Montgomery?"

"No," I said firmly. "Mr. Montgomery is dead. Mr. Lyons lives on."

She smiled and rocked contentedly on the swing in silence for several minutes before asking solemnly, "Shall we pray?"

We bowed our heads and did so.

Chapter 23

Some people say the human conscience is God's voice, providing inner guidance. Perhaps that's true. I prefer to believe my conscience is my own voice—inspired by God—to act in accordance with what I already know to be true. This time, my conscience came from the voice of a small-framed woman in an old, faded frock, rocking contentedly on a weathered porch swing in the Lower Ninth Ward of New Orleans.

What she said of Roger Lyons wanting to change his life convinced me. I realized that if I wanted a successful conclusion to this snowballing case, I needed Detective Robicheaux as my ally. I had been unfair to him. I was arrogant to think, just as Portier had told me, that I could investigate Lyons' death better than he and his staff. I had impeded Robicheaux's investigation by withholding the finial and other information until a time I saw fit. It was no wonder the detective was all too through with my meddling, as he called it.

I was weary of it myself. It was time to make amends.

I returned the Golden Hawk back to Portier, parking it in front of the cottage on Ursulines where the sun glittered in all its glory off the car's shiny chrome. I clasped the keys in my hand and entered the cottage to find Portier sitting in his chair with his book.

His reading glasses slid down the bridge of his nose as he looked up at me. He must've noticed my reflective disposition because he asked, "Are you okay?" It was a sincere question, void of insults or quips to one-up-me with his wit.

"Yes, thank you, my time with Miss Cora was fruitful, but now there's something I must do. I'm going to see Detective Robicheaux and apologize for my behavior during this investigation. Even though I only met Roger Lyons for less than ten minutes, Lyons continues to have a profound effect on me and how I'm living my life. Most of what I'm reflecting, Portier, I don't like, but only I can change that."

Portier closed his book and took the glasses from his nose. "I could say the same of myself if I'd be honest. I've done a lot of thinking since you've been here. I've behaved like a schoolboy—jealous and angry of the time you've spent on this case."

"We could go fishing after this," I said, half-jokingly.

"Or I could realize how important this case has been to you," he replied. "That's a more plausible resolution. It's been important not only in how you regard human life for Roger Lyons, but it's been important to you regarding that young man named Donnie and his correlation to Toby Markle's memory."

I nodded. He was right, and it was comforting to know he recognized it. "Is that an apology you're making?"

"Certainly not!" he joked. "You know me better than that. I have a reputation to maintain as a staunch, old Cajun, and I intend to keep it that way."

"You're just as Genny said you are, Portier. You're an oyster—hard and crusty on the outside, soft and mushy in the middle."

"That'll never be repeated," he said, lifting his finger to make a point. "You, on the other hand, need to clear the air with Detective Robicheaux." He rose from his chair and went to a side table where several goldenrod envelopes sat in a stack. He picked them up and walked toward me, extending them proudly into my hands.

"What are these?" I asked.

"All the evidence he'll need to back our theories. Mostly, it's the documentation from the Secretary of State's office and other research I was able to glean, using my accounting and auditing skills. You'll give them to Detective Robicheaux for me, won't you? Explain to him what we've learned. More importantly, invite him again to Manny's open house. Don't insist but beg him to come if you have to."

"Do I need to look through these papers before I give them to him?"

"Only if you're curious. The documents should be self-explanatory, but I included a note to have him call me if he had any questions."

I thanked Portier and left the cottage. Clutching the envelopes tightly under my arm, I walked toward the precinct station.

The noon-time sun was bright and warm on my face as I walked down Burgundy Street. A pleasant breeze assured me that spring was just around the corner, and I welcomed its symbolic hope for new beginnings. I took a deep breath and allowed the fresh air to lift my spirits.

Tourists, strolling the residential section of the Quarter, stymied a rapid pace, but I didn't allow them to diminish my purpose. By the time I reached St. Ann Street, however, I became aware of more than just the presence of sightseers. Ahead of me, leaning against a wrought-iron fence in front of a building of pied-a-terre residences, stood a man, cleaning his fingernails with a pocketknife. He watched me approach, and I could tell by the way he looked at me that I was the reason he was standing against the fence.

I got a good look at his face, being in the bright sunlight versus the dark shadows of Bienville Street or the smoky haze of the Clover Grill. His eyebrows just below his fedora gave him away as the man in the grill who'd told me about Miss Cora and who'd followed Glen Balfour while I passed out chocolates to the homeless. He was younger than I'd thought, but his eyebrows were unmistakable—just as bushy and pronounced as I remembered.

"How did you know I'd be coming this way?" I asked him.

"It's the route to the precinct," he said, smiling.

"You must've followed me from Miss Cora's."

"And I knew it was just a matter of time before you'd go to the police," he added.

I wasn't afraid. In fact, this time I felt empowered in the light of day to continue walking despite his protests. "I assume you've been hired by someone in the Lyons family to follow me and to be here," I said. "Well, you can report back to them that you trailed me successfully, confronted me, and I told you to step aside. You did your job."

"Not exactly. I'd like the envelopes, please."

I stared at him in disbelief. "You wouldn't rob me in broad daylight."

"It won't be robbery because you're going to give them to me."

I didn't have a chance to rebut. We both turned to the sound of a beat-up Chevy half-ton barreling up Burgundy. Jeffrey, a Kool hanging between his lips, screeched to a halt beside me and gestured me to hurry inside. I jumped into the cab, and he took off, appearing unfazed and apathetic to the confrontation just avoided.

I tried to explain what had transpired, but he raised his hand and said he didn't want to know. All he wanted was to drop me safely at the police station and to get back to the garage where the love of his life waited for him. I knew he meant a car—most likely a tidy Thunderbird convertible with fender skirts and a Continental tire.

"How did you know I needed help?" I asked.

"I didn't," he replied, taking a long drag from his smoke. "Mr. Charles called. He had second thoughts about letting you go with important papers in your hands. He said you don't have a good track record when you're by yourself."

"I'm sure he had more than that to say."

Jeffrey smiled. "You mean something like you're arrogant, naïve, and still don't know the ways of this town?"

"Yes, something along those lines."

"You're right, he did. I wasn't going to tell you."

~

Detective Robicheaux sat at his desk, scribbling a note into a file. Several more reports and requisitions for his review and signature sat on his desk than the last time I'd seen him, but he appeared to be taking the work in his stride. He signed the note and set it to the side before addressing me simply by looking up. No words, no facial expression, just eye contact.

"Detective, if you'll excuse the intrusion."

He invited me to sit.

I began by announcing the purpose of my visit—to apologize for my indignant behavior during the investigation and for not believing he would take the death of Mr.

Montgomery seriously based upon the man's appearance and socioeconomic status.

"You mean homelessness, don't you?" the detective inquired. "You don't have to use fancy words with me, Reverend. I know you believed I didn't give a damn about the man because he was homeless. I don't fault you for that. Look at my desk. Any number of loved ones represented by the unsolved folders on this desk say the same thing. They think I don't care. Why should you think any different?"

"Because I should've been better than that, and I do apologize."

His eyes focused on the goldenrod envelopes I held in my hands.

"Oh, these. Yes, Detective, in addition to my apology, Mr. Portier wanted me to give you these documents based upon research he did at the State House and at the bank where Roger Lyons did his business. I don't know exactly what's in them, but we hope it clarifies our thought processes."

Robicheaux's eyes softened, and the creases around his lips gave way to a sigh. He extended his hand, and I gave the envelopes to him. His interest in their contents appeared to be genuine. He pulled out the first set of documents and scanned them quickly, then he set them aside and did the same with the next envelope, not saying a word. He did mutter a "hmm" once or twice and raised his eyebrows on other occasions as he perused what Portier had provided. "A lot of work went into organizing and writing an explanation of each document," he finally said. "Please extend my appreciation to Mr. Portier, if you wouldn't mind."

"Better yet," I said, "you could tell him in person. We hope you'll change your mind about attending Manfred Lyons' open house. The entire cast of characters will be there."

"I assume there's a basis for your invitation. You said the first time you invited me that you wanted Officer Betz, the officer who interviewed you at the scene, at the open house, too. Do you still need him?"

"Yes, if he's available. I can explain why your attendance is important. Do you have the time?"

He gestured with the palm of his hands that the floor was mine. Over the next several minutes, I presented the facts of the case as I saw them, most of which were circumstantial. "I hope, however, that Mr. Portier's documentation turns what's circumstantial into solid evidence."

The detective rose from behind his desk and extended his hand to shake mine. "From what I can see so far, the information will help us a great deal. I need time to verify the facts, of course, but I appreciate the information, and your apology is accepted. It took a great deal of courage and integrity for you to apologize as you did."

"And the open house?" I asked eagerly.

"Oh, the open house. Yes, Reverend, Officer Betz and I will attend." He grinned. "In fact, we wouldn't miss it for the world."

Chapter 24

Portier and I arrived at Manfred Lyons's new company about thirty minutes after the ribbon cutting. The reception was in full swing. It appeared that everyone who was going to be at the reception was already delving into the appetizers and cocktails.

The renovated building smelled new, a combination of oiled machinery and fresh paint. A section of the work area had been cordoned off for the guests to enjoy themselves, and several of the administrative offices were open for private conversations.

Portier ordered a gimlet, and I ordered a club soda with a twist of lime before we mingled with the staunch array of businessmen and their wives. The Lyons family was interspersed with Manfred's guests, talking in cliquish groups.

No one talked to us.

"Did I break out into smallpox on the way here?" I asked Portier.

"No, but perhaps we should've packed a couple of gris-gris bags to put in our pockets to ward off the curses they're spouting under their breaths."

"As long as they keep them under their breaths, I'll be fine with that. Wait, we've spoken too soon. Here comes Reginald Falgout. I wonder if he's come to give us a complimentary toaster from the bank."

285

"Mr. Falgout," Portier said lightheartedly when the banker stood in front of us. My friend extended his hand to shake his.

Falgout ignored his greeting and said, "What was the meaning of your coming to see me in my office yesterday, Mr. Portier? You said it was to look into the bank transactions of your client. You had a different motive. I'd like to know what it was."

"I'm flabbergasted," Portier said, accentuating each word with his finest condescending Cajun accent. "Being the fraud examiner of your institution I can understand being skeptical. It's a part of your nature and your business to do so, but you truly do midjudge me, sir."

"Midjudge, my ass. I believe you came to my office under false pretenses. I should report you to the police. I've close ties to the Commissioner."

"There'll be plenty of time to explain your actions to the Commissioner."

"I'm not talking about me."

"But I am. We've invited Detective Robicheaux to this fine affair. He should be arriving in a few minutes. He'll be interested in what you have to say because I doubt very seriously that preventing fraud is all you've been doing for the bank. My inquiries to Mr. Alemand's account relationships proved what I suspected after I made a trip to the Secretary of State's office in Baton Rouge."

Falgout paled. It appeared that he suspected Portier knew more than what he'd revealed but was too afraid to ask exactly what it was.

"Shall I refresh your drink for you?" Portier asked. "How about a double this time?" He lifted his own glass to show Falgout it was empty. "If not, then I'll leave you with that thought, Mr. Falgout. Enjoy the party."

"That was very bold," I said as I walked with Portier to the bar.

"Nonsense."

"Premature then. I'm not quite sure we want any of these people to get an inkling of what we suspect. They may leave before the detective arrives."

"I'm sure their curiosity won't allow that to happen."

"In that case, I do hope Angelle comes through for me again."

"Why is she helping you anyway?" Portier asked. "She's opened the door to her family, provided photographs, called you numerous times, told you her deepest thoughts of her father, and now this. It doesn't make sense."

"I'll admit it shouldn't, but in another way it does. If we believe her behavior is out of guilt, her cooperation and openness may be nothing more than a disguise."

"Whatever the reason, you've exploited her assistance superbly. It's worked to our benefit."

We grabbed our drinks and turned to see Joyce Nicolet and Andre Lyons walking towards the bar. Our presence obviously surprised them—at least Joyce anyway; she couldn't hide her expression of alarm.

"I'm shocked the two of you would have the audacity to show your faces here," she said. "You and Reverend Fountain have caused my family great angst and heartache. Please tell me you're here only for the free drinks and food."

"I'm here to support my client," Portier replied.

"Are you now?"

"And I'm here for closure," I said.

She looked at me with disgust. "Closure? Surely you don't suspect one of us as having killed my father. Yesterday, you infringed upon our financial privacy. Are you telling me that

287

today you plan to accuse us of murder? Come now, gentlemen. Where do you two get off?"

I started to answer her, but Portier grabbed my coat sleeve in an attempt to hold my words.

Joyce Nicolet left us for the bar, leaving her brother Andre to defend the Lyons name. "You'll have to forgive my sister, gentlemen. Joyce is quite an independent and strong-willed individual as you may have gathered. You may even think she's cold and uncaring when it comes to my father, but I assure you she's taking his death rather badly. The two of you are easy targets given recent events. I hope you understand that."

"Yes, I can see where that might be one theory," I said.

"What are you insinuating? Are you telling me you believe my sister's distraught state of mind is a farce?"

"No, not at all. What I'm saying is that her distraught state of mind may not be related to your father. She may be distraught because the world she's controlled for so long is starting to unravel before her."

"That's preposterous."

"Is it? I bet she knew well in advance of your father's death that he was in New Orleans, living modestly within the camps of the homeless. He'd been spending a great deal of money on his new spiritual passion that he called Labreville. He was bleeding the family fortune. Besides that, she knew exactly the kind of man he'd been all of his life, and she resented him for it. She resented him politically, socially, and personally. Suddenly, he's become benevolent and spiritual. It was too little too late for your sister to stomach. I believe your sister had a huge motive for wanting your father dead."

"I did, too, for that matter, Reverend. You might as well include me on your list of suspects. I resented my father more than she did. I had a well-developed business plan for a successful stock theater in the Quarter. All I wanted was affirmation from my father in terms of financial assistance to help me with The Landalia. Did I get it? No, I didn't get a damn thing. He snubbed me completely. Then who do I discover is the recipient of The Lyons Foundation assets? Some nobody in the Ninth Ward who doesn't know a hill of beans about running a charitable operation, that's who. My father chose a complete nobody over his own son. How do you think that makes me feel?"

"Like killing him?"

"You're damn right like killing him, but that satisfaction was taken from me. Someone killed him before I had the guts to do it myself." Andre Lyons's face reddened with anger. I found him very convincing that he wanted his father dead, but equally convincing that he couldn't do it himself.

"So what do you plan to do?" I asked.

"As you've probably heard, the change in our father's will didn't happen. I'll have enough funds to pay my creditors and to give my investors a tidy return on their investment. That should please your client, Mr. Portier, and afford me the opportunity to bring in higher quality productions."

"So all's well for you after all."

Andre looked at me and said, "If that's what you want to call it. If you have any plans for interfering in my good fortune, I ask that you reconsider for my sake. Now if you'll excuse me, I'd like to get something to wash this bad taste you've given me out of my mouth. Good afternoon."

Before Andre left, I noticed his attention being diverted. I turned to look. His brother, Manfred, greeted a striking older woman in a fashionable belle-poque skirt and floppy-rimmed feather and net fascinator. He kissed the side of the woman's cheek. She carried a celebratory air as if everyone in the room wanted to kiss her cheek.

"The prodigal mother returns," Andre said blandly. "Goody. Just what we need today."

As soon as he left, I asked Portier, "Is that Alexandra Lyons?"

"Apparently. I've never met her."

"She's dressed as if she's just returned from the Kentucky Derby."

"No doubt. Her reputation has it she's interested in studs. What a remarkable woman, though, isn't she? If I didn't know better, I would take her for Joyce and Angelle's sister rather than their mother."

I thought the very same thing.

I scanned the room to find Joyce and Angelle. I wanted to see their reaction to their mother's entrance. I saw Joyce first, then spotted Angelle. Both women watched Alexandra out of the corner of their eyes. They didn't appear they wanted to give their mother the satisfaction that they cared she was in the room. Neither one of them left their conversation partner to welcome her.

"This is a bit awkward for dear Alexandra, isn't it?" Portier joked. "Being snubbed by her daughters the way she is."

"On the contrary," I replied, "her daughters' reaction appears to be just what Alexandra hoped they would be."

"What are you talking about?"

"Haven't you noticed?" I pointed towards Manny. Even though he greeted her, Alexandra's attention hadn't been on him since she'd arrived. In fact, she looked away from him several times during their conversation to focus on her daughters. "I'd say there's a bit of competition between the three women for attention."

"That's absurd. Do you really think so?"

"Oh, believe me, Portier, I've had plenty of opportunity to study the female psyche between mothers and daughters in my congregations. I'm not getting a good feeling here. There's definitely some bad blood going on between these women. And to think I thought Joyce and Angelle's issues were solely about the bad blood between them and their father."

"Is there an angle we're missing? I thought we had everything worked out."

"Not so fast. I believe what we're seeing is just another interesting facet to the dynamics of Roger Lyons' family."

"I think what we're seeing is more than a facet," Portier said. "Alexandra Lyons is an absolute gem. She's an intriguing and compelling woman. There isn't a man or woman in this room who doesn't have their eyes upon her."

"Except her daughters."

Portier looked at Joyce and Angelle. "You're right. They're not fazed by her presence at all. I say, Fountain, it's been worth coming to this little shindig just for this moment alone. This calls for another drink. In fact, I think it calls for a good Kentucky bourbon mint julep if you ask me. Woodford Reserve, eh? Shall I get you one?"

"No, go ahead. I see Detective Robicheaux and another officer coming through the entrance right on cue."

Portier left my side, but before I could approach the men, Reed Alemand called my name. I turned just as he grabbed my arm, pulling me close to show how angry he was.

"You brought the police to this affair? Are you out of your ever-loving mind? Have you no sense of decency or respect whatsoever? This is highly embarrassing to say the least."

I jerked my arm from his grip and told him to calm down.

"I will not calm down. Their presence is your doing, don't deny it."

"Is there something about it that has you unnerved?"

"Me? No, of course not. I'm thinking of Manny. I'm thinking of the entire Lyons family."

"Are you sure it has nothing to do with your conversation with Reginald Falgout the other day? Something you don't want the police to find out?"

Alemand's expression turned to one of genuine surprise. "I don't know what you're implying, but whatever it is, it's nonsense."

"You were seen speaking with Mr. Falgout. Was he delving into your accounts? Was he getting close to unraveling an intricate fraud you were perpetrating under Portier's nose? Is that why you're so nervous to see the detective?"

"You have no idea what you're talking about. I wasn't angry about Falgout's investigation into my accounts, you nincompoop. I was concerned about Manny. I was very concerned about my partner and his involvement with that Falgout and his crooked ways. He's a fraud himself, that Falgout. I was angry, and I confronted him. Yes, right there in front of the bank, I confronted him. I told Falgout he was a fraud. I demanded he make it right to keep Manny from civil and criminal investigations."

"Criminal?"

"Didn't you hear me? Yes, I said criminal, and I suggest that if you don't know what I'm talking about, you discuss it with Portier who's going to be my ex-accountant very soon if the two of you don't clear matters up right away."

"Mr. Alemand—"

He raised his hand in the air to stop me. "I want no excuses from you, Reverend. I want you to clear this matter immediately, then what I want you to do is to pack your bags and to leave on the first train out of town."

"Mr. Alemand—"

"Do I make myself clear?"

I conceded and said that he did.

Alemand walked away, leaving me alone with the feeling of egg dripping from my face.

Chapter 25

"Cheers, old man," Portier said, extending a julep to me. "I took the liberty of having one made for you. It's a stiff one. I thought you might need it. Ol' Alemand didn't look like he was in a particularly good mood."

"And neither am I at the moment. Why didn't you tell me Alemand wasn't the focus of your inquiries when we talked to Falgout at the bank?"

"I thought it was obvious."

"It wasn't, and it also wasn't obvious that Falgout was a fraud."

"I'm sorry you missed that point, too. I thought you knew."

I took a hefty sip of my drink to clear my head. The bourbon burned the back of my throat. I tried my best not to cough, but I couldn't help but do it anyway.

"You okay?" he asked. "I don't need you kicking the bucket on me."

"Don't make fun of me or this situation. I need to know what's going on."

"You already know what's going on. You know who killed Roger Lyons."

"Yes. Moline, the princess."

"There you have it."

"But I need to know who paid Moline to kill Lyons and why. That's where you come in. I'm counting on you for the motive when we present the killer to Detective Robicheaux, but you have me so confused right now I'm about to tell him we have to delay."

"I'll spell it out for you. What do you want to know?"

"Everything. From the beginning."

"It's simple. Roger Lyons wasn't killed because his family was afraid he changed his will. Oh, they may have been concerned at one time, yes, but it wasn't enough to drive them to murder. They also didn't care that much that their father was spending his fortune on the homeless. His murder wasn't about his political leanings or who his children were dating or the fact that he was not there as a father when they were younger. It wasn't even about not giving them money to start a two-bit stock theater."

Alexandra's gregarious laughter suddenly bellowed from across the room.

"Pay attention, Fountain. His murder wasn't even about her. It had nothing to do with his two-timing alcoholic wife who was known to carouse the countryside in search of a good time."

I raised my hand for him to stop. "Enough. Do you know who the murderer is?"

"Yes. It was Moline just as you said, but there's more to it than that. Someone paid Moline to kill Roger Lyons."

"But if none of the theories you just mentioned were the motive for why someone paid Moline to kill him, what was the motive? Was it something financial that involved Falgout?"

"Yes, Fountain, it was all in the packet of information I gave to Detective Robicheaux. I didn't explain it to you, but I documented it very clearly for the detective. I'm assuming it was my indisputable documentation, not your heart-warming apology and confession, as to why he decided to join this affair."

"Then explain it to me now—briefly, of course."

Portier raised his glass as if he'd be happy to oblige. "It's true that Roger Lyons's disappearance caused a strain on the family's financial situation. The family wanted and needed money for a variety of reasons, but it was tied up. They needed Roger's authorization or approval to get at it. It was too much to have him gone for such a long period of time. What the family failed to realize, however, was that he still maintained tabs on the family. I suspect he wanted to see how his family would survive and conduct themselves in his absence."

"Knowing what I know of Roger Lyons that sounds very plausible. So what happened?"

"He discovered a flaw in his family's integrity. They were willing to circumvent Federal IRS and charitable foundation laws to get the money they wanted. Manny's business, for instance, was funded using illegal funds transferred from The Lyons Foundation to his business. The Landalia was being sustained through similar transactions. Likewise, with Angelle. She lied to you if she told you that her father resumed payments to her. No, she obtained her allowance illegally from funds earmarked for charitable purposes from The Lyons Foundation."

"And Joyce?"

"Joyce simply took the money from the foundation because she wanted it."

"How were they discovered?"

"Roger kept close tabs on the foundation because he was using the foundation's bank account to fund the organization's mission established by the board. One of their projects was

Labreville. He found out about his family's illegal transfer of funds and put a stop to it. He had the board of directors dissolve the foundation and transfer the assets to a new foundation specifically dedicated to help Labreville."

"That put a kink in the siblings' waterhole."

"For a short while. They simply continued their illegal ways by using a different foundation."

"Atchafalaya Preservation."

"Exactly. It was a stroke of genius on your part to have me go to the Secretary of State's office when you did. I not only found out about the closing of The Lyons Foundation, but was able to determine there was another foundation with close ties to the family. In fact, the board of directors of the Atchafalaya Preservation Foundation consists almost entirely of Lyons family members. Now, who do you suspect is the chair of this foundation?"

"Manny?"

"Obvious guess, but no."

"Joyce?"

"Another obvious guess, but another no. Try her stunning look-alike."

"Alexandra?"

Portier winked and took a celebratory sip of his mint julep in response to my correct guess.

"I still don't understand how Falgout fits in," I said. "He's a fraud examiner. Surely he identified these fraudulent transactions through his review of their bank accounts. Why didn't he stop it? And what about that IRS audit Manny went through? He was cleared of wrongdoing with flying colors."

"Of course he was. That's because Falgout didn't use his capacity as an auditor and fraud examiner to protect the banks' interest. He was hired by the Lyons siblings to cook the books between the foundations and Manny's new business, Andre's stock theater, and personal accounts that Joyce and Angelle had. Who better to fix transactions and to hide illegal activities than an auditor who knew what IRS agents would be looking for? The family hired Falgout and paid him a great deal of money to have him work it all out."

"So who is technically guilty of this crime?"

"Ah," he said, lifting a finger for patience. "There'll be a better time to discuss that. It appears your detective and officer friends have arrived and are interested in getting this production underway."

Detective Robicheaux crossed the room to where we stood. An officer followed, appearing as if he'd rather be anyplace but where he was. "Reverend Fountain, I assume you remember Officer Betz, the officer who interviewed you the day Mr. Lyons died."

I extended my hand. "Yes, sir. Good to see you again. Thank you for coming."

Robicheaux turned to Portier and said, "I appreciate the information you provided through the Reverend here. I didn't have much time, but I was able to verify the most important facts you presented in your envelopes. I'd like to get everyone together to discuss your findings if I may." He turned from side to side and evaluated the room. "But I'd rather not do it here in the middle of this reception. Do you know if there's a conference room or other place where we can meet?"

"Yes, I believe there's a room down the hall, Detective," I said. "The reception will be winding down soon."

"No doubt. It appears people are starting to leave. I hope our presence hasn't spoiled their fun."

Officer Betz smiled at the detective.

"Officer Betz and I will go to the conference room and wait," Robicheaux added. "I assume the two of you will be joining us. I'll start things off, but I'd prefer the two of you to present the evidence because you know it better. It will also give me a chance to stand back and watch their reactions."

Portier and I agreed. I showed the detective the way to the conference room and stayed with him while Officer Betz requested the family's presence.

~

Portier soon entered the conference room followed by Reed Alemand and Andre Lyons. Reed continued to look angry, but Andre's face had softened. He looked more nervous than angry.

Glen Balfour entered with Carmen Nicolet on his heels. Glen appeared glum. Carmen looked stoned. I glanced at Detective Robicheaux. He'd clearly noticed her red eyes and faraway look.

Joyce Nicolet came into the room by herself, refusing to look anyone in the eyes. She and her stepdaughter sat down in unison across from each other at the table.

Reginald Falgout entered with a drink in his hand. He tripped once as he tried to maneuver around a chair but composed himself, appearing not the least bit embarrassed. He took a spot leaning against a wall on the other side of the room.

Laughter came from the outer hall as Manny's personable voice called out to a departing guest, thanking him for attending the reception. He stopped in the doorway and studied everyone's faces before walking into the room. His mother, Alexandra, clung to his right arm to steady her balance. Like Reginald Falgout, she had indulged too much. Manfred led her to a chair where she tried to sit gracefully, but

299

her legs got tangled with each other and she collapsed clumsily into her seat.

Joyce didn't look at her mother. She closed her eyes in disgust then opened them slowly as if hoping that the bad dream in which she was living would disappear.

Robicheaux took control. "Gentlemen, there are plenty of seats with the ladies if you'd care to sit down."

They didn't. Only Reed Alemand took the detective's offer. He looked as if he needed to sit down before he passed out.

"Is this everyone?" Robicheaux asked.

"Angelle isn't here," someone said.

"Yes, where did she go?"

"She'll be in directly," I said. "I asked her to do something for me before she came in. We can go on and get started."

Detective Robicheaux began by saying that the disappearance and subsequent death of Roger Lyons was an odd and mysterious case from the beginning. It baffled his department and frustrated him personally by what appeared to be an apathetic attitude on the part of the Lyons family. He had never seen so many people in one family so disinterested in uncovering the truth about a loved one's death.

"If it weren't for the reverend here, I dare say Mr. Lyons would still be on a shelf in the city morgue," he said, "and you people would be absolutely keen with that. It's unfathomable to me." He turned to me and asked if I had anything I wanted to add regarding opening statements. I said I didn't. "Then let's get down to why we're all here."

"Will this take long?" Alexandra asked. "I do plan to stay to hear you out, but I must tell you I have dinner reservations with Niccolo Machiavelli at the Monteleone. He's not the real Machiavelli, obviously, but he pretends to be and his commentaries on the benefits of political corruption and immoral leadership are entertaining to say the least."

"Mother, shut up," Joyce Nicolet said.

"Ma'am," Robicheaux added bluntly, "I need everyone's focused attention, if you wouldn't mind."

Alexandra sat back in her seat. Joyce's disdain didn't appear to upset her. In fact, she smirked as if the annoyance amused her.

Robicheaux looked at me. "Reverend, I now turn the floor over to you."

"Thank you, Detective. I appreciate each of you attending this impromptu meeting. Mr. Portier and I will make this as brief as possible to allow Detective Robicheaux and Officer Betz to get on with their duties and to put this affair of Roger Lyons's death to rest. This case must be explained in two parts. There's a financial aspect leading up to his death that Mr. Portier will explain first. I'll then review the murder itself. We cannot discuss one without the other so we ask for your patience while we explain." I gestured for Portier to begin.

He prefaced his presentation by reviewing his professional background and saying that he had experience with awkward and complicated cases of forensic accounting. The conclusion he was about to present regarding the motive for Roger Lyons' death required concentration and deductive reasoning only an educated man such as himself could accomplish. He exuded such a condescending air of superiority over the attendees that when he glanced over to me for my reaction, I glared at him with disapproval. The telepathic waves coming from my head, telling him to drop the theatrics and stick to the facts, must have reverberated with him because he stopped immediately, cleared his throat, and began again.

"We all know how much of a financial burden Roger Lyons's disappearance placed upon the family," he said. "Although each of you are or should be wealthy in your own right, you did have this co-dependent reliance on his benevolent nature."

"Benevolent?" Joyce Nicolet blurted out. "You must be joking. It shows just how little you know of our father and of this family. I can tell already this conversation is going to be meaningless. If you suspect one of us as the person who killed him, you'll have better luck putting our pictures on the wall and throwing a dart to find your suspect."

"And I suggest you listen to what Mr. Portier has to say, Mrs. Nicolet," Detective Robicheaux said.

"Even if you didn't need or want his money," Portier said, addressing Mrs. Nicolet, "your father's political leanings were enough for you to want to ensure that he didn't contribute to capitalistic candidates."

"I couldn't care less about politics, and I certainly wouldn't ruin my life over them."

"There was also a fear that your father had changed his will."

"It wasn't a fear. It was just one of those irritating tactics father used to watch us squirm. It didn't work on me."

Portier raised an eyebrow. "Not even the amount of money he was spending on Labreville?"

"I didn't know about Labreville until recently."

"Didn't you? If not, your siblings did. Glen Balfour did. Even your stepdaughter did. That was enough motive to kill him. Manny, you could have used your father's financial assistance to open this business. It's an interesting story how you obtained the necessary funds without borrowing or having investors." Before Manfred Lyons could speak, Portier turned to his brother. "And, of course, there's the inequitable treatment you received from your father, Andre."

"Father treated us all inequitably in different ways," Andre said.

"But yours directly affected your livelihood and dreams. It affected your self-worth. It angered you."

"I'm angered by many things in life. Father's inequity prepared me for the inequities in life. It was a life lesson for lack of better words. That's how I look at it, and I'm sure that's how my father intended it. I don't harbor a grudge strong enough to kill him."

"You, on the other hand, Miss Nicolet," Portier said, changing his attention to the young woman.

Carmen filed her nails. She lifted her head upon hearing her name.

"Your immaturity exacerbated the greed you had for a fortune that didn't belong to you."

The young woman stared wide-eyed across the table as if she had no idea what Portier had just said.

Portier finally turned to Alexandra Lyons.

Alexandra smiled. "There's nothing to accuse me of, Mr. Portier. I wasn't here when he died. I'm rarely here."

"I have to differ with you. His financial restrictions kept you from going to the exotic places you wanted to go."

She laughed. "This is where your absurdity has gotten out of hand. My husband rarely dictated where or when I went on my trips. He didn't care. He was happy when I was gone."

"Off to New York or Paris recently?"

"Recife. I went to the beach then stayed in Olinda. I'd much rather spend Carnival in Brazil. So, you see, your theory is completely off base."

"Nevertheless, Mrs. Lyons, you had a need for funds just as each of your children and their associates had a need."

Portier elaborated on the illegal withdrawals from The Lyons Foundation and how Roger soon became aware of what they were doing. He then explained how the family used another foundation when they got wind of their father's knowledge.

Some of the men shifted uneasily on their feet.

"Then something unfortunate happened," Portier said. "The IRS requested financial documentation related to your father, The Lyons Foundation, and transactions related to the opening of this business. Before turning over the documentation, the family had to work quickly. That's where Reginald Falgout came in. What better person to hide fraudulent transactions from the IRS than to hire a professional fraud examiner who worked for the bank in which the transactions occurred?"

Falgout stepped forward to protest.

Detective Robicheaux lifted his hand for him to stop. "Don't try to deny it, Mr. Falgout. You were paid very well. Your own bank ledger shows hefty deposits made into your account. They were deposited to your account while you did the work. The payments continued even after you finished your work to ensure you kept your mouth shut. If you're wanting to disagree, I should have you know that I verified this transaction directly with the appropriate individuals at your bank." Robicheaux stopped and looked about the room, studying the ashen faces and eyes of those who looked at him intently. "Please proceed, Mr. Portier."

My friend took the floor again, addressing the siblings around the table. "Your father was becoming a changed man recently. He was becoming the kind of person he always wanted to be. You may not have seen it in him or refused to see it in him, but he was questioning the value he'd placed upon his life and the value he was offering others and their lives. He developed a need to help the unfortunate in our city. He was changing his life, but he realized the rest of you weren't changing yours. He knew what was happening with your illegal transactions and how you were hiding those transactions from the IRS. He realized you were never going to change. You continued your manipulative and materialistic ways. Something had to be done to stop you. That's why he dissolved The Lyons Foundation to stop the flow of money to you. As a result, each of you determined that something had to be done to stop him."

"Something was done," I said as I stepped forward to replace Portier. "On that morning when I was taking my walk, someone pushed Roger Lyons on Decatur Street. He hit his head upon the iron fence, dazing him. He stumbled to the park bench where I thought he'd been bludgeoned. I found his walking stick in the bushes nearby. The finial was broken from the main portion of his walking stick. I thought it was the murder weapon, but Detective Robicheaux found no traces of blood on the finial. I later learned his head wound was from the fall against the fence. He didn't die from being bludgeoned. He was strangled, but I couldn't see the ligature marks because of the way his head was bent down over the park bench. He was strangled, using a gold cord, I learned later."

"Strangled? That doesn't make sense," Manfred Lyons stated. "He couldn't have been strangled. He was alive when you found him."

"That's true. I did find him alive, and I talked him through to the other side. I believe the strangler was interrupted, but they'd done enough damage for him to eventually succumb to his injuries.

"A curious thing about his death. After he died, I noticed he had a playbill to Andre's play, *Dickies, Stocks & Jabots.* It interested me because I'd been to the play just the night before with Portier. A woman stood behind me on Decatur Street while I talked to Roger. This woman saw me taking the playbill out of his satchel to look at it. She told Officer Betz I was stealing it. She also told him I'd killed the man, but I wasn't the person who killed your father. Moline killed him that morning, just as I said it was done, using the gold cord from Victorius' toga. In the process of doing so, though, her arm cuff, the one she was accustomed to wearing, fell off from her skinny forearm."

"Skinny?" Glen Balfour asked. "Then she couldn't have overpowered him."

"But she did. I'm proof that she could surprise and overpower an older man in her drug-induced state. It didn't take much to push your father into the fence. It also didn't take much to strangle him as he slumped over the arm of the park bench. A small person could have overpowered him just as effectively as a large person."

"So what happened to the cuff?"

"In the course of the violence against your father, the serpentine cuff came off her arm and rolled into the hedge. Moline told me, when I asked her about it, that she gave it to her partner, Victorius, because he'd lost his, but that couldn't have been true. Victorius didn't wear cuffs, and his arms were thick and muscular. Her cuff could never fit him. The next thing I know, however, she has her cuff back.

"I surmise that Moline was in such a hurry to leave the scene after she killed Roger Lyons that she didn't have time to look for the cuff that fell from her arm. Perhaps it was me she saw coming. I didn't see her, so we may never know, but I suspect it fell off her arm, and she told the person who paid her that there had been a glitch during the murder. The person she told was close at hand to make sure Moline did the deed. It was this person who ingeniously got the cuff back for her."

"Do you mean one of us?" Andre asked. "Are you implying that one of us found a way to get back to the scene of the crime to retrieve the cuff?"

"Yes, I am."

"But I doubt any one of us cared that much to go to the trouble of doing that."

"Oh, but one of you did. She was the woman at the scene who stood behind me as I spoke to your father, helping him cross over to Heaven. That woman said to me, 'You killed him.' She also bent down and picked something up from the bushes. I didn't see what it was, but I suspect she found Moline's arm cuff and then hid it in her clothing."

"But how do you know it was one of us? That woman could've been anyone."

"Except that Officer Betz interviewed the woman after he interviewed me. I recommended to Detective Robicheaux later that he interview her again, but the address she gave him wasn't hers. In fact, the address she gave was the homeless community Roger Lyons built named Labreville."

"That's silly," Joyce said. "Why would one of us, if we're trying to throw suspicion off ourselves, give an officer of the law an address tied to our father?"

"You tell me. I suspect the person didn't think she'd be asked that question. She had to think of an address quickly. The best solution was to say she was homeless and living among the homeless at Labreville. Whatever the reason, it was a huge mistake because I then realized there was a connection between Roger Lyons and the woman at the scene with me. And then there was something else I saw—a picture."

The siblings looked at each other as if they had no idea what I was talking about.

"What sort of picture?" Manfred asked.

"A picture that was once placed on a mantle in Joyce's library. It was of each of you dressed in your Mardi Gras costumes for the Krewe of Acadia ball in Lafayette. You were all in the picture; even you, Mrs. Lyons."

Alexandra glared at me and shook her head. "It couldn't have been me, darling."

"Yes, it was definitely you in the picture. You weren't out of the country as you claimed."

Alexandra opened her mouth, presumably to make a quick comeback, but closed it again without making a sound, then she sighed. "All right, I admit I was at the krewe ball, but I wasn't here in New Orleans when my husband was killed."

"Yes, you were. That can be easily confirmed."

"Perhaps by Niccolo Machiavelli," Joyce chided her mother.

"Show us the picture!" someone demanded.

I raised my hand. "The picture was in Joyce's library the first time I visited. When I returned, it was no longer there."

"There you have it," Andre said. "You have no proof of your claim."

"No, but I asked Angelle to find it. When she couldn't, she brought other photos she found of that evening at the ball. I found one costume strikingly familiar—at least the wig." I turned towards the closed door to the conference room and called, "You may come in now."

Angelle Lyons entered the room dressed in one of the women's ball costumes.

"That's her!" Officer Betz blurted. "That's the woman I interviewed."

"Look carefully, Officer. Are you sure it's the same woman you interviewed the day Roger Lyons died? Could it have been Joyce Nicolet? Or Alexandra Lyons?"

The policeman looked at each of the women.

"It wasn't me," Angelle said, taking off the dark wig.

"It wasn't me, either," Joyce responded, "and I'll not put that nasty thing on my head to prove it."

"Well, don't look at me," Alexandra said. "I didn't want to be in Lafayette or New Orleans in the first place, but Niccolo wouldn't take me to Recife."

"It can't be blamed on me," Carmen said, slapping her nail file on the table. "I don't look like any one of you, thank goodness."

"Put it on and let's see," I said to her.

She turned and looked at me to see if I was serious. Her smug expression disappeared.

"Angelle, give your niece the wig," I said.

Angelle walked to Carmen and held out the wig for her to take.

Carmen shivered and shook her head. "No! Get that thing away from me!"

"Miss Nicolet, put the wig on for Officer Betz to see," Detective Robicheaux said.

"I won't do it. I don't have to do it."

"For crying out loud, Carmen," Manny pleaded. "If you weren't the one who was there, you've nothing to worry about. Put on the wig."

She looked at me defiantly, then reached for the wig. Angelle handed it to her.

Carmen put it over her head slowly and clumsily. I didn't know if it was on purpose or nerves, but she made an ordeal of putting on the wig. When it was on, hair covered her face. She flipped back the dark strands, rubbed her fingers through the sides, and looked toward the head of the conference table.

Officer Betz nodded but didn't exclaim an identification. All he said was, "I can't rule her out."

"You may remove it, Miss Nicolet," Robicheaux said.

"That wasn't conclusive, gentlemen," Manny said. "In fact, it was a waste of our time. We still don't know the truth."

Detective Robicheaux agreed. "That's true, we don't. We seem to be getting nowhere fast."

I noticed the family appeared relieved. When I looked at the detective, however, I saw nothing on his face that indicated they had anything to be relieved about. In fact, the gears inside his head appeared to be turning quite rapidly.

"What are you thinking, Detective?" I asked.

He turned abruptly to me, as if coming out a trance, and said, "I'd like to give everyone an opportunity to make a statement."

"A statement?" Joyce asked defiantly. "There's nothing more to say. I suggest you go about your business and do what you must do, but statements from any of us are out of the question."

"It's not that simple, Mrs. Nicolet. There's the question of who paid Moline to kill Mr. Lyons and which one of you was the woman who tampered with evidence at the scene of the crime. Those are not solved to my satisfaction."

Joyce gave Manny a quick glance.

He shook his head and said, "All I've heard is talk, Detective. You've talked of payments to Mr. Falgout. You've talked of payments to this Moline woman. You've implicated all of us, but you've shown us nothing."

Detective Robicheaux stood motionless before slowly turning to Portier and me with a subtle wink that I was sure no one but Portier or I could see. "Manfred is absolutely correct," he replied to us. "We'll have to show him the documentation."

My eyes widened with alarm. Unless Portier had provided him with evidence I was unaware had been obtained, I didn't know what he was talking about.

"You do have the documentation in your possession at Mr. Portier's cottage, do you not, Reverend?" he asked.

I didn't know what to say. I turned to Portier. He gave an almost imperceptible nod and I read his expression to indicate that I should play along.

"Yes," I said with reluctance. "It's in a briefcase in the parlor."

"Unfortunately, we were planning to be out this evening," Portier interjected quickly. "Would tomorrow morning be early enough to stop by the precinct?"

I looked again at Portier who was apparently more in tune to the detective's ploy than I was.

"Yes, that will be fine," Robicheaux said.

"Then I take it we're through here," Joyce responded snidely, rising from her chair.

"Until tomorrow, yes."

"Good," she added. "After all, I wouldn't want Mother to be late for her date with Machiavelli."

~

Dusk glided across the French Quarter much earlier than I anticipated. Portier's cottage was eerily still and void of light.

Robicheaux's officer hid within the gloomy corner of the parlor. Two more officers concealed themselves in the shadows of the kitchen. Bentley stayed next door, keeping Genny company, while Portier and I sat nervously in the guest room with the detective.

"You're being good sports about this," Robicheaux said. "I appreciate you following my lead at the meeting this afternoon."

"Glad to do it," Portier said. "Aren't we, Fountain?"

I wasn't as gracious. "It seems we're being placed in undue danger," I said.

"It's danger you're concerned with now, Reverend?" Detective Robicheaux chided, a slight chuckling tone in his voice.

"I don't find that funny."

"Don't you now? For several days, you've done nothing but put yourself in danger with no one between you and your threat to protect you. Now, there's several officers here to protect you, and you suddenly feel in imminent danger. Funny, perhaps not. Ironic? I can't think of anything more ironic."

"Touché, Detective," I said. "Point taken. Still, I'm not sure what you're hoping to gain."

"My documentation to the detective only went so far," Portier explained. "I didn't have access to all of the Lyons' account information at the bank that I needed. I had to give him my hypothesis as to what he'd find if he inquired."

"It could take days going through all of the bank's records of each family members' accounts," Robicheaux added. "I'm hoping this exercise will immediately tell me where to concentrate my efforts."

"If that's what this trap is for, I could've given you a recommendation on whose accounts to look at," I said.

"What do you mean?"

"I know who'll break in and try to find the briefcase I said contained the documentation."

Before Detective Robicheaux could ask further, we heard a subtle creaking of a gate outside of the cottage.

"They're coming through the alleyway that leads to my courtyard," Portier whispered. "There's an outside door to the kitchen from there."

I held my breath and listened, but heard nothing. I imagined footsteps creeping along the alley under the cottage's windowsills. Soon, however, we heard faint sounds of someone tampering with the backdoor lock. I had faith that the officers in the parlor and kitchen were attuned to the sounds and were preparing for the intruder's entry.

The back lock unlatched.

My heart raced with each slow, methodical creaking of the door being opened. I cupped a hand over my ear towards the bedroom door to try to listen better, but it didn't help. I couldn't tell when the door opened. I couldn't hear them enter. I couldn't tell how many intruders there were. All I knew was that the detective's hunch was right; someone would come for the evidence we said we had in the cottage—and that someone was here now.

My heart pounded faster.

It felt like several minutes of silence occurred, though it was probably only seconds. Nevertheless, nothing happened. No searching. No ransacking. No combing our belongings. Just silence. I found the silence more frightening than if I'd heard them searching.

Suddenly, we heard movement again. My imagination exaggerated every creak upon the floorboards as they entered the parlor. Someone flicked on the lights, and I heard officers wrestling an intruder to the floor. Detective Robicheaux bolted from the bedroom and took command, ordering the man on the floor to rise.

Portier and I left the bedroom as well and entered the parlor eager to see who'd been captured. Just one person stood between two officers, his presence looming.

"Victorius!" Portier yelled.

The man turned towards Portier's alarmed voice, and I saw immediately that he wasn't Victorius.

"Glen Balfour," I said solemnly. "I hoped it wouldn't be you, but I suspected it would be."

Portier, seeing he was mistaken, turned to me and asked, "What are you talking about, Fountain? He's a damned crook! A murderer! He's the one who paid Moline to kill you! Why would you be disheartened to have his sorry ass captured and placed in jail?"

I didn't answer immediately. I looked toward the kitchen where an officer came through the doorway, clutching another hand-cuffed culprit by the arm. I shook my head sadly and said, "Because I knew Angelle wouldn't be far behind."

Portier's mouth gaped. He gave her a once over, his eyes widening in alarm. I could see why. Fine lines and blotches etched her porcelain skin. Make-up couldn't disguise a life that was harder than she allowed others to see. She'd replaced the pastel taffeta dress that used to swirl like a cloud around her with dark, jagged pants that hung loosely around her hips. A black leather jacket draped from her shoulders as badly as The Landalia's theater curtain draped from its stage.

She gave me a sharp, piercing glare before turning away. I knew at that moment, she hoped to never see my face again.

I said nothing. I didn't have to say anything. She could see my disappointment in the reflection of my eyes.

Chapter 26

Portier and I took the St. Charles streetcar to Napoleon Avenue and walked the three blocks to Pascal's Manale, one of my favorite restaurants in the Garden District. For over forty years, the Uptown landmark served Louisiana-Italian dishes in an unpretentious atmosphere. I looked forward to the eggplant appetizer stuffed with ham, shrimp, crabmeat, and a blend of seasonings accompanied with a paper bag filled with warm bread.

We entered the building and the restaurant's aroma teased me immediately. While Portier went to the host podium to announce our arrival, I heard a familiar laugh and saw Genny Duval sitting at the bar with a gentleman whose facial features, fedora, and dark zoot suit reminded me of a Chicagoan mobster. Genny wore silk stockings, but they were bunched terribly around the knees. She introduced me to the gentleman—not a mobster from Chicago but a sweeper salesman from Shreveport. They weren't laughing about a recent hit he'd made on one of his rivals but about a nutria that had crossed Genny's path on her way to the restaurant.

"Can you believe some people eat those things?" she asked. She looked at me and said, "Oh, Richard, guess what? This gentleman has heard me sing! And he loves me!"

Her laugh made me smile. "Everyone loves you, Genny," I said.

Portier joined us.

"I know," she continued, "but I think this guy really means it. Is our table ready, Chuck?" When he said it was, Genny turned to the man from Shreveport and said, "I never forget a face, sweetheart. Next time you're in the club, be sure to get my attention. I'll have Tomas make you a special cocktail on the house." She gave him a hug and we were off to our table.

"You never offer me special drinks on the house," Portier stated with a straight face.

"That's because you never compliment me. Say something nice."

"Your hair is bigger than usual."

She laughed and shook her head in wild abandon. Curls flung around her face. "It is, isn't it? I don't know what happened. You'd think I fell into a clothes dryer."

Our host seated us toward the front of the main dining room.

Genny's eyes widened with excitement. "There are just four questions I have to ask before we get started. First, may I have a cocktail tonight?"

"Of course," Portier said, taking the menu from the host. "You may have as many as you like. It's a celebration."

"Are you buying?"

"Of course, again. You must be a secret daughter of Roger Lyons the way you ask for money."

"I'll move on. What're y'all having to eat?"

"Genevieve, we just sat down."

"Barbecue shrimp," I said without hesitation. "Now what's the fourth question?"

"How did you know it would be Angelle who'd show at the cottage, Richard?"

"I didn't, exactly, because at first I thought it'd be Joyce Nicolet. Then, like Portier, I thought it could be Victorius, finishing off Moline's dirty work. After all, the gold cord that strangled Roger came from his toga. Something happened earlier today, though, that changed my perspective on who paid Moline to kill their father. A detective was waiting for me on Burgundy as I walked to the police station. He had followed me from Miss Cora's, and he suspected I'd be going to the police with more information."

"What detective was that? One of Robicheaux's detectives?"

"No, a private detective hired by Angelle to follow her boyfriend around and to find out about her father. I believe Angelle wrote the demand note for Miss Cora to return The Lyons Foundation's money. She knew me well enough to know from our meetings that I'd go see Miss Cora to warn her."

"But I thought Angelle was being so helpful," Genny said. "She gave you photographs. She told you about her relationship with her father. She brought the wig. She even modeled it. I don't understand."

"It was all a façade, Genny. It was all part of the masquerade for her not to appear as she was. No one was who they appeared. Fortunately, even though I was enamored by Angelle's charm and beauty, I never lost sight that her helpfulness was just a ploy to throw me off track."

"Damn!" she said, slapping her hand on the table.

The outburst was so sudden and unexpected, I laughed. Portier scolded her.

"Well, Chuck, you'd slap the table, too, if you just lost five bucks. I bet Tomas it was Joyce Nicolet who was behind it all."

"Who did he bet on?"

"Angelle, of course. I can't believe it. How would *he* know? He just serves drinks."

"He's a bartender, Genevieve. He knows more about what makes people tick than psychoanalysts do. He can see through people, even women like Angelle Lyons."

"I could've used an extra five bucks. I can't believe I have to turn it over to him. So what's she looking at? I mean, what kind of charges? What are they all looking at, do you think?"

I took a deep breath and tried to recall what Detective Robicheaux had told me. My understanding of criminal law was practically nil, and I didn't follow him completely. "Let me see," I said. "There are definitely some first-degree murder charges in the works or conspiring to commit first-degree murder against the Lyons siblings."

"All of them?"

"Yes. Joyce, Manny, Andre, and Angelle. They all benefited and had a hand in their father's demise to cover up their financial fraud."

"The ol' woman, too?"

"Alexandra, too. Glen Balfour has been implicated in the charges. So has Carmen Nicolet. On top of that, they're facing Federal fraud charges and other punitive penalties by the IRS."

"Reginald Falgout is facing serious charges regarding his role in the fraud," Portier added. "I understand the bank relieved him of his duties as soon as he returned to the office, Fountain."

"As well they should've."

Genny turned to Portier and asked delicately, "What about your friend?"

"You mean Alemand? He's my client, Genevieve. He's guilty of being a fool, not a criminal. He made a bad investment, that's all. He'll do well to find another partner and to stay away from the theater for a while. I won't let him forget this ordeal any time soon."

Genny turned her attention to me. "You've been very quiet about one part of the mystery, Richard. Who confessed at being on Decatur Street to pick up Moline's arm cuff when you were with Mr. Lyons?"

"How much do you have riding on this one, Genevieve?" Portier asked.

She gave him a side glance and replied casually, "I could get my five bucks back. Tell me, should I make it double or nothing with Tomas?"

"Depends on who you bet it was," I replied. She started to say, but I lifted my finger. "I'm teasing you. We don't know yet, Genny. You'll have to wait with the rest of us. All four women remained completely silent. They didn't confess or implicate the guilty one."

"So you really don't know which woman was at the scene with you? How will you be able to find out?"

"Robicheaux and his men will have to do more investigating unless we get a lucky break somewhere."

Genny sat back in her chair and asked solemnly, "Does this mean you're returning to the Midwest?"

"Not immediately. I'm still hopeful something will turn up."

"You're not a man who waits patiently, Richard. Detective Robicheaux will continue with his investigation, yes, but what are *you* planning to do?"

I shook my head. "I honestly don't have any plans. I don't know what I can do. I've overturned every stone I can think to overturn. I'll have to get lucky I suspect."

She patted my hand with empathy.

"I think I'll have Oysters Dante," Portier announced as if we'd been sitting on the edge of our seat until he decided.

He looked at us without expression, then added, "I've been thinking. Who'd like to go to the theater tonight?"

He wasn't joking.

Portier said he was tired of talking about the Lyons family. He was disinterested in the case now that it was solved, and he would very much like to get back to some form of normalcy. "So who would like to go with me? I need something to rid me of the look Reed Alemand gave me as we left the conference room. Good Lord, did you see his face, Fountain?"

"No, I was too busy wondering if one of the wait staff from the reception had been hired to kill us as we exited the building."

After dinner, Genny and I accompanied Portier to the theater. We saw a quality production and were thoroughly entertained. It was the first genuine moment of fun and relaxation since my arrival.

～

It was late by the time we got home. Bentley had been in the back garden and was ready for a treat and some attention. I rubbed his ears and scratched his back. Portier remembered he hadn't brought in the afternoon mail. He went after it and when he stepped back into the cottage, his eyes were wide with alarm.

"What is it?" I asked.

"Another note in the letterbox." He lifted it up for me to see. My name was the only thing written on the outside.

My heart sank into the pit of my stomach. I took the letter from Portier's hand and noticed immediately that the envelope differed from the previous one. The paper was translucent. I held it to the light. Writing from a blue-ink pen was clearly visible through the paper, although the words were illegible.

I opened the flap and removed the note. "It's from Miss Cora."

"What does she want? Is it threatening?"

I ignored his nonsensical comment and read:

Dear Rev. Fountain,

The Labreville community has come together in our hour of sorrow to plan a second-line from the Presbytere to Congo Square in Treme. At that time, a candlelight vigil will be held for Mr. Lyons to honor his memory and to give thanks for the blessings he gave us. The ceremony has been hastily put together, but your presence would be appreciated. We would be grateful if you would say a few words on Mr. Lyons's behalf. Tomorrow at dusk.

Regards,
   Cora,
   The Friends of Labreville

I gave the invitation some considerable thought. There was no doubt in my mind that I'd attend and speak. I'd only known Roger Lyons a few, brief minutes, but those minutes were eternal to me. My words would be few, but I'd have a lot to say.

~

The next evening at dusk, Portier, Genny, and I joined in the revelry of the second-line parade at the Presbytere in front of Jackson Square. A brass band led the way, followed by a lone snare drummer. *When the Saints Go Marching In* had been requested, and it was performed with all the gusto a second-line could muster. The sound echoed off St. Louis Cathedral and out to the Mississippi. What the line lacked in numbers was compensated by the energy of Genny's boisterous voice and raucous dance moves behind the drummer along the festive streets of the Vieux Carré.

Darkness fell quickly over Congo Square when the line reached Treme. What had, just moments before, been a loud celebration of a man's life became reverent and still in the somber gathering. Two men, one old and one young, shabbily dressed, distributed candles wrapped in aluminum foil. Another man passed around a cigarette lighter.

Portier lit his candle, and Genny and I placed our wick in his flame.

I scanned the square and saw a variety of people from different walks of life. Ministers and elders from area churches attended, and I heard someone mention the presence of a representative from the mayor's office. Portier recognized some businessmen and their spouses from Lafayette. Of course, I recognized faces from my evening jaunts around the Quarter. They recognized me, too, minus the dollar bills and chocolate.

Dampness from the Gulf made our stand in front of a makeshift stage increasingly uncomfortable. Others seemed to feel the chill, too, as they put their hands closer to the flames of the burning candles to warm the tips of their fingers. I focused on my discomfort so much that I didn't see a young man approach or sense his presence next to me.

"Want a Lucky?" he asked.

I turned to see Donnie's face, glowing from the reflection of his candle. He didn't have any cigarettes to offer. I knew the greeting was his way to offer amends.

"No apologies necessary," I replied.

"I think so. I'm sorry I left you at the lake as I did. I'm sorry you got stabbed. I'm sorry I wasn't there to help you

323

when you needed it. You were always there for me, just like Mr. Lyons was."

I reached around his shoulder and gave him a hug to let him know it was good between us. "Everything is working itself out. The detectives have almost everything they need to take the charges against the Lyons family to trial so that Mr. Lyons will receive justice."

"Almost?"

I lowered my head. "There's a matter of the mysterious woman who took evidence from the scene. The police haven't been able to identify the individual, and I haven't been able to give Detective Robicheaux any additional information that could help."

"You mean the woman who took Moline's cuff?"

"Yes, exactly," I replied. I looked at Donnie and saw the light from my candle flickering off his eyes. "Wait a minute. Did you see someone? Do you know who I'm talking about?"

"Of course. Remember? I ran up to the ambulance to see if the man being taken away was Mr. Montgomery. When I turned around, you were there and so was that woman dressed in a black wig."

"Yes, the woman! Did you know her?"

"Sure. It was Karen—the woman, that is."

"Karen? You mean Carmen."

"Karen, Carmen, yeah, what's the difference? Same chick."

"No, Donnie, you have to be exact. Who did you see?"

"I saw Carmen Nicolet. I know her as Karen, but her real name is Carmen. She was standing near a policeman. I saw her about the same time I saw you."

"Did you see her well enough that you could make a positive identification for Detective Robicheaux?"

"I'm sure of it."

I laughed out loud, relieved the final piece of the puzzle had fit into place. "I can't believe I didn't think about you being the key to the mysterious woman, but I remember now. You were very upset that Mr. Montgomery had died. We went to that café to have breakfast to talk about it. As we were talking, you said a woman looked through the window of the café, and it spooked you. You ran out the door. That woman was Carmen, wasn't it?"

"Yes, but she didn't spook me, Mr. Fountain. I spooked her. She saw me at the scene just like I saw her, and she followed us to the café. I'm sure it worried her that I saw her there with Mr. Montgomery. I didn't run out of the café because I was spooked. I ran out so I could catch up to her to find out what she was doing there and to find out what happened to Mr. Montgomery, but she gave me the slip on the street. It was too crowded for me to catch her."

Inexplicable joy leapt from my heart. He smiled at me, knowing he'd done something good and atoned for what happened at the lake. For a fleeting moment, I saw the image of Toby Markle reflecting from his face, reassuring atonement for me, too, reassuring me that the Lord who knew all and loved all, would make everything right—not in my timing, but in His perfect time.

"Say, did you come with someone tonight?" I asked.

He shook his head as if embarrassed. 'Naw, I'm by myself."

"No, you're not." I placed my hand on his shoulder and directed him to a spot between Genny and me just as the program started.

Miss Cora spoke a few words on behalf of the people of Labreville, and an a cappella group sang a spiritual hymn, then Miss Cora gestured me onto the stage.

325

The attendees stood scattered in small clusters, but drew closer as I looked out among them. They held their candles in such a way as to cast a golden glow upon their weathered faces. Donnie moved to the front so he could see and hear me more clearly. His smudged face and ragged clothes were the only impetus I needed to say what I wanted to say.

I started with a prayer, praising God and giving thanks to Roger Lyons's life, then I looked at the crowd again and said:

"How do you eulogize a man like Roger Lyons? I was there when he died. I saw him take his last breath. Surrounded by the horror of what had happened to him was a peace I'd never before experienced. Before he died, I talked with him. I asked him if he saw the Lord, reaching for his hand to bring him home. He resisted, but I continued to encourage him. He appeared destitute, homeless, hungry, and suffering in a world forgotten by most of us. So I told him to take God's hand and go to a better place. But I didn't know him, and I didn't understand him. Roger wasn't resisting because he was afraid of dying. He resisted because there was so much that still needed to be done. But what? He'd already built his fortune. He'd initiated and developed more projects and left his family with more wealth and possessions than any one of us could imagine. What more could there be?

"To answer that I'd like to introduce you to someone. His name is Donnie. Some of you know him. He sings and plays the guitar. He's charismatic, thought-provoking, and funny in his own way. He works here and there, doing what he can whenever he can, and sometimes he oversteps the boundaries of what he knows is best for him. He's made mistakes. He's also homeless, and hungry. He hasn't eaten a solid meal in days. He can't find work. He tries to help others, but sometimes he needs more help than the help he's able to give. He can't seem

326

to cross the threshold in front of him that'll give him his first break. That's because even though he's paid his debt, did his services, and repented of his ways, he can't shake the demons that remind him he's no longer worthy of such luxuries as a home and a meal like you and I receive each day.

"I'm not saying he shouldn't be held accountable when he is irresponsible. And I'm not saying we should overlook what he's done, but how much punishment must someone endure before that person earns forgiveness? What is our hope if there's no amount of punishment that can make a wrong right? What is our hope if there's only a limited amount of forgiveness to help a person out of his or her despair?

"I have no answer. There may not even be an answer. If there is, it isn't an easy one to comprehend let alone to implement. This is Donnie's story, however. It's a story seldom told and rarely listened to because we don't want to hear it. It's a story that should touch the soul of every human heart— especially if that heart wonders about the safety in trusting someone like Donnie when all logic says we shouldn't.

"I have to ask, however; if we don't trust him and it's okay not to trust him, then where does compassion enter? Should it enter at all? And at what point does compassion turn into enabling? Does our compassion have the propensity to know the difference? If you believe Donnie made his bed the moment he decided to steal, and you believe he deserves no compassion, then how will it ever be possible to stop the cycle of hurting and being hurt, of wanting and needing, and creating felons? Without compassion, when will the hurting stop and the healing begin? At this point, the answer is simply bringing the topic into the open and discussing it.

"I'm standing here because, for better or worse, right or wrong, there's not enough punishment, rehabilitation, correction, compassion, and forgiveness in our society to heal our hearts and to stop the plight of the homeless. And because of that, Donnie's not only here, but he's also hungry. So I stand before you to ask: What do we do with him? What do we do with the men and women like him? Roger Lyons asked those questions. He was a man more compassionate than me. He was a man uncomfortable with the situation and was much more insightful about what needed to be done. That's because Roger Lyons became one of those people he was trying to help so that he would know how to help them better. He was a man more Christ-like, more compassionate, more uncomfortable, and more insightful than any one of us at this gathering. That's because we forget our Lord didn't feed, clothe, or heal the multitude because they deserved it; He did it simply because they were hungry, cold, and hurting.

"So the question isn't how do we eulogize a man like Roger Lyons? It isn't even what do we do with a man like Donnie. The real question, ladies and gentlemen, is what do we do with us?"

$\mathcal{A}$ note to my readers

M*asquerade of Truth* began on the bright, cool morning of 19 August 2006 as I walked through King's Square in St. John, New Brunswick, Canada. I wasn't disappointed in my stroll through the Trinity Royal Heritage Conservation Area. Victorian buildings built after the 1877 Great Fire of St. John contained house shops, restaurants, pubs, art galleries, and private homes along picturesque streets of yesteryear.

In a roundabout way of returning to my hotel to join my family for breakfast, I came across a man in King's Square just as I wrote in this book. He appeared to have slept overnight on the park bench where I found him. His beard was scraggly. His overcoat was unkempt but appeared to have been of good quality and appearance at one time. He had been struck violently on the back of his head. Blood had coagulated but not before oozing down the side of his face. I was amazed he was still alive. He was breathing, but barely. I encouraged him to hold on until medical help could arrive.

Being the forensic auditor that I was, I perused the area around him to provide any assistance I could to the police. Nothing struck me odd except that his sole possession—a backpack—lay under the park bench upon which he slumped. It had been rifled through as if whoever assaulted the poor man believed they would get something of value. I noticed some items protruding from the bag that suggested the man was of above average intelligence and had an interest in the arts. I didn't think of him as having a past—perhaps even a glorious and successful past that included the arts. I only saw him as he was at the moment—ragged, unkempt, slumped over a park bench, and near death.

It took what seemed to be an hour for emergency personnel to arrive even though it was probably closer to minutes. In the meantime, I noticed the man's breathing was becoming more labored. My words for him turned from physical encouragement to something more spiritual and eternal. I gave him the Gospel and suddenly, as if peace and forgiveness welcomed him, he died before me.

I stood slowly and prayed momentarily, contemplating what had just transpired when I realized for the first time that a woman was standing behind me, watching the event unfold.

"You killed him," she said bluntly.

It was the most horrifying thing anyone had ever said to me. Nothing could have been farther from the truth, and should anyone believe her, I knew I could be in serious trouble. I corrected the woman, but she wanted to hear nothing of my explanation. She was adamant that I had killed the man by my words. In fact, she reiterated her mistaken observation to the police when they arrived. An officer questioned me, of course, and although he gave me no assurance that he didn't believe the woman's accusation, the situation unnerved me until I was back at the hotel with my family.

There, I began to think more rationally. My thoughts returned to the poor man who died before my eyes. My imagination also grew. Creative thoughts conjured scenarios surrounding the man and what had happened to him.

What if he wasn't who he appeared to be?

What if he wasn't bludgeoned for his meager possessions?

What if he was killed for a more sinister and compelling motive?

Masquerade of Truth began.

Of course, I moved the setting from St. John to my beloved New Orleans simply because I knew New Orleans better than the historic city on the Bay of Fundy. Readers may first believe my descriptions of the Big Easy are unflattering and paint a tainted view of the city and its people. Readers may believe I wasn't fond of New Orleans at all. Again, nothing could be farther from the truth.

The descriptions and issues in this book are not confined to New Orleans. Homelessness, hunger, addiction, and mental health are components of every city in the world. We, as residents, simply choose to ignore that they are a part of the city in which we live. In addition, we forget that behind every issue in every city are human beings who have stories to be told related to that issue.

I often wondered what was behind the story of the man I found in King's Square.

This book was written for him, I suppose, as my way to acknowledge that at least one person found his life worthy to be written about on that bright, cool August morning.

If you enjoyed this book, I would be very grateful if you could write a review and publish it at your point of purchase. Your review, even a brief one, will help other readers to decide whether or not they'll enjoy my work.

If you want to be notified of new releases from myself and other AIA Publishing authors, please sign up to the AIA Publishing email list. You'll find the sign-up button on the right-hand side under the photo at www.aiapublishing.com. Of course, your information will never be shared, and the publisher won't inundate you with emails, just let you know of new releases.

Gary Lee Edward Kreigh
19 May 2020
New Orleans, Louisiana